M000284516

BY GABRIELLA BURNHAM

It Is Wood, It Is Stone

Wait

Wait

Wait

A NOVEL

Gabriella Burnham

ONE WORLD
NEW YORK

Wait is a work of fiction. Names, characters, places, and incidents are the products of the author's imagination or are used fictitiously. Any resemblance to actual events, locales, or persons, living or dead, is entirely coincidental.

Copyright © 2024 by Gabriella Burnham

All rights reserved.

Published in the United States by One World, an imprint of Random House, a division of Penguin Random House LLC, New York.

One World and colophon are registered trademarks of Penguin Random House LLC.

Grateful acknowledgment is made to Penguin Books, an imprint of Penguin Publishing Group, a division of Penguin Random House LLC, for permission to reprint an excerpt from "The River" from *Dream Work* by Mary Oliver, copyright © 1986 by NW Orchard LLC. Used by permission of Penguin Books, an imprint of Penguin Publishing Group, a division of Penguin Random House LLC.

LIBRARY OF CONGRESS CATALOGING-IN-PUBLICATION DATA
Names: Burnham, Gabriella, author.
Title: Wait: a novel / by Gabriella Burnham.
Description: First Edition. | New York: One World, 2024.
Identifiers: LCCN 2023033500 (print) | LCCN 2023033501 (ebook) |
ISBN 9780593596500 (Hardback) | ISBN 9780593596517 (Ebook)
Subjects: LCGFT: Novels.
Classification: LCC PS3602.U76377 W35 2024 (print) |
LCC PS3602.U76377 (ebook) | DDC 813/.6—dc23/eng/20230724
LC record available at https://lccn.loc.gov/2023033500
LC ebook record available at https://lccn.loc.gov/2023033501

Printed in the United States of America on acid-free paper

oneworldlit.com
randomhousebooks.com

2 4 6 8 9 7 5 3 1

FIRST EDITION

Book design by Ralph Fowler

Lighthouse illustration by Gerilya/Adobe Stock

For my mother

Home, I said.
In every language there is a word for it.
Deep in the body itself, climbing
those white walls of thunder, past those green
temples there is also
a word for it.
I said, home.

—MARY OLIVER

The difficulty with waiting, Rosalie thought,
is that one can rarely wait in absolute stillness.

—YIYUN LI

PART I

Home

Elise sits cross-legged on the dorm room floor, absently twirling a sheepskin rug as she watches Sheba dress for the party. A window on the far wall has been propped open with a textbook; the night's tranquil air eases into the room. Sheba searches through a heap of hangered clothes on her bed and pulls out a slinky shift dress that resembles the one Elise is already wearing—black, spaghetti straps, a neckline that drapes like molasses. She slips the hanger over her head and pins the fabric to her hipbone. Yes, no doubt, go with that one, Elise tells her. The identical dress she has on is borrowed from Sheba anyway.

I can't stay out late tonight, Sheba says. Like, physically speaking, I cannot. My body will revolt.

Will I know anyone there? Elise asks, sipping from a plastic goblet. They're going to a party for a friend of Sheba's from Dalton. Sheba said she had to go for convoluted social reasons that were lost on Elise.

Me, I'll be there, Sheba says, batting her eyes through the vanity mirror.

It's the night before graduation and Elise's mother, Gilda, and her sister, Sophie, are traveling from their home on Nantucket

Island to attend the ceremony tomorrow. They planned to take a 6:30 A.M. ferry, then rent a car and drive thirteen hours from Cape Cod to Chapel Hill. Elise tilts her phone to see if they have texted her back. The screen illuminates, revealing a thread of unanswered blue bubbles. Have you passed through Baltimore yet? Elise wrote to her mother at ten A.M. It's the first time they're coming to visit her on campus. At two P.M.: Did you stop for lunch or are you eating gas station food? At five P.M.: I'm worried if you drive straight here you're going to be exhausted at graduation. She thumbs over to Sophie's text message box and types: Hi. Where are you? Mom isn't answering.

She wedges the phone into her wristlet and retrieves a drugstore eyeshadow compact from the side pocket.

Oh, can I use that too? Sheba asks. Elise wipes her ring finger on the underside of the rug and passes the compact to Sheba.

Sheba swabs the lilac shadow into her lid creases. Is your family close? she says.

Elise presses her chin into her shoulder and massages the bone. Yeah. They should be here by morning.

After drinking four proseccos mixed with Chambord and ice, Sheba requests a car at the dormitory pickup point. When they arrive at the party close to midnight, Sheba doesn't say hello to anyone and immediately finds a clearing in front of the audio system. The woman whose music is plugged into the speakers wears a round, fuzzy hat and has a thin blunt tucked behind her ear. She plays the entirety of Robyn's album *Honey,* followed by Frank Ocean and LCD Soundsystem, in glittering, psychedelic succession. Sheba places a hand on Elise's collarbone and snakes her torso to the music. Elise mirrors her moves, mesmerized by the copied dresses skimming at their thighs. She offers Sheba a finger, coyly, as if to beckon, and Sheba closes her lips around it, which startles Elise, the balmy inside of Sheba's mouth. The pad of her finger touches the hard ridge on her palate and the fleshy bumps on her tongue. Surely her finger must taste bitter, like sweat and vanilla moisturizer? But Sheba cackles and so Elise plays it off too. She spins and brushes the saliva onto her forearm, leaving a wet, chilly trail. The strap of her dress falls down her shoulder and she lets it hang there: a dare. It feels good for Elise to feel like Sheba, for Sheba to feel like Elise. They've enmeshed so intimately, they see themselves in another person who shares no resemblance, no common history, not even many interests. Sheba, the Heiress, with an attractively large mouth, milk-white skin, and dandelion-seed hair. Elise, the Child of Immigrants, with a soft, easy body and a complexion the color of oversteeped chamomile tea.

Elise returns to her dorm room around three A.M. after eating a cup of mashed potatoes. Sophie tried to call her earlier in the night, but Elise's phone died while they were at the party. She kicks off her ballet flats and falls asleep belly down, a blot of cherry gloss smeared across her pillowcase. She wakes at nine A.M., Graduation Day, and plugs in her phone. Instantly, Sophie's name lights up on the screen.

Are you here? Elise answers, rubbing her forehead. I just woke up.

Elise, I've been trying you all night, Sophie says.

What's going on? My phone was dead.

I can't find Mom.

She sounds hurried and a little hoarse.

Where are you? Elise sits up, bracing her shoulders against the wall.

I'm still on Nantucket, Sophie says. She never came to the boat.

Elise pauses, trying to assess whether or not she's joking.

Very funny, she says, and peeks over the windowsill at a girl in a blue baseball cap. Ha ha. There you are. I can see you prancing around the parking lot.

Sophie's breath scratches against the receiver.

I'm not kidding, Elise. I'm still on island.

Elise reaches for a water bottle on her bedside table and takes a hard sip.

Sophie—my graduation is in two hours. Have you tried calling the restaurant?

They haven't seen her, Sophie responds. The pitch in her voice rises. She didn't go to work yesterday because we were supposed to drive to see you.

When was the last time you talked to her?

The night before last. She told me she'd meet me at the ferry in the morning. She had to do some prep work in the kitchen before we left. So I waited and waited for her by the docks. Our boat left, and then the next one left. After a while I called Mr. Wagner and asked for a ride, thinking maybe she'd gone home.

Why didn't you call me sooner?

I did call, last night! You weren't answering. Sophie sighs stiffly. Don't blame this on me. I was ready to come. I can't drive all that way by myself. I'm not even old enough to rent a car!

Elise drops the phone against her chest.

I'm not blaming you, she says into the speaker.

They are silent for a long time. Elise kicks off the covers and pulls Sheba's dress over her head. She wouldn't be shocked to learn her mother had panicked last minute and decided she couldn't come. Except that she had been animated about the graduation for weeks; she had said she wanted to pack homemade beijinhos and pão de queijo—Elise's favorite—and she kept sending her photographs of a stuffed bear wearing a cap and gown. Elise presses her thumb into her temple.

Let me call you back, she tells Sophie, and they hang up.

She tosses her phone to the bottom of the bed, holds the water bottle above her face, braces herself, and pours a trickle onto her forehead. The cold lingers on her cheeks, drips into her mouth. She had heard stories about twins, miles apart, one waking in the night if the other twin was hurt, the alarm transferred between their bodies. What did it mean that she hadn't sensed that her younger sister had been calling her throughout the night, trying to reach her?

Elise wraps a bath towel around her body and palms the hallway walls down to Sheba's room, enters the security code, and curls up on the sheepskin rug. Sheba shifts in her bed.

Are you dying of a hangover? she says, squinting.

Elise shakes her head. Sheba pushes the curtain open an inch, letting in a strip of sunlight.

Did you shower already?

Elise flicks a drip of water off her chin.

Sophie called. She can't find our mom.

Sheba tosses her duvet aside and crawls onto the floor. They hook arms while Elise explains to her what happened. Sophie waited. Not at work, not at home. A boat left, then another. Do you have any idea where she could be? Sheba asks. Elise takes a deep breath and says: I don't. My mom's good at hiding.

She confesses to Sheba that she only has eighty-six dollars in her bank account. Sheba reaches under her bed for her laptop and opens up an internet browser.

What do you need? Sheba says. A plane ticket?

Elise trains her eyes on her lap, not wanting to ask. Sheba goes ahead and purchases the next available flight from Chapel Hill to Boston. From there, Elise will board a Peter Pan bus to the coast, where a ferry will deposit her back on Nantucket, her childhood home, for the first time in four years.

Are you still coming to graduation today? Sheba asks, though she knows Elise can't. Her voice sounds suddenly fragile. She closes her laptop and places her palm over Elise's knee.

I need to pack and get to the airport, Elise says.

I'll come with you. I don't want to graduate alone.

Your whole family is here, Sheb. Elise's throat clenches. You can't leave.

My family is unbearable. Sheba lowers her head. Just stay a little longer. For me?

Elise smiles, then covers her face with the crook of her arm.

Take lots of pictures. I'll photoshop myself in later.

Fuck, Sheba says. She presses her hands against her stomach. This is heavy.

Elise feels it too—her ribs, a slab of concrete.

✦

Outside on the ferry's deck, Elise huddles on a pockmarked metal bench next to a puddle of stagnant saltwater spray. The air smells strongly of seaweed and gasoline and the ferry's rumbling engine drowns out the plash of waves against the hull. She searches the clusters of twentysomethings in fleece vests and regatta hats, trying to find a local she might recognize, someone she grew up with, but all she sees are summer people. A few take selfies together with small, curly-haired dogs, posing against the passing harbor view. One woman wearing a waxed hunting jacket hurls a coin over the banister into the ocean, instructing her boyfriend to make a wish. As the ferry picks up speed and the wind whips blond strands into her mouth, she gathers her dog and retreats inside. Elise considers if she should move inside too, except she can't stomach the smell of boiled hot dogs, the same ones they've sold since she was a child. Boiled hot dogs, subs wrapped in cellophane, beer on tap, and cartons of orange juice. She watches as the other passengers pile into booth seats torn down the middle, as brazen and ragged as unstitched scars.

An hour into the ride, only Elise and an older man with a frizzle of white hair remain on the deck. They have reached the point of their journey where there's no land in sight, the ocean a sheet of water adjoined to the open horizon. The man crouches into a corner to light a cigarette, smoke billowing from underneath his armpits. Elise approaches and asks if he has one to spare. At first he doesn't hear her over the engine thrum, so she has to repeat herself, louder: A cigarette, can I have one? She places the filter between her lips as he cups his hands and strikes the flint, the smoke barely hovering before the wind churns it away. Elise leans her belly against the handrail and awakens her phone screen. A new text to her mother is already open, the message drafted and poised.

Elise: Are you there?

She presses send, but a red error mark appears. Scrolling up, she counts the number of messages (Are you there?) that have gone unsent (sixteen) and returns the phone to her pocket.

The day before Gilda and Sophie were supposed to leave for Elise's graduation, Gilda called Elise in a flustered state, upset over their aunt Beth's favorite dog, Clinton, who escaped through the front gate and was hit by a car.

Soon you'll get to see my dorm room, Elise interjected an hour into the phone call, trying to redirect the conversation.

The dog was named after Bill Clinton, Gilda continued, which somehow made it sadder for her.

Elise felt silly insisting that her graduation ceremony was a more pressing topic than Clinton's demise, but she couldn't get her mother to concentrate on anything else. Elise has never even met her aunt Beth; she can't picture the road lined with gold medallion trees in Atibaia where she lives. Only recently have Elise and Sophie discussed the possibility of saving money to buy tickets to Brazil to meet their mother's family, their family, for the first time.

Elise taps the cigarette, ashes scattering into the crested waves. Her gut aches whenever she imagines stepping foot in Gilda's homeland when her mother can't leave the country, replaying a loop of seasons that turn on and off. Gilda once spent three consecutive years on Nantucket without leaving the island once, through bitter, desolate winters, biding time for another chance at summer income. Then one day in the spring, she escaped on an early morning ferry and didn't return for days. They learned she had slept in a sleeping bag on the beach in Barnstable, only to wake up and stroll around the shopping mall, free of the worry of being recognized.

Hey! Elise hears a ferry worker shout from across the deck. No smoking! She apologizes, tamps out the butt on the heel of her shoe, and places it in a trash can. When the ship's bow knocks against the wharf, Elise gathers her bag and joins the long line to disembark. Swarms of passengers in pastels and florals flood the parking lot, flummoxed by the rows of self-service trolley carts filled with luggage. She looks for their next-door neighbor, Mr. Wagner, who offered to pick her up from the boat. He's reading a newspaper in his cherry-red F-150 truck as his dog, an American Eskimo named Suzie, frantically tries to fit her snout through the cracked car window. She waves and hoists herself into the passenger seat as he places her suitcase into the truck bed.

Did you learn a lot in college? Mr. Wagner asks, turning onto the road. Suzie is balanced on Elise's lap, the dog's paws digging into her thighs. She's never had a one-on-one conversation with Mr. Wagner before. All she really knows about him is he works for the Department of Sanitation, and once, when a sewage line burst, sending gallons of feces into the harbor, he made the front page of the local newspaper.

I'd say I learned a fair amount, she answers.

He turns his head and glances at her.

It's been a while since I've seen you. Were you here for Christmas?

Elise shakes her head. I haven't been back in four years.

Shoot, Mr. Wagner says, smoothing his goatee. And how's your mom doing? Still working a lot?

She's good, Elise says, telephone poles flickering across the window. Still working a lot.

Mr. Wagner pulls the truck up against her front lawn. Elise can already see the wear on their small, square cottage, like a once-taut spiderweb now sagging between branches. The shingles are black and splintering. The lawn is mostly crabgrass and dandelions. Her eyes meet Gilda's bedroom window and travel up to her and Sophie's room in the attic.

Before I forget, Mr. Wagner says as they step out of the truck. He places Elise's suitcase on the pavement. Sarah is making dinner tonight, if you're hungry.

Oh, Elise says. She doesn't particularly want to eat at the Wagners', but she can't think of an excuse that doesn't include her mother's absence. Thanks. We'll let you know.

He drives forward a few feet and turns in to his house next door as Elise hauls her suitcase across the lawn. Inside, Sophie is in repose on the green futon sofa in the living room, a biology textbook covering her face. When she hears a thump against the steps and the front door opening, she drops the textbook and rushes over to embrace her sister. Elise is surprised by her sudden affection—Sophie usually needs to warm up to a hug. Even as a child, her muscular body would wriggle free if she was picked up too fast and she'd run as soon as her feet hit the floor.

I'm sorry I missed your graduation, she says. I feel really bad about it.

It's OK, Soph, Elise responds. It's only a ceremony.

Sophie's wearing a gray sweatshirt that hangs down to her knees, the edges brown with wear. Its outsized proportions make her look very sweet, Elise thinks, which has always been Sophie's style: to refine the hand-me-downs she inherited from Elise, or the free leftovers she finds at the Take-It-or-Leave-It. Even after these years apart, their sisterly resemblance is obvious—deep moon creases that bracket their mouths, cheekbones as hard and smooth as shells, and lashes so dark, they seem wet. Standing beside her sister, though, Elise feels somewhat embarrassed by how college-fussy she's become. Before leaving for the airport that morning, as hurried as she was, she made sure to flat-iron her hair, singeing her scalp to smooth out the wavy ripples close to the root. She had been convinced these behaviors were required to be taken seriously, to be seen as attractive, but they appear frivolous next to Sophie, who pushes up her gaping sleeves and play-jabs her sister's arm.

I see you're parting your hair differently, Elise says.

Sophie touches her hairline. It's always been like this, she says, even though Elise is sure it's slightly more to the left. Sophie lifts the heavy suitcase and places it on the attic steps.

You want to take this upstairs? she says and ignores Elise when she offers to carry it up herself.

Sophie has left their attic bedroom as Elise remembers it: the sheets they pinned to form a makeshift closet, their parallel twin beds, basketball ribbons tacked to the pitched roof on Sophie's side, antique botany posters on Elise's. The smell of dried wood, like honey, permeates the cool air. Sophie drags the suitcase with both hands across the carpet and drops it at the foot of Elise's bed.

Are you hiding a body in there? she says, breathless. If Mom pops out I'll scream.

Very funny, Elise says and laughs, though the joke unsettles her, the idea of their mother's body folded into luggage.

Sophie falls across her bed, propping her head up with her palm. Speaking of Mom, she says. Should we place bets on when she'll be back?

Part of me thought I'd walk into the house and she'd already be here.

Just, like, at her computer playing solitaire, Sophie says. Sorry I missed your graduation. I've been waiting for an ace of hearts to appear.

Elise forces a yawn. I feel like you're being funny because you're worried something happened.

No, Sophie says, unconvincingly. I'm not worried yet. Are you?

Elise is worried, but she's more worried about expressing her concerns out loud, like the fact that her text messages aren't going through. She probably got overwhelmed, Elise says after a moment. Mom doesn't do well with big emotions, even when they're positive emotions.

I think she'll be back tomorrow, Sophie says, sitting up. And she'll have a whole dramatic explanation as to why she left.

Elise eyes her sister, unsure how to read her confidence, but Sophie does appear genuinely calm, happy even. Do you want to see something cool? she says and reaches behind the closet sheet

to retrieve a shoebox. She brings the box over to Elise and reveals
a trove of school report cards and letters from teachers expressing
how wonderful a student she is. Sophie explains to Elise her high
school trajectory through these crinkled and folded documents—
how, after Elise left for college, she entered freshman year unmo-
tivated and rebellious, until her favorite English teacher lent her a
book filled with magical realism, showed her a clever way of organizing her binders, and let her complete homework in a quiet
classroom before basketball practice. Elise experiences a strange
confluence of feelings as Sophie reveals what hadn't translated
over text messages and video calls: that she is doing well; that she
is capable of caring for herself.

Are you hungry? Elise asks as Sophie tucks the box away. The
Wagners invited us over for dinner.

I heard. . . . Do you want to go? Our fridge is pretty empty. All
we have is ketchup and Worcestershire sauce.

So it's either condiments or a dinner conversation with the
Wagners? Kind of a toss-up.

Sophie shrugs.

Fine, Elise says, heading for the door. Let's go to the neighbors'. I'm just going to splash some water on my face first.

Downstairs, Elise finds a bleach-stained towel and takes it into
the bathroom. Her eyes are bloodshot from travel and she's gone
so long without eating, she's lost her appetite again. Her tongue
tastes sour. She presses and rubs the loose skin under her eyes,
then washes her face with a bar of soap.

Did you miss me? Sophie says as Elise reemerges, the collar of
her shirt dampened. Elise is unsure if she means just now, in the
bathroom, or since she left the island. She swings her arm over
Sophie's shoulders. Of course, she says, and they exit through the

back door, crossing a flattened path in the sedge grass bordering the Wagners' lawn.

Mrs. Wagner is seated in a recliner in the living room stitching a needlepoint, her glazed fingernails clacking against the thimble. Suzie barks erratically as Elise and Sophie enter.

Suzie, stop it! she says and taps the dog's head with her embroidery hoop. Come in, girls! Don't listen to her.

Elise notices that the dining room table is set with silverware placed on top of leftover Thanksgiving napkins. In the center is a casserole dish covered in tinfoil.

Are you starving? Mrs. Wagner says, hugging Elise. She's slender and short, and Elise has to bend over to accept her embrace. It's late—why don't we start eating. I'll reheat the eggplant lasagna in the oven.

Mrs. Wagner returns to the dinner table wearing red oven mitts, struggling to carry the heavy casserole dish. She places it on a silicon mat and serves Elise first, the mozzarella clinging as she plops it onto her plate. Elise takes a small discreet bite while Mrs. Wagner serves Sophie and Mr. Wagner, but it's too hot to taste anything. Some of the condensation from the tinfoil has dripped onto her slice, dampening the cheese. As they eat, Mr. Wagner talks about his plans for tomorrow, saying he'll take the truck to the dump in the morning before work, and that he wants to swing by the beach on his way home to do some fishing.

That's fine, honey, Mrs. Wagner says. I'm off from the hospital tomorrow.

Oh, you work at the hospital now? Elise asks, nudging a piece of eggplant with her fork.

Mrs. Wagner pours herself a glass of Diet Coke and nods enthusiastically. I'm an insurance manager. I started last year. I love it so much—it's exactly the kind of work I'm suited for. I love the people I work with, and I don't have to deal with patients.

I've been wondering, hypothetically speaking, Elise says and clears her throat. If I called the hospital to ask if a patient has checked in, would they be able to tell me?

Mrs. Wagner licks the soda bubbles off her lips.

You know, I'm not sure about that. It might be a HIPAA violation. She stares down at her plate. Oh dear. Are you thinking your mom might be in the hospital?

Elise drops her fork and slices a glance at Sophie, a blade of skepticism. Had she told the Wagners their mom had gone missing? Sophie continues cutting a bite of lasagna.

No, I was only curious, Elise says, twisting the skin on her knuckle.

Well, if someone were to call and tell Nancy at the front desk that they know Sarah Wagner and need a favor, I think Nancy might provide some off-the-books information. Hypothetically. She smiles and adjusts the napkin on her lap.

Sophie cough-laughs and covers her mouth.

Got it, Elise says. Thanks. She picks up her water glass but places it back down without taking a sip.

Mr. Wagner changes the topic to the local election, and when they finish eating, Mrs. Wagner packs up several slices of lasagna for them to bring home. Elise and Sophie cross the sedge grass path in silence, but as soon as they enter the house, Elise drops the lasagna onto the kitchen counter, tomato sauce bursting through the foil.

Did you tell them about Mom? she says.

Sophie balances one hand against the refrigerator and peels the socks from her feet.

No, I didn't tell them, she says. Why would I do that?

Then how did they know?

Come on, Sophie says, sounding suddenly grown. I don't have to tell them—they know about Mom. They know she disappears. It's like a fifty-fifty chance she'll pick me up from school or basketball practice on the days she says she will. When she doesn't show, I have to ask for a ride home from Mr. Wagner. They see her headlights in the driveway late at night after she's been sitting at the bluff alone, drinking beers after work, staring out at the ocean or whatever she does. I don't have to spell it out for them.

Elise pulls a chair out from the kitchen table. Of course, she says. Everyone seems to know about Mom except me. She picks up an ashtray balanced on the windowsill brimming with cigarette butts. Gilda had told her she'd quit months ago, assuring her over text messages and phone conversations each time Elise asked. She empties the tray into the garbage pail next to her, the eruption of stale cigarettes seizing at the center of her throat.

♦

Money was too scarce for Elise to shuttle up and down the East Coast after she left for college, so she found a job at the campus library during the summers, and spent winter holidays with a group of international students on F-1 visas who came from countries halfway around the world. They would cook dishes like lamb haleem and mango sticky rice, which they ate in a circle on the floor of the student center while listening to Broadway musical soundtracks. Students and professors returned in droves over Labor Day weekend, populating the shuttered buildings and empty stretches of lawn, noses sun-kissed, hair salt-sprayed, eyes rejuvenated. Did it bother Elise that she didn't spend months away on summer break with her family, cultivating separation between home and work, education and identity, like most of her classmates? Not really. She had observed this formation her entire life, every summer, when tens of thousands of visitors occupied the island, only to return to their real homes before the Northeastern gales began to blow.

When Elise arrived at her college campus four years prior, traveling solo on a Greyhound bus, she hadn't anticipated there would be mothers and fathers who would stay for the entire orientation week, sleeping at a nearby hotel or in their child's dorm room, to help decorate, buy groceries, locate campus classrooms, and teach them how to use a washing machine. When classes finally began and these parents begrudgingly vacated, they continued to call every day to ensure their children woke up in time for class and ate regular meals. Elise felt grateful Gilda did not hover over her shoulder and offer opinions on her every move. But she also felt embarrassed her mother had only called a few times since Elise left: once to ensure she caught the bus, once to ensure she arrived in Chapel Hill, and then one unexpected call, a clue indicating Gilda did in fact miss her daughter.

Gilda was twenty years old and had only been in the United States for eight months when she got pregnant with Elise. When she told her mother she was having a baby with an Irish bartender she met at work, whom she said she had fallen in love with, no less, her mother told her she'd better pray her baby would be born with ten fingers and ten toes, hung up the phone, and didn't speak to her until she went into labor. Four years and several expired work visas later, Sophie arrived. In some ways it was easier when they were infants—babies are always happy to see their mother. It was when they got older, and Gilda had to work longer hours because their father had vanished to Ireland that they became more desperate for her attention, less satisfied with what little time she could give them. Gilda's favorite moments were when they piled into bed to watch *Law & Order* together, and the girls would fall asleep tucked into Gilda's armpits. They always looked like little cherubs when they slept, even as they lost their baby faces.

The first time Gilda left the girls alone overnight, Elise was ten years old and Sophie was six. By that point Gilda had accepted the fact that she didn't have any friends her own age, only co-workers in the kitchen who were mostly male and spoke Spanish so quickly she couldn't understand them. She longed for her teenage years, when she and Beth and their best friend Marina would go dancing in São Paulo until dawn. Then one day Gilda opened up her email to find a message from Marina herself, whom she hadn't heard from in a decade. The email explained she had been granted a tourist visa to come to the United States to celebrate her thirtieth birthday and planned to stay in Boston for a few days. When Gilda told Elise and Sophie she would be meeting her friend Marina on Cape Cod, that she couldn't believe her old childhood friend would be in the United States, they responded by asking how she was allowed to take time off from work. She had started a new job as a cook at a French-fusion restaurant on the harbor that sold sixteen-dollar cups of vichyssoise and paid five dollars more an hour than her last job. Sometimes she would get home at two A.M., only to wake up at seven, put on her chef's coat, and return to the restaurant. They thought the only day she got off was Christmas, and that was because no one else in the kitchen had young children.

Are you spending the night? Sophie asked. She and Elise sat perched on the edge of Gilda's bed, watching her get ready. Gilda had laid out a few items—toothpaste, Oil of Olay, an underwire bra—on top of her bedsheets.

I'll be back tomorrow morning, Gilda said. It'll be a quick trip, I promise.

But what if something happens while we're asleep? Elise said. What if Sophie leaves the sink running and it floods?

I wouldn't do that, Sophie said.

You do it all the time, Elise muttered.

Gilda spun a tube of brown lipstick and began to apply it in the mirror. It will be like when I work a double and you don't see me until the next morning, she said. Just pretend like I'm coming home while you're still sleeping.

She took a balled-up receipt from her pocket and scribbled on it with a bank pen. Here's the name and address for the hotel where we're staying, she said. I'll leave you the phone number too. You can call me there if anything happens.

You're staying at a hotel? Sophie blurted out. Again, they didn't know Gilda could stay at a hotel—whenever they asked if they could stay at the hotel near the airport because they wanted to swim in the pool, she told them they couldn't afford it.

Marina got a room. It has two beds so she's letting me stay in one.

Elise could feel that her mother was nervous, the way she kept wiping the edges of her mouth and swallowing air in knots. It made Elise want to reassure her that she and Sophie would be fine through the night, even though her skin had a tingling feeling that she didn't want to be left alone.

There's chicken breast in the refrigerator, Gilda continued. And lettuce for a salad.

We can take care of the house, Sophie said, perhaps sensing Gilda's anxiety too. She enjoyed being in charge of things like setting the thermostat or making sure the living room windows were latched at night so the morning dew didn't dampen the carpet.

Gilda placed her hands over Sophie's ears and kissed the top of her head. She squirmed, banging her toes against Gilda's shins. Elise picked up the receipt from the dresser where she had written the hotel details, ironing the wrinkled paper over her knee. Gilda had written in dashes and loops, Elise noticed, which is how she wrote when she was in a hurry.

Elise and Sophie took the bus to school soon after their conversation, and Gilda called for a taxi to catch the noon ferry to Hyannis. In the summers, the passenger line for the boat would border the entire parking lot and sometimes spill out onto Easy Street. But on a Tuesday in October, there were only about twenty people waiting, mostly tradesmen heading off island to collect supplies. Gilda waited alone with her hands in her pockets and her face tucked behind her sweater collar. She exhaled softly to warm her nose, which the winter air had bitten cold. After ten years in New England, she still didn't own a proper winter coat. Maybe it was because of the thick, stifling chef's coat she wore every day, or maybe she wanted to convince herself every winter was her last. There was something about the punishment of the cold—stiff neck from contracting her shoulders, perpetual numbness in her toes—that felt appropriate. Honest. She handed the dockworker her ticket and found an empty booth seat near the concession stand inside. The Plexiglas windows were fogged along the edges, but she could make out a slate of ocean water swallowing up the gray sky.

As the boat ambled out of the harbor, foghorn blowing, Gilda asked herself the question she had been avoiding: Had it been wrong to leave her daughters alone for the night? Gilda's mother, Frieda—a surly Austrian woman who worked as an aesthetician—used to leave her and Beth alone for weeks at a time when they were even younger, to visit her guru at an ashram in the countryside. The rule was, when Frieda was gone, Gilda and Beth weren't allowed to leave their apartment. The military dictatorship in Brazil had been kidnapping children from families who they believed to be dissidents. Frieda worried they would be targeted, so their housekeeper walked the girls to and from school, and when they returned home they were ordered to stay inside. They couldn't even go to the back stairwell where they liked to play Rumpelstiltskin on the railing. Gilda never forgot how trapped she felt, powerless, too young for the society in which she lived.

Growing older became a study, then, in avoiding confinement. By the time she was eighteen, Gilda worked as a stagehand at a concert venue that had wet concrete floors and a cigarette machine. When Gilda stumbled home late at night, rummaging through the refrigerator for leftover potato-and-clarified-butter soup, Frieda would fling her bedroom door open and yell: Vá embora, chata! She wanted her daughter, the chata, out of the house, but her Catholic family thought Gilda's rebellious behavior was a reflection of Frieda's bad mothering. If Gilda spent a summer in another country, however, as a cultural immersion, she would come back independent, disciplined, and return to God.

Gilda had heard about a magical place called Nantucket Island from a friend who had worked at a restaurant in Miami and knew other waiters who spent their summers there. He kept saying she could make thousands of dollars in a few months from wealthy tourists like the fashion designer Tommy Hilfiger and Teresa Heinz, the ketchup heiress, who owned vacation houses on the island. One bus trip and three flights later, Gilda landed on an island thirty miles out to sea off the coast of Massachusetts. She stepped off the nine-seater plane directly onto the tarmac and thought, This looks nothing like Miami. The air tasted like unsalted rice. She ended up renting a room from a retired sculptor and found a job at a steakhouse built inside an old whaling merchant's home—a wide brick building with white shutters and a widow's walk. She barely knew how to scramble an egg, but they told her they wouldn't consider her for a job in the front of the house. Those jobs were reserved for skinny white women from Bulgaria and Poland. The manager put Gilda in the kitchen, on the line, where she flipped burgers with a metal spatula. Whatever, she thought, rolling her eyes, trying to avoid dripping sweat onto the simmering flattop. I guess Americans are too stupid to understand when I ask, Would you like a booth seat or a table?

Gilda was the only woman in the kitchen, working side by side with cooks, dishwashers, and food runners from El Salvador, Jamaica, and the Dominican Republic. When they taught her how to juice the burger before scraping it, a grease pocket popped onto her wrist, leaving a hard purple bubble. She didn't dare cry; she climbed up the widow's walk for a cigarette and pretended to send smoke signals across the Atlantic to her family. Help me, Mãe, she said into the air. I promise I'll be good. But she never received a signal back.

She met Peter, the bartender, after their first dinner shift. She was seated on a barstool, pressing a sliced tomato into her burn— a trick one of the dishwashers had taught her—when Peter slid her a gin and tonic. She slid the glass back and asked for a Pilsner. I get angry when I drink gin. Are you trying to make me angry? Maybe I am, he beamed. Elise liked it when Gilda told this story about her father. She thought it demonstrated the special relationship they had—how they could tease each other in the tender way only people in love can. Peter would watch the gap between Gilda's two front teeth and the flush that brightened her cheeks after a few sips of beer. She had different levels of freckles, he thought, some above the skin's surface and some below, a multilayered pigment that made her look like no one he'd ever met before.

Gilda had never met anyone like Peter either. He looked like he'd been handwashed and left out to fade on the clothesline. He chewed on a peppermint-flavored toothpick he kept in his front shirt pocket, along with a soft-pack of cigarettes, a golf pencil, and a condom. Were all the Irish like him? she asked. Brazen, impish, quick to temper. Peter reiterated that he was properly Irish—born and raised in Charleville, County Cork—whereas the blue-collar New Englanders on Nantucket who claimed their great-grandparents' birthright probably hadn't even been to Ireland. This jaunty nationalism amused Gilda. She grew up in the fourth-largest city in the world with punk boys who rode skateboards on the backs of buses, coiffed their hair into careful swoops, and worshipped bands like the Clash and the Sex Pistols. The New England not-quite-Irishmen she encountered had rough, honking accents, wore rust-colored pants, and drove two-door cars. Who were these confidently bucolic men, she wondered, who didn't own a mirror or a comb?

A group of them boarded the ferry she was taking to see Marina on Cape Cod. She tore the corners off a paper napkin, trying not to stare. They were construction workers commuting back to the mainland. It had become common on Nantucket for teachers, nurses, electricians, and construction workers to find housing off island and commute to their jobs on island. Gilda had considered it herself when she couldn't find a place to live for herself and the girls after Peter left. But she couldn't afford to quit and look for a new job, nor could she risk being stranded because of precarious ocean conditions or lingering dinner guests who sat with their dessert for too long.

One of the construction workers, the one with a dimpled chin and a large forehead, took a seat directly in her sight line. His hand passed over his mouth, to wipe coffee from his five-o'clock shadow, and Gilda's gaze briefly connected with his. She feigned a thought, pretended she hadn't noticed him noticing her, and instead watched Brant Point Lighthouse as it shrunk on the horizon, into the distance.

When Elise and Sophie returned home from school, they squeezed together on Gilda's swivel chair in her bedroom and powered up the desktop computer to search for the hotel where she was staying. Sophie steadied her leg on top of Elise's as she wiggled the seat back and forth, waiting for the screen to load. The website displayed images of a bright sign for OCEAN WAVE, a motel with bedroom doors that opened directly onto an outdoor pool. Around the pool deck was a wire fence with faux ivy plants woven through the spokes, an attempt to disguise the two-lane highway on the other side.

Do you think Mom is staying on the bottom floor? Sophie asked. She could open her door and cannonball right into the pool.

Maybe. But the pool isn't open. See, it says here—Elise pointed to the computer screen—Pool closed September 1.

Sophie leaned closer to the monitor.

Maybe Mom will take us there when the pool is open, she said, and used her toes to twirl the chair around. I'm going to ask her for it for my birthday.

Elise grabbed on to the desk edge and halted the spinning chair. In the folds where her underwear met her hip creases, she felt a deep prickling sensation, like when she laid on wet, fertilized grass and it made her itch.

Why are you squirming? Sophie said.

My underwear is uncomfortable, I think. Elise stood, rubbing her thighs together. I'm going to get changed.

She hurried upstairs to their bedroom and retrieved a flashlight from underneath Sophie's bed, then opened her bedsheets and burrowed inside, tenting the covers with her knees. She shimmied off her underwear and shined a light onto her groin. Are they bug bites? she thought, trying to pinch a red bump to see if one would pop. Then she remembered with regret what she'd done that morning, before school, and before Gilda announced she would be leaving them alone overnight. Elise had crept downstairs, locked the bathroom door behind her, undressed, and turned on the shower faucet, waiting for it to get hot. Sometimes she took lukewarm showers because she didn't have the patience, but she'd read in a women's magazine that the water had to be hot in order to open up your follicles for a closer shave. She was only ten years old, but already small, black pubic hairs were developing, and she'd overheard an older boy telling his friends in the cafeteria that girls were more attractive with clean-shaven crotches. Elise soaked and lathered her groin, then ran Gilda's plastic Bic over her pubis. Black fragments clung to the razor's underside, then glided down the drain.

Elise returned to Gilda's bedroom and stood in front of Sophie, covering her pants fly with her hands. The more she concentrated on her groin, the more intense the prickle became, until her hand reflexively dug into her underwear and scratched.

Can I show you something, Soph? she said. Sophie was playing *Minesweeper* on the computer. She spun around in her chair and eyed Elise scratching her crotch.

All right, she said.

Elise began to unbutton her pants and then paused.

You have to promise you won't tell anyone.

Sophie drew an X over her heart with her finger. I promise I won't tell.

Elise unzipped her pants and dropped them to the floor, then pulled her underwear down far enough to reveal a swath of skin dotted with scarlet pinpricks.

What is that? Sophie said and rolled the chair closer. Poison ivy?

I shaved this morning, Elise confessed. With Mom's razor. And I think it did this.

Sophie inspected the bumps as she'd seen doctors on television do, then looked up at Elise and shook her head.

Mom's razor doesn't do this. I've tried it once and it didn't happen to me.

Elise pulled up her underwear. You tried to shave?

I was testing it out. I don't have hair yet or anything. Sophie tapped her finger against her chin. I'd say it's either fire ant bites, poison ivy, or a bacterial infection.

A bacterial infection? Elise glanced down at her crotch. She lifted her pants from the floor and buttoned up. Well, how do I get rid of it?

Sophie reclined in the chair and crossed her arms high on her chest. Let's see what we've got in the medicine cabinet.

At this point in her life, Sophie was an aspiring medical doctor. She had written on her kindergarten worksheet that she wanted to be a karate instructor, but her ambitions soon changed into professional basketball player, then a chef like her mother, until, at age six, she realized she needed to earn a lot of money to buy a house with a swimming pool, and so she decided she'd become a doctor. Her favorite pastime lately was finding injured butterflies in their backyard and dabbing them with a tube of ointment. She instructed Elise to remove her pants and sit in the bathtub bare bottomed while she searched for a topical treatment. The slick porcelain tub was a cool relief against Elise's skin—she propped her arms against the sides and stared at the red rash puckering above the surface. Sophie exclaimed that she'd found the bottle of calamine lotion from when they had the chickenpox. Elise used her finger to plaster on a thick coat while Sophie dried it with their mother's blow-dryer. The pink crust smelled chalky and cracked like desert fault lines. After a few minutes, Sophie asked Elise if the itch had subsided.

She waited for a moment and then declared it had.

Great! Sophie said. Then do you want to run around the maze before it gets dark?

They biked to their favorite empty summer mansion, the one with an elaborate boxwood maze in the backyard, and navigated its gnarled, overgrown pathways until their fingers and noses went numb. They picked dried leaves from flowerless rose bushes and called them foxglove, wormwood, and hollyhock. Put these in the jars for medicine, Elise instructed Sophie, and Sophie crammed the crispy leaves into a frilly sock strung to her belt loop. When a blue dusk swept across the island sky, they hurried toward the maze entrance, retracing their steps, and gripped rubber handlebars with cold, aching hands. They returned home in time to cook dinner just after sunset.

As the ferryboat ambled over the ocean's hard waves, Gilda strained to hear the construction workers when they called the dimple-chinned one by his name. Damn it, Adam, they said as he flexed his biceps after winning a round of rummy. He slyly checked to see if Gilda was watching him. Gilda examined her lap, avoiding his eyes, then pressed her thumb into her wrist bones, a remedy for seasickness Peter had taught her many years ago. Adam smirked and stood from his seat, stretching his arms to reveal a sliver of abdomen.

I'm going to get a beer, he announced, and strutted to the concession stand. As he passed by her, he touched his index finger to her table and dragged it for several inches, as if to swipe a layer of dust, his hands crusted with small scabs.

Gilda pinched down on her wrist harder. A Bloody Mary would be nice, she thought. Did seasickness work like a hangover? Maybe the hair of the dog would settle her stomach. She bundled her purse into her arms and joined him at the cash register.

Up close, Adam appeared much younger than she had originally thought. From a distance the illusion of parched skin and brawny shoulders made her think he'd crossed over into his thirties like her, but standing adjacent to him in line, she recognized the newness of his beard, the bounce in his sentences. He must have been close to twenty-five, she estimated. He probably didn't have children either. Roommates, more likely. A hairy lotion pump and a stiff towel.

The woman working behind the counter handed him a wheat beer in a plastic cup, the foam brimming above the edge. He arched his neck to take a careful sip, then turned to Gilda.

You know, when I first saw you, he said, I thought you were my ex-girlfriend.

She chuckled. I'm too old to be your ex-girlfriend, she said, and read the menu posted above them. A strong wave crashed port-side and Adam saved the beer from splashing onto her chest.

What would you like, dear? the woman working the cash register asked, wiping down her counter.

Bloody Mary, please. With extra pepper.

My mom always drinks those, Adam said, shaking the drip from his fingers.

Gilda rolled her eyes. Who am I, then? Your mother or your ex-girlfriend?

Well, you're nothing like my mother, he said.

You're sure about that?

He nodded and took a large gulp of his beer.

I found a celery stick for you, the cashier said and handed Gilda the Bloody Mary. That'll be fifteen dollars.

Adam reached into his jeans pocket and pulled out a folded leather wallet. Allow me, he said.

Gilda rubbed her cheek, trying not to blush. Normally she wouldn't allow someone to pay for her drink. She didn't like to feel indebted. And yet, fifteen dollars was a lot of money for a Bloody Mary.

Thank you, she said, and lifted her cup into the air, tipping it toward his.

That night, Elise removed the chicken breast from the refrigerator and punctured the plastic wrap with her finger. It smelled faintly astringent, like a clean factory floor. She peeled back the wrap, lifted the poultry out of its Styrofoam bed, and poured the pink chicken water into the sink. Gilda taught Elise how to cook meals like top ramen with feta cheese or crispy sliced Spam with fried potatoes, so she and Sophie would have dinner when Gilda worked a double shift at the restaurant. When she first began cooking, Elise used to handle raw chicken flesh with plastic bags over her hands, especially if it had white strings of fat or a purple vein. That was years ago, though. By now she was used to it. She rinsed the skinless breasts and patted them dry on paper towels, then poured salt into her palm and sprinkled it over the top. She liked to put a lot of black pepper on her chicken, and sometimes she added garlic powder too, a spice she had discovered on her own, without Gilda's direction.

Gilda usually worked six days a week, often doubles, and on the seventh day she stayed in bed and slept. Rest was a job in and of itself. Sometimes Elise would find her on her rest day and beg her to make them breakfast—omelets, she was so good at making omelets—and sometimes Gilda would get up and cook on the day she wasn't supposed to be cooking. Elise would run to find Sophie to pass the news along (Mom is making breakfast) and the three of them would spread across their small kitchen table, laying out jars of fancy jam Gilda brought home from work. But then, the following morning, the clock would reset: Gilda's callused hands, scarred with burns and knife cuts, reached for the door yet again.

How's the homework going, Soph? Elise said over her shoulder.

You just asked me that five minutes ago, Sophie said, focused on a math problem at the kitchen table, brushing her hair from her eyes.

Elise stood on a chair and heated canola oil in a pan, then rested the chicken in the bubbling slick. She monitored the flesh as it transformed from pink to white to golden brown, juices sputtering. This was the part of cooking Elise enjoyed most, the science behind it, activating molecules and proteins and sugars. When her sixth-grade biology teacher taught them about bone marrow, how it produces blood cells in the body, Elise flung her arm into the air and proudly announced that her mother loved to eat bone marrow on toast. It's good for you, Gilda had told her. The teacher was astounded—she didn't know humans actually ate bone marrow. She decided to tell every science section that day that in Brazil, people like Elise's mom eat bone marrow with bread. The taunts resounded down the hallways. Hey, Elise, are you a bone marrow eater? Bone marrow eater, bone marrow eater. Elise's mom is a bone marrow eater. Even then Elise knew that her mother had a better palate than the rest of them.

OK, now I'm done, Sophie said, and pushed her math homework aside. She opened the refrigerator and removed a head of iceberg lettuce from the drawer, tossed it into the air, then jumped up onto the counter and stabbed it with a steak knife. Elise used a spatula to slide the chicken onto two plates. They sat at the kitchen table and Elise waited as Sophie took a first bite, observing her face as she chewed. What do you think? she asked finally. Very good, Sophie responded. Very good or great? Elise prodded further. Very good is my highest rating, Sophie explained. Below very good is good. If it's terrible I would tell you. Elise exhaled slowly and took her own bite. You're right, she said. It's very good.

After they finished eating and rinsed their dishes off in the sink, the telephone rang.

Hi, Mom, Sophie answered. We finished dinner. Elise made chicken and I made salad. Have you been to the pool yet?

Elise turned off the faucet so she could try to hear her response. When are you coming home? Sophie asked. And then, several seconds later: OK. I will. Love you too.

Sophie handed Elise the phone, flipping it around like a pair of scissors, its long, curly cord skimming the floor. Elise pressed it against her chest and walked to the back door near the stove.

Hi, Mom, she said, watching her reflection in the storm door. Are you with your friend?

Gilda glimpsed across the hotel room, where Marina sat on the maroon floral duvet. Adam was sitting next to her, leaned over as she showed him a photo of her Yorkshire terrier.

Yes, sweetie, she's here, Gilda said. Do you want to talk to her?

Elise could hear the vodka mixed in with Gilda's voice, the slightly higher register, the dragging vowels. Gilda began to ask if Marina would come say hi to her daughter, but Elise stopped her.

When are you coming home? she said, twisting a piece of hair on her forehead.

She thought of telling Gilda about the rash she'd developed. She could feel an itch attempting to break free from the calamine lotion. But her mother was distracted—Adam had sauntered over and rested the rim of a beer can against her bottom lip. I have to work the dinner shift tomorrow, she said, the beer dripping onto her chin. So I'll be home before then.

OK, Mom. I'll see you tomorrow.

I love you, filha, Gilda said before hanging up. Call me if you need anything.

Around nine P.M., Elise convinced Sophie to stop playing *Minesweeper* and to brush up for bed. The attic wasn't insulated or heated, so in the wintertime they wore thick socks and beanie caps to sleep, their noses and cheeks frigid when they woke. Elise read *The Secret Garden* out loud, testing if Sophie had fallen asleep by stopping midsentence to see if she'd react. When she no longer did, Elise rested the book across her stomach and closed her eyes. She dreamt she was falling into a pit of broken teeth and bolted awake. She and Sophie hadn't closed the curtain in their attic room and the moonlight shone in, illuminating the ashen dark with a lacquered sheen.

Elise stood and pulled the curtain shut, then began to walk downstairs to the bathroom. She'd learned that when she woke suddenly in the night it was usually because she had to pee, but when she reached the bottom of the stairs, she began to cough. She pressed her fingertips against her eyelids, her eyes stinging in the thick, bleary air. What had woken her wasn't the bad dream, or her bladder, or the glaring moon, but the smell of a burning pan. She hurried over to the kitchen and realized she hadn't turned off the electric stovetop. In the dark, the coils glowed fluorescent red, dotted with black spots where Gilda lit her cigarettes. Elise rotated the burner knob until it clicked and used a dishrag to toss the pan into the sink. It sizzled against the stagnant beads of water.

Elise remembered from her school's fire drills that smoke inhalation can lead to delirium and dropped to the linoleum floor. She held her breath and crawled down the hallway, her eyes pinched shut, feeling her way with her hands. She stretched her arm up to reach the handle on Gilda's bedroom door, then gasped and sealed it shut, shoving a discarded shirt into the bottom crack. Elise lifted Gilda's bedsheets and folded herself underneath.

What if we die? she thought. What if I murdered my sister? As these thoughts gripped her into a ball, tensing tighter and tighter, the bedroom door creaked open. For a moment she thought it might be Gilda and peeked her eyes from behind the covers.

Why aren't you sleeping upstairs? Sophie said, standing in the doorway in a holey, oversized T-shirt, holding her stuffed tiger by the tail.

Close the door, Soph, Elise said and scooched over to make room. Sophie slipped under the covers and placed a foot on top of Elise's.

It smells bad out there, Sophie said.

I forgot to turn off the stove from dinner. Mom is going to be so angry.

Oh no, Sophie said, her voice slippery. Did you shut it off?

Elise nodded.

Don't worry. The smoke will disappear before the morning.

Sophie's eyelids relaxed and her mouth went slack. Elise listened to the whispering sound of her breath as she began to fall asleep. She held her mother's pillow against her face, her wet mouth and eyes leaving impressions in the fabric. It took her a little while longer than Sophie, but Elise managed to detach from her worst thoughts. She held a loose fist against her heart and fell back to sleep.

The following morning, the lower deck on the return ferry to Nantucket was entirely occupied by a group from Ohio, Texas, who called themselves the Nantuckophiles because they were obsessed with novels set on Nantucket. Gilda walked onboard and discovered them trying to stage a photograph with foam whale hats strapped to their heads. She sighed and made her way upstairs, where she tucked herself into a corner next to three quiet girls traveling home from a soccer match, their jerseys streaked with dirt and grass.

Gilda's night hadn't gone as she'd expected. Instead of showing Marina the best clam chowder in Hyannis, they ended up at the

Brazilian Grill, where they feasted on rodizio, coxinha, farofa, kibe, sushi rolls, and brigadeiros for dessert. Adam joined them—he hadn't left Gilda's side since they'd strolled tipsily off the boat together. Gilda was feeling a little responsible for him, but Marina didn't seem to mind Adam tagging along. She was as bubbly and fluid as she had been as a teenager, always giggling at the end of her sentences, always prodding Gilda at the waist. When they reunited at the ferry pier, Marina whistled an old nickname at Gilda before she'd even exited the ramp: Gatinha, Gatinha, Gilda Gatinha! It awakened a part of Gilda that had been dormant for years.

After the Brazilian Grill, they saw live music at an Irish pub on Main Street, and as they were dancing, Adam kissed Gilda on the mouth. She tasted bittersweet cocoa powder on his lips. Marina insisted Gilda go home with him instead of sleeping at the hotel, but Gilda felt sick from the food and beer and dancing, and besides, she wanted to spend the rest of the night with her childhood friend. Marina kept saying she would fall asleep as soon as she got to the hotel anyway. It would be a waste of her time. This entire back-and-forth took place while Adam waited on the street corner, kicking the curb with his heel.

OK, I'm coming with you, Gilda decided finally, careening past Adam and to the cab line across the street. She blew Marina a kiss goodbye through the taxi window, and as they pulled away, a sharp thought sliced through her beer haze: not even her own daughters could share in her history like Marina could. They couldn't reminisce about the wild horses eating brush on the top of Pedra Grande, or how she and Beth would collect bruised kumquats from Marina's backyard.

The taxi pulled up to Adam's duplex and he led her across the yard. Wet plywood and a garden hose were strewn by the door.

They walked inside and found his roommate slouched at the kitchen counter, so they immediately retreated into Adam's bedroom, locking the door behind them. At least the room was tidy, Gilda thought—recently vacuumed, not enough clothing or objects to cause a mess. Adam kissed the crease of her neck, his teeth skimming her skin. She tipped her head to the side to offer him more surface area, and he took the opportunity to glide her shirt off in one expert move, then found her cleavage with his mouth. She tried to reach for the hem of his shirt, thinking this would be the moment she finally beheld his strong, broad shoulders, but he stopped her. He kissed her on the palm and removed the shirt himself, doing a little dance as it came off. She laughed and reclined into the desk chair behind her. He kneeled and pulled the seat lever up to its highest setting, then opened her pants, button by button, slid them off, and placed each of her legs on the armrests. Gilda thought the pose was slightly too gynecological, but then his warm, moisturized lips encountered her pubic hair, and she stopped with the extraneous thoughts. She let him do what he had set out to do from the beginning, and she enjoyed it, thoroughly.

He offered up his phone number as they lay beside each other—maybe they could continue this again sometime on the island? She accepted his offer sincerely, though it would never come to pass. Before she left, she snuck into the bathroom, and by the time she'd flushed the toilet, Adam had fallen asleep naked, his feet dangling off the bed.

Gilda arrived at the hotel by taxi and opened the door with her spare key. Marina, she whispered. Are you asleep? A rerun of *Baywatch* was playing silently on the television, flashes of red and yellow blanketing Marina's sleeping face.

Meu deus, Gilda, she said, blinking. You're back already?

Gilda lay next to her on her stomach, propped up on her elbows.

There are still a few hours left before you leave, she said.

Marina shielded the television from her eyes. I had a dream, she said, and in it I remembered I was supposed to tell you something. She paused and placed her palm over the back of Gilda's hand. I saw your father a few months ago, in Atibaia.

Gilda squinted and tilted her head. That's not possible. You know my father is dead.

I swear, I didn't see a ghost. He was sitting alone at the bar where the paragliders fly overhead. I wasn't sure it was him—he's much older now, smaller than I remember him—but I recognized the scar on his biceps from the motorcycle accident. So I asked him, senhor, are you Gilda de Oliveira's father? He seemed shocked. He said, I am. Or I was. I haven't seen her since she was a little girl.

As she said this, Marina lifted a finger into the air, then let it fall on her lap. Gilda felt a bubble of vomit creep into her throat. She swallowed to keep it down, but her stomach felt limp. She had been convinced her father was dead when her family didn't hear from him after Frieda died three years ago. Gilda couldn't leave the country to attend her mother's funeral because of her immigration status. She had waited by the phone for a call from her father that never came.

Does Beth know? Gilda asked.

Marina frowned. I don't know if Beth knows. You should talk to her about that.

Gilda turned onto her back and stared at the textured hotel ceiling, trying to recall in her memory the shape of her father's face. She asked Marina to tell the story again, but slower. How did she come to recognize him at the bar? Though Marina did not have much more to add, she told the story again and again, until it was etched into Gilda's mind, until the morning sun began to filter through the translucent curtains.

When the ferry to Nantucket arrived at the docks, Gilda waited until the Nantuckophiles disembarked before she stood from her seat. Outside, she was met with a milky blue sky and a breeze so cold it felt brittle in her nostrils. She decided she would walk the eight miles home, not out of punishment or loathing but because she needed to think. It was rare that she could drill into her thoughts without the interruption of a dinner ticket or an alarm clock or the whine of hungry children. She took comfort in knowing she could up and leave with her own two legs and feet, that her body could carry her away if she needed it to. As she walked, she tried to remember details about her father. She knew his name was Manuel and he was a musician from Bahia. He and Frieda were still teenagers when they first fell in love. She only met her father a few times, all before she turned ten years old. Frieda's parents pushed her to marry Beth's father, a white man who looked like Chico Buarque, with light eyes and flowing brown hair. He had a stable job working for the post office, Frieda's father argued, whereas Manuel was a Black man with a thick mustache and made money gig by gig at bars in São Paulo. Gilda could still remember how much she loved it when her father visited, how he would lift her by the waist and throw her over his shoulder, and drum on her butt like a bongo. Compared to Frieda, who could be vain and dismissive, she felt her father was the only person who truly understood her.

Gilda entered her home through the back door and nearly tripped over her work clogs, which were placed where she had left them. She opened her bedroom door and found her chef's coat and pants draped on the stool next to her bed. She sniffed them to check if they were clean, or clean enough, though they always smelled of brown vats of fryolator oil, no matter how many times she washed them. She put her purse down on the bed and undressed to take a shower. She only had another hour or so before she had to be at work. But when she tried to push open the bathroom door, it was locked.

Filha? She knocked. It's Mom. Open the door.

She heard the shower curtain trail shut and then the knob click. Elise opened the door and wrapped her arms around her mother's waist.

You're home, Elise said, the shaving razor tucked away in her back pocket.

Why did you lock the door? Gilda said, patting her back. You know you shouldn't do that.

In this moment, Elise realized there would be parts of her life her mother would never know about, a lesson Gilda had learned about her own mother many years before. It's better to live in ignorance, Gilda thought as she prepared to go to work, than suffer with the pain of knowing.

◆

An invisible rain falls across the island, undetected through the windowpane but strong enough that when Elise walks outside to inspect the flat tire on Gilda's car, her hair and pajamas soak through as though she's radiating an indelible mist from within. Sophie will graduate from high school next week and Elise has decided she will not rely on the Wagners for a ride to the ceremony. She wants to drive Sophie herself; she wants to go to the grocery store to buy a vanilla sheet cake with pink rosettes along the border, and ask them to inscribe it with *Congratulations Sophie!* in purple frosting. There will be no mistaking to whom this cake belongs. Elise wipes the rain off her forehead with the hem of her shirt and pops open the trunk. Gilda has always loved this car, she thinks. A co-worker gave it to her for free when he needed to move back to Colombia in a hurry—a bluish-gray stick shift with leather seats and a six-disc changer. Sophie told her it's been sitting in the driveway with a flat tire for months. Elise pushes aside the items in the trunk—an extra pair of chef's pants decorated with red chili peppers, two worn-down black clogs, a shovel, several dented Bud Light cans, and a pair of jumper cables. She lifts the hidden compartment in the trunk floor and there, staring back at her, is a brand-new spare tire. Elise laughs in disbelief. Did her mother not know the solution was here this whole time?

Three weeks have passed, and they still have not heard from Gilda. Elise tried to call the hospital the day after their dinner at the Wagners' to see if she had checked in, but when the receptionist answered she said the system was down, so she couldn't access the patient list.

How long will it take to fix the system? Elise asked, seated at the kitchen table.

Hmm. I don't know, the receptionist said. Sometimes it's a blip, other times it's out for a few hours.

OK, she said. I can wait.

She endured thirty minutes of ragtime music before the receiver clicked and a dial tone flatlined. They hung up on me, she said out loud. This was why Sophie, the youngest, had always been in charge of calling customer service lines or front desks. Elise redialed and the same receptionist answered. I called about a half hour ago, Elise reminded her. My mom may have checked in yesterday or the day before. She's missing and we're worried she may be at the hospital.

Oh yes, yes, you're right, she says. Sorry about that. The system's back up. Are you the patient's family?

Yes, I'm her daughter, Elise responded. And also, if it makes a difference, I'm neighbors with Sarah Wagner.

Who? the receptionist said.

Yes, I'm the patient's daughter, Elise said again. She heard clicking and the occasional blurry exhale, until the receptionist said, Hmmm, I'm not seeing anything. Have you tried the police station?

Elise thanked her for the suggestion and hung up. Refusing to call the police, under any circumstances, was perhaps the only rule Gilda enforced. When Elise came home from the first grade and announced she wanted to be a detective when she grew up, Gilda took away the plastic badge the school officer had handed out to the students. Absolutely not, she said. They arrest people like us.

But, after two weeks without any word, Elise broke down and decided to involve the police. They told her they would contact her if they had any leads and advised her to complete a missing persons report. Elise seriously considered it but feared that, when she did reemerge, Gilda might never forgive her for offering up her personal information to law enforcement.

Sophie! Elise calls up the attic stairs, shaking the rain from her shoulders. She can hear her sister's footsteps creak across the ceiling.

Yeah? Sophie replies.

I found a spare tire in Mom's trunk.

Sophie descends a few steps on the staircase, her hair stringy and slick with grease. She hasn't showered since classes ended last week, and they've been washing their underwear with dish soap in the bathtub.

Do you know where a car jack might be? Elise asks.

Sophie shrugs. Maybe try the cellar?

Elise hasn't gone to the cellar since she's been home. She's always disliked it down there—the single, bare lightbulb hanging from the ceiling, cobwebs strung across the cinderblock walls. She walks down the wooden plank steps and the smell of rotten garbage hits her nose. She covers her face with one hand and uses the other to flick on the light. In the corner, two months' worth of trash bags are piled in a bulging heap. Houseflies whirl around the stench, landing in the brown liquid pooled underneath.

Sophie! Elise calls again, futilely, not wanting to uncover her mouth.

She searches the workbench against the wall, rummaging through damp cardboard boxes filled with loose screws and washers. A family of silverfish scurries out and Elise coughs and gags, wanting to give up, when a metal object shaped like a car jack appears in her sight line.

She runs up the stairs holding the jack and a box of miscellaneous tools and calls out her sister's name again. Sophie is standing by the car outside, pulling the spare tire from the trunk. Elise steps barefoot onto the wet grass and drops the jack next to the tire.

You were right, Sophie says. I don't know why Mom never checked here. Maybe she didn't know this compartment existed.

Sophie, Elise says. Why are there bags of garbage piled in the cellar?

Ah, she says, squeezing her face into a pinch. I forgot to tell you. We couldn't go to the dump with the car broken.

It smells disgusting down there. I nearly vomited.

Sophie stares at her toes, her shoulders slumped over.

Hey, she says, gesturing toward the jack. At least for once we own a tool we actually need.

They search the internet on their phones for a video demonstration of how to change a flat tire and find one of an older man from Alabama who is changing the tire on an electric-blue Mustang he's rebuilding. They loosen the tire with a lug wrench from the box and Sophie insists she wants to be the one who lies underneath the car to place the jack. Take a picture of me! she shouts to Elise when she's halfway under, her legs protruding like the flattened witch from *The Wizard of Oz*. She centers the jack on the metal frame, then shimmies out and cranks the tire off the ground. They remove the flat tire and push the spare tire into its place.

Sophie remarks on how unbelievable, inconceivable, it is that they had the parts and tools required, and that a man from Alabama guided them through the instructions. They finally have an automobile to drive—the freedom of mobility—something they have lacked for weeks.

Should we take it around the block? Sophie asks, opening the passenger-side door. Elise swipes her hand across the windshield, clearing the wet pollen. Gilda had taken her out to learn how to drive the stick shift several times, but she was an impatient teacher and didn't know how to articulate the details of what to do. She felt it was more intuitive than a matter of instruction and told Elise to feel for when the car was unhappy, listen for the sound of the correct gear. Elise managed to change from second to third gear and third to fourth while the car had momentum, but whenever she reached a stop sign and had to coax it into first gear, the car spasmed and rumbled to a halt.

Everyone in Brazil knows how to drive a stick shift! Gilda told her. If you want to get around in Brazil one day, you have to learn.

She meant it as encouragement, but it was too much pressure for Elise. She opted to take the school bus instead and left for college without having driven beyond the confines of their neighborhood.

Maybe in a bit, Elise responds to Sophie, concealing her worry. I want to clean up first.

Elise is in the shower reviewing the steps in her mind, hot water beating against the crown of her head (clutch down, shift, feather the gas, release the clutch, clutch down, brake, shift down, release the clutch). Finally, the telephone rings. As soon as she hears the sound, she grabs a towel and runs to the kitchen phone, her feet leaving dark impressions on the beige carpet.

Mom? she says as soon as she picks up.

Sophie is upstairs folding the piles of clothes that have accumulated at the foot of her bed. When the word *Mom* reaches her from below the floorboards, she tramps down the stairs and retrieves the wireless receiver in Gilda's bedroom.

Oi, filha, her mother says.

Where are you? Elise asks.

I'm at your aunt's. In Atibaia.

The way she frames her response (to imply she is safe, at a family member's, in the town in Brazil where she grew up) is intentional, so as not to frighten her daughters. But as soon as Sophie says hello, with her sweet younger-sibling voice, Gilda can no longer suppress her tears. Elise sits on the tiled floor in the kitchen, her towel cinched underneath her armpits. They can hear their aunt Beth in the background, running the faucet, closing cabinets, quieting her dogs.

Don't cry, Mom, Elise says.

We're fine. You don't have to worry, Sophie says.

They ask her to explain to them what happened, where she's been the last few weeks. Gilda, her voice bewildered and drained, wants to know if they have seen the stuffed bear she bought Elise for graduation. Elise finds the question strange, but her mother persists. Did you see it, she asks, in my bedroom? Elise confesses she had found the bear when she searched through the duffel bag Gilda had packed for her graduation. She thought about how she would have grumbled when Gilda handed it to her, but how she would have saved the bear for decades to come, carefully packing it in cardboard boxes every time she moved to a new apartment, a new state, a new house, a new country.

Yes, we found the bear, Elise says. Why?

Days before they were supposed to leave for the ceremony, Gilda explains, she posted a photograph of the bear to her Facebook page, leaned against a pillow in its cap and gown. She wrote in the caption: My baby graduates from college on Thursday!! I am a proud mama bear! The post had forty-three likes, mostly from relatives in Brazil. Gilda would periodically check to see if the like count had gone up and if anyone else had commented. This was a normal American thing to do, to post life updates on social media channels. Gilda had been in the United States for more than twenty years. She paid taxes and utility bills, received a paycheck from an employer, sent her two American-born children to public school and occasionally to the doctor, where they used state-run health insurance. When Gilda bought her used moped on Craigslist for two hundred dollars, she applied for a driver's license and then posted a photo announcing she had named the moped Elaine after Julia Louis-Dreyfus's character on *Seinfeld*.

What Gilda didn't fully appreciate was that, like most average Americans, the government had access to her data: they knew where she lived and worked, what car she drove, what time her kids went to school and came home. An ICE official posing as a local community member with the handle @frozenack had been monitoring Gilda's social media accounts for months. When he saw Gilda had posted the photo of the bear with a mention of Elise's graduation, he checked the ferry-passenger records to see if she had made a reservation to travel off the island. As he suspected, she and her daughter Sophie were scheduled to leave on the 6:30 A.M. boat to Hyannis, where they planned to rent a car and drive to Chapel Hill, North Carolina.

Gilda's work visa had been expired for three years when a letter arrived in the mail saying she needed to appear in immigration court. She was five months pregnant with Sophie. On the morning of her scheduled court date, her uterus started cramping. She checked her underwear in the bathroom and it was soaked with blood. So she put Elise on her hip and went to the emergency room instead of going to her court appearance.

What was I supposed to do? Gilda says to her daughters. Go to court with a bloody pillow between my legs? I was twenty-four years old—I didn't understand what was going on.

This decision meant that, eighteen years later, ICE still considered her subject to expedited removal. They called the police department to alert them that her car was sitting in the driveway with a flat tire, so she would be leaving her work shift around midnight traveling by moped.

As Gilda neared the rotary and picked up speed, the breeze levitated her curls off the nape of her neck, a welcome relief after ten long hours standing in a sweltering kitchen. She pushed on her blinker to signal she was veering onto Milestone Road, and as soon as she did, she saw the red-and-blue lights flashing behind her, a strobe against the dark island sky. Her heart quickened. They only want to pass, she told herself. No one wants to be stuck behind a moped going thirty miles an hour down Milestone Road.

Elise glances at Sophie, who is folded upside down on the futon, her legs draped over the back.

They arrested you? This can't be right, Elise says, her mind already sorting through solutions. They can't deport someone without a hearing.

Gilda insists she has a plan, she's going to figure out a loophole. She's resolute that she will return home to be with Sophie and Elise. I'm going to apply for a green card, she says, her speech rapid. Elise is twenty-two now, so I can apply through her.

What can we do to make it happen faster? Sophie asks.

You don't have to do anything, filha. Just stay safe for me, OK? I can't have anything happen to you girls.

I think, Elise says, we should find Dad and tell him to help us.

Your father? Gilda responds, as if she's never heard of him.

He can explain he abandoned us and that you raised us alone.

It doesn't work like that, Elise. They don't care about our reasons.

The three of them pause for a long moment, each clutching a phone receiver tight against their ear. Aunt Beth's dogs bark loudly in the background.

Can we come to Brazil? Sophie interjects, still inverted on the futon. She wants to meet Aunt Beth, she pleads, and the rest of the family.

I'm sorry, Sophie, but you can't. Not right now.

Please, Sophie says again. I want to come.

Not now, honey. You girls can't leave the country. It could hurt my chances for returning—you're the only good reason I have for why I need to come back to the United States. If they think you can leave freely, they won't let me back in.

Sophie tilts herself upright.

We're never going to meet our family, she says and pulls the phone away from her ear.

Elise covers the receiver with her hand and tells Sophie it isn't the right time.

Girls, don't argue, Gilda says. It will happen one day. You'll meet them. I promise.

Elise tries to gesture to Sophie to get back on the phone, but Sophie refuses.

Sophie, Elise says. Talk to Mom.

Speak to her calmly, Gilda tells Elise. Don't yell.

Sophie, perhaps hearing her mother's suggestion on how to deal with her, tosses the phone aside and flees to Gilda's bedroom, locking the door behind her.

She left! Elise says to Gilda. I can't believe she's doing this right now.

It's fine, Elise, she needs her space, Gilda says.

She can't throw a tantrum and leave, Elise says, biting on her bottom lip.

Give her time. It's OK.

I'm going to get her to come back, Elise says. She rests the receiver on the floor and adjusts her towel as she heads to Gilda's bedroom. She taps on the hollow wooden door with her knuckles.

Soph, Elise says. Come talk to us.

Sophie doesn't respond.

Elise turns around, eyeing the receiver swinging by its cord.

This is too much. Just come out.

Elise bangs on the door hard, harder than she intends, but Sophie does not budge. She presses her forehead against the wood and can hear a dresser drawer open, then the squeak of Gilda's mattress.

She's not coming out, Elise tells Gilda, her skin dotted with goosebumps. She won't even respond to me.

Gilda says to let her little sister be for a while. She's trying to sound understanding, but Elise can perceive the worried crackle in her voice. I have to go buy a cellphone before the store closes anyway, she reasons. Then we can talk whenever we want.

Wet strands of hair cling to Elise's neck and shoulders. She closes her mouth and her teeth chatter.

I love you girls, Gilda says. Tell Sophie I say goodbye and I love her.

I love you too, Elise responds. She wants to reassure Gilda they will find a way, they will talk to a lawyer, but her mother hangs up the phone before Elise can speak again.

Sophie hides inside her mother's bedroom until after sundown. Elise is sitting on the couch in the living room scrolling through her phone, an attempt to expel the strained thoughts pervading her body. The cuffs of her shirt are rigid with tears and snot. By the time Sophie slinks out of Gilda's bedroom wearing her mother's yellow sweater, Elise has lost the energy to argue with her sister.

I'm going to scramble an egg, Sophie says, her words small. Do you want one?

I'm not hungry, Elise says, eyes glued to her phone screen.

Sophie opens up the refrigerator and pulls out a carton of eggs. She cracks four into a bowl and whisks them into a froth.

What did I miss? she asks.

Mom got a cellphone. It doesn't have video chat, but we can text her now. She called back a while later and sounded in better spirits.

This straightens Sophie's spine a bit. Elise waits for her to say something about their mother's situation, a reflection on how difficult, impossible, it will be for her to receive a green card and return to the United States. They have always known that if Gilda was detained and deported, it would mean she would be banned from entering the country for at least ten years. She says she plans to apply for a waiver to the ten-year bar, but she needs to prove that Elise and Sophie would face extreme hardship without their mother in the country. That was the legal term: *extreme hardship*.

You know, it's pretty fucked up what Dad did to Mom, Sophie says, pouring the egg mixture into a frying pan.

Elise rubs the tip of her nose, feeling for the pop of cartilage.

Yeah. I always thought they had this passionate love affair, but now I think it's kind of horrible, she says.

He got her drunk, Sophie continues. And that's basically the story of how they fell in love.

Then she got pregnant, twice, and he left her here without a visa or any money, Elise says.

Mom would say we were worth it. Sophie hands Elise a coffee mug full of eggs, the plates and bowls all dirty in the sink.

She would, Elise says, and rests the mug between her thighs.

Sophie sits on the futon next to her sister and stares into the distorted reflection of the kitchen in the living room window. Then she turns and wraps her arms around Elise, clutching her in a tight sideways embrace. Elise can feel her sister's warm face against her shoulder.

It's OK, Elise says, stroking the side of her head. We'll talk to her again soon.

✦

Elise searches for Sophie in the congested hallway, blocked by matching bodies sheathed in blue polyester caps and gowns. She finds her pressed against a cement wall that has been painted white, clutching her yearbook against her chest. The Wagners appear a moment later—she hadn't realized they had been trailing her. She hands Sophie a bouquet of sunflowers and asks if she wants to attend the school-organized after-party. An usher had informed her it would be held underneath a giant white tent on the football field.

I don't know, Sophie says. I kind of want to go home.

Come on, Mrs. Wagner says. Let's go for a bit. You only graduate high school once. Well, if you're lucky.

Would you want to come? Elise asks Gilda.

N-o, it—you—I love— she says, appearing in a blur of pixelated squares on Elise's cellphone, transmitted from a webcam at an internet café in Atibaia.

I think she's saying goodbye, Sophie says, waving.

Elise holds the phone above her head to try to improve the signal, but Gilda complains Elise is shaking the camera too much and they decide to end the call. They walk down to the football field and the four of them, Sophie, Elise, and the Wagners, stand together in a semicircle near a buffet of chocolate strawberries, cut cheeses, and cantaloupe slices. Mr. Wagner sways in place with his hands in his pockets and makes small talk with a passing father while Mrs. Wagner drinks sparkling water through a paper straw. Elise wonders if anyone assumes they've adopted her and Sophie as their own children. She inches away when Mrs. Wagner tries to lean over and fix the tag on her shirt collar.

After about half an hour, Sophie asks if they can leave the party. Her favorite English teacher has already signed her yearbook, she says, and everyone else can sign it another time. Elise agrees and, as they cross the parking lot, admits it was hard to feel celebratory when she had to carry their mother around on video call, tilting her toward the stage as Sophie collected her diploma, moderating her volume and searching for better reception.

Yeah, and I'll forever be known as the orphan girl who isn't going to college, Sophie says, tossing the sunflowers and her yearbook into the back seat. Even Tommy O'Connell is going to community college.

You're smarter than Tommy O'Connell, Elise says. And you're not an orphan. You're going to work for a bit, make a lot of money this summer, and apply next round. There's nothing wrong with that.

Elise sits behind the wheel and pulls down her skirt to protect her thighs from the sun-scorched leather. She adjusts the air-conditioning and a vague scent of chicken soup permeates from the vents. The parking lot is crowded, so she eases the car into first gear and stops to allow a family to cross in front of them. The father is wearing a camel suit, the mother an A-line floral skirt. The graduate son spots Sophie and flashes her a wide, proud grin.

That guy has never spoken to me before, Sophie says. But now that we're wearing the same outfit he thinks we're friends.

Elise glides around the curb and approaches the four-way stop outside the high school swimming pool, but when she attempts to make a right turn, the car stalls sideways across the intersection. Sophie unzips her robe, revealing Gilda's yellow sweater underneath.

Try again, she says and places Elise's hand on the gear stick. Elise can feel the heavy impatience from the other drivers, their eyes trained on her. She pushes the clutch in and rotates the key in the ignition, then presses down on the accelerator. The car jerks and stalls again.

Fuck, Elise says. I don't know if I can do this, Sophie. We might have to push.

A black Range Rover creeps a foot past the stop sign behind them, vying to move his car around Elise's, but the road is too narrow and he has to reverse. On the sidewalk, a group of male students stops to spectate. One makes a heckling sound in their direction.

Shut it, Jeffrey! Sophie yells, rolling down her window, and the boys huddle together and howl with laughter.

You can do it, she says to Elise. You drove perfectly this morning.

In the rearview mirror, Elise can see Mr. Wagner's cherry-red truck three cars down. She pushes on the clutch and turns the ignition again.

Easy, Sophie whispers as Elise touches the accelerator. The car rumbles forward and Elise completes the turn.

Yes, keep going, Sophie says and grips her sister's shoulder, but Elise brushes her hand away and flips the AC vent. At the rotary, she encounters another stop sign but manages to idle momentarily and roll while the car still has momentum.

You know the cops will pull you over for that, Sophie says.

Yes, I know, Sophie. But if you want to make it home we're going to have to take some shortcuts.

They are relieved when Elise pulls into their shell driveway and cranks the emergency brake. Sophie balls up her robe as they walk through the front door and tosses it onto the green futon. Elise slides the *Congratulations Sophie!* vanilla sheet cake with pink rosettes from the refrigerator and places it on the kitchen table.

Cut me a massive slice, Sophie says, reclining on the futon, her feet rested on the armrest. I want to eat the *Congratulations* and get sick off sugar.

Elise passes Sophie a plate over the back of the sofa. She takes a bite and drops a dollop of frosting on Gilda's sweater, the cotton fabric already speckled with food stains. Sophie hasn't changed her clothes since they spoke to Gilda last week. She's also stopped sleeping in the attic with Elise, instead curling up in their mother's bed at night. Elise hasn't confronted Sophie about it—she understands well enough that they are processing in their own ways—but she cannot fathom falling asleep in their mother's scent, surrounded by their mother's artifacts, the bedroom a Chernobyl of the day she was taken.

Elise presses her fork into a rosette and watches the frosting splay through the tines.

What are we going to do with this house? she says after a moment, seated behind Sophie at the kitchen table.

What do you mean? Sophie says.

I mean, what are we going to do about the house now that Mom is gone?

Sophie frowns and takes another bite of cake.

What kind of question is that? We live here, she says.

But we don't own the house or any of the furniture. Everything is rented, and it's falling apart.

Sophie looks around.

No it's not.

Soph, the bathroom sink stopped working yesterday. And everything smells like mom's stale cigarettes.

So? We fixed the car. We can fix the sink.

What about the piles of garbage in the cellar? Who's going to drive them to the dump? Me?

I'll drive, Sophie says. I can figure it out.

Elise laughs and looks at Gilda's bedroom door.

It's not so easy, she says, and licks the pink frosting off her fork.

Sophie decides not to respond and instead ducks behind the futon and continues eating her cake. Elise scrapes the rest of her slice into the garbage, turns on the faucet, and scrubs the dishes, clattering her plate and fork loudly to try to make a point, though what the point is she isn't quite sure. She stacks the dishes in the drying rack on top of the dishes that have been there for days, then removes the broom from the gap between the refrigerator and the counter and sweeps the floor. After she finishes sweeping, she takes the condiments from the refrigerator door and sprays a bleach solution on the spills that have hardened against the plastic.

Sophie peeks her eyes above the back of the futon.

All right, she says, standing. I'm going to the dump.

I'm not driving again, Elise says, shielded by the refrigerator door. We just got home.

No, *I'm* driving, Sophie says.

Elise continues to scrub, calling Sophie's bluff, but Sophie marches across the living room and opens the door to the cellar.

If you want to come, then help me move the garbage bags. I'm going either way.

She stomps down the wooden cellar stairs and props open the metal hatch door that leads to the backyard. Elise can see the top of Sophie's head through the living room window as she drags two garbage bags to the side of the car, then disappears around the back of the house and returns with two more. Finally, when she's brought all fifteen bags of trash to the front lawn, Sophie steps into the driver's seat and fidgets with the ignition. The clutch, Elise thinks, peering from the edge of the window. Sophie, you need the clutch. The car engine stutters. You're going to burn the transmission.

Gilda had once told them a story about a time when Sophie was a toddler and she threw a water glass onto the kitchen floor to see it smash. Gilda hurried to clean up the shards, but she missed one, and Sophie stepped on it several days later. She fell back onto her diaper and stretched her foot around to see where she had been pierced, then fainted at the sight of her own blood.

Elise turns away from the window and throws her arms into the air.

Fine, she says to the silent, empty house. You win.

They can only fit eight of the fifteen trash bags in the car: five in the back and three in the trunk. Sophie takes the sunflowers and yearbook inside and lays out towels across the seats to protect them from the unidentified seeping liquid. She does not comment when Elise sits in front of the wheel and turns on the car. They drive with the windows rolled down to circulate the air and a Top 40 station playing on the radio. Elise relaxes into the bends, finding a rhythm with the gears. The roadside shrubs pass in a whirl, and the clouds blanket a gray-lit sky.

It almost looks like a mountain, Elise says as they approach the landfill's chain-link gates. Seagulls circle and caw over the rolling hills made of grass-covered refuse. Elise backs in front of the recycling chutes and they each haul a rattling translucent bag to a cement platform where glass has to be tossed and shattered into a dumpster below. Sophie digs into the bag and pulls out a wine bottle.

Try to hit that green one, she says, pointing to a jagged emerald cylinder jutting on the far side of the bin. Elise winds up and tosses a marinara jar, but it lands short. Sophie nails it with the wine bottle in one flawless shot, sending a spray of glittering glass across the dumpster. The eruption startles a flock of gulls nearby.

This is kind of therapeutic, Sophie says, and throws another.

I can't believe this trash was sitting in the cellar for months, Elise says, shaking off a pill bug crawling up the bag. She understands it sounds accusatory, but she has a clawing need to point it out.

Sophie turns to face Elise, pressing her back against the hand railing.

I get it. You don't like the house. You want to move to New York City with your college friend. So leave. I'm not holding you back.

Elise can see a glossy shine forming across Sophie's eyes. She laces her arm loosely through her sister's.

I'm not going to leave you, Elise says. I'm not going anywhere until we figure out how to bring Mom back.

Sophie sighs deeply and stares down at her feet. A man wearing khaki overalls carries a bag of brown bottles onto the platform.

He stops a few feet away and overturns the bag into the dumpster; the sound of the crash burrows into Elise's spine.

Mom hates living here, Sophie says. Why would she want to come back?

Elise glances at Sophie, confused. Because, she says. She's been taken from her children and the country where she's lived for most of her life. Of course she wants to come back.

Then what do we do about it? File paperwork with the same system that deported her in the first place? Sophie drops another glass bottle into the dumpster.

It's the only option we have, Elise says. We have to try.

They retrieve the rest of the garbage bags from the car and throw them into the bin for noncompostables. Elise closes the trunk and Sophie declares she wants to drive back to their neighborhood. They sit facing forward, Sophie in the driver's seat with the keys dangling from her finger, a rotten-vegetable scent hanging in the air. She inserts the key into the ignition. Clutch, Elise reminds her. Sophie shakes her head and releases her hands from the steering wheel. You're never going to learn if you don't try, Elise says and realizes the tone is her mother's. It is enough to break Sophie's confidence. Actually—can you do it? she says. Elise waits for a moment to check if she's sure, then Sophie climbs over the center console and watches from the passenger seat as Elise crosses around the hood.

When they arrive home, Sophie retires into Gilda's room and closes the door. Elise ascends the attic stairs holding her cellphone. Their room isn't as it was—the makeshift closet they built out of blankets has fallen to the floor, and Sophie's twin bed is stripped bare. The humid summer air has intensified the saccha-rine smell of the wood. She sits on Sophie's bed and smooths the quilted mattress with her palm. She thinks: If this was my last hour inside this house, would I miss it? The thought builds its own house inside her mind, until the sound of a ringing cellphone jangles from her hand.

Hey, Sheb, Elise says, answering. Did you make it to Saint-Tropez?

Yes, I'm at the hotel, Sheba says, a little too enthusiastically. It's so nice here.

Elise sighs and stares up at the rafters. It was Sophie's gradua-tion today.

How are you two feeling?

I don't know. Anxious, Elise says. This house is making my skin crawl. It's reminding me of my mom . . . in a bad way.

You always have an open invitation, you know, to my family's house on island.

Elise wipes her nose with her wrist. She had a faint awareness that Sheba's parents recently inherited her grandfather's summer house on Nantucket. Elise wanted to know more, but Sheba wouldn't directly say where it was or what the house looked like, only that the division of assets had been contentious.

But you're in France, Elise says.

It's not a big deal—I'll give you the code to the gate. Let your-self in.

Your moms won't care?

No, not at all. They think you're a good influence on me.

I don't know, Elise says. I'll have to think about it.

Whenever you want, Sheba says. Just let me know so I can have the people open it up for you.

Elise thanks her for the offer but is unable to conceive of it as real, the idea of an empty house on the island available for her usage. They talk for a while about how affordable everything is in Europe and how, if the United States elects another fascist president, Sheba will find a way for them to move there together. In the months leading up to graduation, Elise had been searching for jobs in New York City related to her environmental studies major, maybe something in policy work, but she was finding it difficult to secure an interview without a local address. Elise couldn't confront this paradox on her own (she needed to find an apartment in order to land a job, when she didn't have a job to afford an apartment), so Sheba had offered to get a place where they could live together as roommates, an apartment with an elaborate fireplace and parquet floors, she said, and a terrace that faced the Hudson River.

She and Sheba say their goodbyes and Elise tosses her phone onto the mess of clothes in her suitcase. The sun is burying itself in the earth, lighting up the backs of trees. It's in these transient moments, Elise thinks, that her house and the island feel most familiar, as though the years she's been gone can fit into a small, contained memory. She didn't know when she left for college that she wouldn't return for four years, that in that time her desire for home would stretch and contract, strengthening in some ways, weakening in others. The day she left to go to Chapel Hill, Sophie and her mom drove her to the ferry, and as they said goodbye, Elise made Sophie promise she'd call and tell her what she did every day, even if she didn't do anything. Call me and tell me anything you want—your homework assignments, which teachers you like, which you don't like, what books you read, what you eat for breakfast. Gilda stood behind them, waiting for her turn to give Elise a hug. When the foghorn blew and the dock workers began to untie the ramp, Elise ran out onto the deck and waved as the ferry left the harbor. She kept trying to spot Gilda and Sophie among the other waving people as the boat exited onto the open sea, but they were too far away, a compilation of colors, fragments of light reflected on the island's shore.

PART II

The Guest

A fleet of wooden boats approaches the island's western shore, sails beating against the spotty gusts of wind like outstretched chests crying out for battle. On the docks, onlookers slosh IPAs in plastic cups, pugnacious from the mix of beer and salty air. They cheer for the *Alerion,* an underdog yacht that has nudged ahead with an early starboard tack. The crew lets out the sheets, their cheeks red and chafed, trying not to wobble the boat in the still sea. Overhead, a herring gull releases a blue crab from its clutches, dropping it onto the dock. Its back cracks from impact. Clouds drift across the sun, doling out warmth by the spoonful. These are the signs that summertime on Nantucket has officially arrived. The ferry schedule is up to five trips daily, the rotary is plugged with traffic, and store windows that have been vacant through winter are decorated with island-branded tote bags, needlepoint pillows, and floppy hats.

It's nearing seven A.M. and Elise can still hear the tambourine rattle of crickets in the brush, the slick pavement against her tires. Her phone is wedged between her legs as she drives, and Gilda is talking on the other end, her voice broken up by exhaustion: As soon as you can, Elise, will you text me your social security number? Sophie's too if you can get it from her.

Sure, Elise responds. What do you need my social security number for?

The immigration forms. It's important you give me your and your sister's exact numbers. The lawyer says if I mess it up, they'll reject the application.

Elise rubs her fingers across the indents on the steering wheel.

I didn't know you found a lawyer? she says.

Your aunt knows him. He does immigration work for people here.

He's a good lawyer! Beth shouts in Portuguese. He helps a lot of people in the neighborhood! Elise sighs, imagining the kind of lawyer her aunt might know: a man in an oversized brown suit with a for-hire ad posted at a bus stop.

Your aunt is driving me nuts, Gilda says, her hand cupped over the phone. This is how loud she talks all the time.

I'm not loud, Beth yells. Your mother is too quiet! She's lost her voice after all these years.

Elise pulls into a beach parking lot on the west side of the island and sees her boss, Steve, sitting in his Jeep, knees propped up on the steering wheel, playing a blinging jewel game on his phone.

I have to go, Mom. I just pulled into work.

OK, my love. Don't forget about the social security numbers.

I won't, she says.

Good luck on your first day. Say hello to the little birdies for me.

Elise walks over to Steve, who passes her a small cup of black coffee from Cumberland Farms and moves a pile of deer antlers from the front seat to the back. Steve took the doors off his Jeep years ago and he couldn't put them back on if he tried—the hinges have rusted into a dusty orange oxide. Welcome back, he says as Elise climbs inside. You can take one of those antlers if you want. I found them in the moors yesterday. She sips her coffee, noticing the craggy, red-speckled beard he's grown since the last time she saw him. Nice beard, she says.

He rubs his knuckles against it. I've had this thing forever. How long has it been since you saw me?

Not since I was in high school.

Damn, he says, and drives onto the beach. A lot has changed since you've been gone.

He guides his wheels along two tracks in the sand, the ocean's skin flickering on one side, silky glares of dune grass on the other. The stretch of land leading to the estuary has eroded to a jagged strip, bitten like a watermelon rind. She takes her phone from her bag and turns it off to preserve battery, since there isn't cell service on this part of the island. When they reach a dinghy anchored to the shore, Steve dons a pair of black rubber waders and pulls the boat up so Elise can step inside. He steers them across the yellow foamy waters—the sun awake and vibrant—to a smaller strip of sand.

Don't forget to wear a hat today. He wipes his forehead with the back of his hand. It's August in June, apparently.

Elise jumps off the bow. He passes her a cooler, a tackle box, a beach chair, and an umbrella, and then he says goodbye, explaining he has to get back to the office or he'd stick around for her welcome party. You already know the ropes, he shouts. Just keep an eye on those little buggers! Then he motors the puttering boat to the other side of the water.

Elise sets up her beach chair and umbrella and retrieves a notebook and pencil from her backpack. Her fingers tremble as she writes the date at the top of the page. Like peering through a fish-eye lens—that's how she feels about returning to work as an endangered species monitor, the same job she had when she was in high school. She knows Steve is doing her a favor letting her work for him, especially on such short notice. The endangered piping plovers she will keep watch over have migrated to a secluded area where there isn't much risk of loose dogs and tourists interfering with the eggs. He said he could only offer her one dollar more an hour than what she earned in high school. She had no leverage to negotiate, especially now that she and Sophie have to split the rent. At least it's somewhat related to her degree, she told herself.

She scans the beach, searching for the birds. They always appear indistinguishable at first: bobbling gray spheres, smaller than her fist, their legs twittering along the sand. When she first started monitoring, she'd try to follow and memorize a single bird, but the exercise felt like a parlor trick, where a ball is hidden and shuffled among overturned, rotating cups. After about a month her eyes adjusted to their subtle differences, the way identical twins, over time, reveal their individual features. She spots one by the shore and raises her government-issued binoculars, following it as it patters by the shoreline. She observes the way the wind tousles its thimble body, the nimbus-gray feather-shell on its back, its protracted footprints, indented in the wet sand like the inside of a peace symbol.

A wash of tide teases up the shore, enveloping open-mouthed scallop shells and horseshoe crabs bellied up to the sand. The birds have laid eggs. Four butter-beige, black-crackled spheres that are mostly, but not completely, indistinguishable from the sand. The pair have already chosen their ideal territory to sit and brood— about ten feet from the tide line—though none of these locations are actually ideal. Building a nest in the middle of exposed sand, as these birds do, means the eggs must hide in plain sight. In wide, sweeping glances, the eggs are sand, until sunlight flickers against their sleek edges, and then they are not sand, they are found.

Elise vibrates her lips together, exasperated by how confidently they've chosen the worst place to procreate. Steve has already hammered in a fence around the area where the eggs are, with stakes spaced far enough apart for the birds to fit through but too close for larger predators or humans. She records the necessary data points in her composition notebook: adult count (four), fledgling count (zero), number of eggs (four), evidence of hatching (N/A), weather (hot & bright). Then she retreats underneath the umbrella and curls her toes into the cold underbelly of sand.

A wind twirls, sweeping up dried dune grass. Elise imagines what would happen if a large wave collapsed over the beach with her out there, alone, no cellphone service, no transportation. A tsunami comes to mind, but she envisions turquoise water, not the dark, jeweled ocean surrounding the island. The wave approaches as a slow, menacing wall that never crashes, only drifts and swallows. In actuality, she knows it won't be something as dramatic as a tsunami that takes her on this beach, but a more stealth and invisible disaster, a persistent chipping away at the sand dunes, until each pine tree, rosehip, deer, and rabbit falls into the sea, from whence they all, we all, originally formed.

Around four P.M. Steve returns to pick her up in the dinghy. How was your first day? he asks, pivoting the boat around. Really good, Elise says, though she feels delirious from spending eight hours in the sun. When she reaches her car, she blasts the AC immediately, pointing the still-hot air at her neck, and turns on her phone. A missed text message from Sophie lights up on the screen.

Sophie: working again tonight :(

Elise types out a response.

Elise: Noooo

Three dots pulsate on the screen.

Sophie: Covering someone's shift. And I have to work again in the am

Elise clicks her phone screen off and tosses it on the passenger's seat. Sophie is waitressing at the Lunch Counter again, a casual restaurant in town staffed mostly with women from Eastern Bloc countries who wear T-shirts of disgruntled cartoon characters, like a Tweety bird who hates mornings and loves coffee. In the past two weeks, Elise has really only seen her sister in the brief period between when Sophie returns from her lunch shift and before she leaves. She dreads going home when Sophie isn't there—the empty house ignites in her a dull panic—even though Sophie spends most of her time in Gilda's bedroom, retiring there after work, sleeping in her bed every night. Sophie recently found a box of Gilda's photographs and letters, a private box that isn't meant for them, and organized its contents in a quasi shrine on Gilda's dresser.

Elise exits the beach parking lot, drives to the rotary, and turns onto Milestone Road. Her hand tenses around the gear stick—she shifts up to third, then immediately downshifts back to second. Sheba has offered multiple times for her to stay at her guest house whenever she needs, but Elise has yet to take her up on it. Sheba even asked the caretaker to prepare the house just in case.

Elise takes a quick left onto Polpis Road, rather than driving straight on Milestone. Just for a little while, she thinks, to see what it's like. She follows the scenic curves to Sheba's summer mansion, slowing to read the numbers on the mailboxes as she drives by. She enters two incorrect driveways before she realizes the house is on the other side of an ornate metal gate, not visible from the road. Elise idles at the top of the stone driveway, Gilda's car sputtering a hard rumble every few minutes. Her mind goes blank—she can't remember the code that Sheba had given her. She'd sent it by text weeks ago, but that message is lost in a conversation about Sheba's economics professor who had grazed her breast after graduation, over her right nipple, after telling her how challenging of a student she had been.

But then Elise remembers—1026. Of course, Sheba's birthday. The bars ache open, revealing sheets of pin-straight grass, cut down the middle by a chevron stone drive. Sheba's summer home—the main house—is a two-story mansion with gray shingles accented by white trim along the gabled roofs. On the top floor are balconies that overlook the tumbling moors, and on the bottom floor is a wraparound porch with weathered Adirondack chairs and matching teak side tables. Though the house meets Historic District Commission requirements, Sheba's moms have marked their modern aesthetic where they can. The landscaping is minimal, forgoing the floral prowess most wealthy summer residents pay gardeners to maintain year-round (even infusing the soil with acid to force a blue, not pink, hue to their hydrangea bushes). The windows do not have lavish, prize-winning boxes. Not even a stray dandelion pokes out from the flat blue-green lawn, and the property is bordered by a meticulous, even privet hedge.

As Elise's car rolls forward, three cottontail rabbits chewing on the grass flee into the bushes. Sheba had mentioned that the house was huge, but Elise never could have imagined the extent to which that is true. She parks in a cul-de-sac at the end of the driveway in front of a stone path to the guest house and pauses to collect herself before exiting the car.

Relative to the main house, the guest house appears petite and shy, though by most standards it is house-sized, larger than Elise's house, larger than most houses she has been inside. Though she was told she would be the only one using the property this summer, her heart is beating like she shouldn't be there, like someone might mistake her for an intruder. She walks up onto the porch and reaches into a lantern where the caretaker has hidden a spare key. The front door pops open and the sickly-sweet smell of stagnant air rushes out, air that has been trapped inside storm windows all winter, cannibalizing on stagnant toilet water and sugar bowls. The guest house is where Sheba's late grandfather's memory has been preserved, through hunting ornaments and a Thoreau color palette. Elise steps into a small mudroom lined with brown tiles. Several rubber rain jackets sag on the wall hooks, mummified in their unworn state. From the mudroom emerges the kitchen, with its olive-green cabinets and an oak peninsula that faces the living room. A calfskin rug is stretched and framed on the wall across from the stone fireplace, and on the mantel is a line of taxidermy animals: a small fox, a guinea hen, a jackrabbit, and a pheasant.

Elise places her bag on the kitchen counter, enters the living room, and sits on one of the washed-velvet sofas. She does not move for several seconds, waiting for a crash or bang to startle her. Elise hasn't slept soundly in days. Every sound her own house emits seeps into her consciousness and multiplies, until all she hears is noise. But Sheba's house remains silent; the startle never comes.

I finally made it to your guest house. It's SO nice, she writes to Sheba, who replies instantly: GOOD! Pierre said he left food in the kitchen and some goodies upstairs. Enjoy it!!! Elise returns to the kitchen and opens the refrigerator, where she finds three cartons of lemonade, a glass jug of almond milk, and a bowl of Meyer lemons. In the cabinet above the espresso and coffee machines is a box of dried spaghetti and a jar of marinara sauce. Sophie won't be home until after midnight anyway, she thinks, filling a pot with water. She prepares the pasta, pours herself a glass of tap water with a squeeze of lemon, and sits out on the porch to watch the sky turn.

When the horizon transforms from blue to pink to a deep purple, she returns inside and switches on the television. The screen beams across the room, lighting up the taxidermy on the mantel. Elise's mind keeps running, leaping over thought after thought. Would Sophie even notice if I didn't come home? Would she care? She hand-washes the pasta pot, bowl, and fork in the sink, dries them with a dish towel, and returns them to the cabinets. I'll see what the upstairs looks like before I leave, she thinks. She ascends the stairs and finds two simple white bed-rooms, each with an en suite bathroom. She sits on top of the goose down comforter. Next to her is a white robe and a pin-striped linen pajama set with a note from Pierre, the caretaker: *Welcome, guest!* She runs her hands over the textured quilt, then stands to remove her shirt, bra, shorts, and underwear, remnants of sand falling onto the floor. One night, she thinks, putting on the soft linen pajamas. She sends a text to Sophie explaining she'll be gone for the night, in a way that unintentionally makes it seem like she's doing Sheba a favor, checking on the house for her. Then she walks to the windows and opens them wide, deciding she will sleep with the outside air in. On the bookshelf in the hallway is a copy of Marilynne Robinson's *Housekeeping*. She retrieves it, then peels back the tightly tucked covers and gets into bed. The house is so quiet, she can hear the air move. She imagines how far she would have to walk before she encounters another human being—through Sheba's lawn, over the split rail fence and into the moors, across scrub oak and tupelo trees, down the fire road and over a small meadow where the closest neighborhood begins. She clicks the light off and turns onto her stomach, then reaches her hand into the linen pajama pants. She pleasures herself, slowly, until her body shakes—for the first time in months—and gives in to a blissful, enchanted sleep.

✦

Elise opens her eyes several hours later and looks at the glowing
mechanical clock on the nightstand. Four A.M. She's unclear
whether she fell asleep and has spontaneously awakened, or if
she's been awake the entire time. Her scent fills the covers with
pancake-batter sweetness. She shifts to click on the table lamp
when an arrow of noise breaks through from downstairs. The
whoosh of compressed air, the screen door clicking shut. A police
siren whirls faintly in the distance. Someone is in the house, Elise
thinks. Sophie doesn't know the address. She wouldn't have been
able to enter through the gate anyway, unless she found a way to
climb over. She taps her cellphone screen. No text messages.
More sounds emanate: cabinets slamming shut, the refrigerator
door opening. Her skin tightens. Had she locked the front door
with the key before going upstairs? The bedroom window is
about twenty feet off the ground, she estimates. There aren't any
bushes to cushion her fall, but there is a lawn, at least. If she broke
her ankle, she would only need to run far enough to reach the
scrub oaks and hide in the moors.

She squeezes her hands into tight fists, an attempt to wake her
body up. On the dresser is a nail file with a pointed tip. It sounds

like only one person is downstairs. Possibly a drunk teenager who was partying in the moors and wandered onto the property searching for his parents' vacation rental. She stands, picks up the nail file, and slowly tiptoes down the steps.

In the blue-moon darkness, she can discern a figure sitting on the floor. Their initial encounter is quick, not more than a few seconds, before the figure mutters, Harry? in a garbled breath, and Elise realizes it's Sheba. She flips on the light. Sheba is in an oversized gray pajama shirt, her legs flopped against the tiles, with a tub of yogurt in her lap.

Harry? Sheba asks, yogurt gurgling in her mouth.

Jesus, Sheba, you really scared me. What are you doing on Nantucket? Elise picks up the yogurt and puts it back in the fridge. Sheba watches her, vacant, then drops the spoon she's holding. She probably decided to take an Ambien to help correct her jet lag, Elise deduces, even though Sheba knows she gets horrible side effects from sleeping pills. In college she once took an Ambien after an all-night study session, broke into the communal refrigerator, and gorged on someone else's birthday cake.

I didn't know you were coming back from Europe, Elise says. Why didn't you say something when I texted you?

Harry? Sheba tilts her chin up. Her eyes take a circuitous route around Elise's face, down her body, and to her feet.

Please stop asking for Harry. It's weirding me out. Elise tugs on Sheba's wrist until she stands.

Is Harry here?

No, Harry's not here. She guides Sheba toward the stairs, one arm steadied around her waist.

I hate Harry. He's *not* your boyfriend. You're *my* friend.

Elise pulls back the covers and maneuvers Sheba's hips onto the bed until she sits, then coaxes her to lie down.

My best friend. Sheba reaches for Elise, hooks her finger into Elise's shirt collar, and yanks down, exposing her right breast. OK, OK. Elise unhooks herself. Time for bed. She tucks Sheba under the covers tightly, in a swaddle. Most sleeping people have a plump ease to them—glistening and vulnerable—but Sheba's face looks contorted and pained, as though her subconscious wants to wake up, but the sleeping pills are holding her in a pressure-cooked slumber. Elise slips under the covers and presses her leg against Sheba's. Finally, she stops fussing and rests.

Sheba and Elise met on the first day of college, in a basement-turned–coffee shop that sold matcha lattes, vape pods, and make-your-own s'mores. Elise had been dazed most of the day, unsure where she was supposed to be, wandering through the campus's alienating beige halls. When she walked into the coffee shop, she found Sheba wearing a sweatshirt with NANTUCKET emblazoned across the front. Normally, tourist love of her hometown would be a sign that Elise should heel turn in the opposite direction, but she was feeling homesick, and so her heart dizzied at the sight of her island's name in an unfamiliar landscape. She walked straight to Sheba and pointed at her chest.

That's my home. I'm from there.

Sheba raised her eyes from her book, a battered copy of M.F.K. Fisher's *Consider the Oyster,* and said: What do you mean *from*?

I was born there. It's where I grew up.

Stop it, Sheba said. Sit, tell me everything.

Sheba was born and raised in New York City by two moms, one of whom was the heir to the Play-Doh fortune and the other a retired hedge fund manager who invested early in cryptocurrency. I'm a test tube baby, she told Elise proudly when they met, which meant her body and her soul were created by science. At the time Elise knew very little about the Tribeca lifestyle in which Sheba had grown up, the seemingly nameless au pair who changed her diapers and taught her French, the self-designed curriculum at her Upper East Side private school, the assets and the trusts, estranged family members and inheritance rifts.

I'm not me when I'm in New York, Sheba told Elise, sipping on an iced espresso through a short straw. I'm me when I'm on Nantucket.

Sheba started summering on the island at her grandfather's house when she was in utero, a tradition that ended abruptly when she turned seventeen and her mother and grandfather decided they were in an all-out feud over something having to do with her other mother, Holly, and the changes she wanted to make to their financial portfolio. Sheba brought up a sepia-toned photo on her phone of her mother Helen, outstretched on the beach, her pregnant belly glimmering in the sun. We probably won't be back until my grandfather dies, Sheba said, a premonition that turned out to be entirely true.

So much of Sheba and Elise's relationship grew, remarkably, around the cracks of their differences. They returned to each other after three summer breaks apart, Sheba's study abroad in Florence, consecutive semesters without one shared class, and now, college graduation. Perhaps it was because they had met early on as freshmen in desperate need of friendship. Sheba grew up as an only child in private-school social networks, with strategic alliances and best friends who doubled as sworn enemies. She had never shared a bed with a friend before she met Elise, and Elise had never spent more than a week off Nantucket before she met Sheba. In the context of dorm rooms and dining halls, where everyone lived in relative squalor and sat in the same rows of rigid metal chairs, it was easy to glaze over the chasms that separated and shaped them.

A few months into college, Gilda noticed her daughter had started to dress in designer clothes, gifted by Sheba, and say things rich people say, like when Elise told her she was going to delegate her dirty laundry to a laundromat so she could better prioritize her schoolwork. Her hair looked different too—Gilda used to give her daughters a trim once a year with a pair of kitchen shears in the bathtub, a story Sheba found so horrifying she took Elise to her first professional hairdresser and taught her how to use a flat iron. Gilda told Elise she needed to pay back the money Sheba gave her, even if it took her ten years, because, according to Gilda, it's against women's rights to live off of someone else's income, even if that someone is also a woman. Neither Gilda nor Elise understood, really understood, how rich Sheba was by way of her parents, who dispensed their daughter's money through a well-monitored trust. Sheba had enough inheritance to live four lifetimes; she didn't have enough room, figuratively speaking, for the money she possessed, so she felt she needed to offload it to Elise as a matter of principle, for her own spiritual cleansing.

Sheba believed their polarity magnetized them together. She loved to remark on how perfect she and Elise looked as a pair in front of a floor-length mirror, like two complementary colors on opposite ends of the color wheel. Sheba used to tell Elise that, if she ever got a nose job, she would bring the doctor a photograph of Elise's nose as a reference. Elise could not imagine her nose on Sheba's face, a nose she saw as her mother's, along with the beauty mark she and Gilda shared on their left cheeks. But she was amused by Sheba's outlandish humor, her hedonism, the ways she impulsively pursued a good time. Sheba's idyllic notions of their fated friendship flattered Elise, especially considering that Sheba's life seemed infinite with possibilities, and yet she chose Elise every time. Sheba often said she trusted Elise more than she even trusted her own family, and Elise would embrace her in response, express gratitude, never able to confess that she couldn't feel the same way; their friendship would never surpass the bond she had with Sophie.

Elise wakes the following morning and feels her leg entangled with Sheba's. She lifts the covers, and at first, she cannot tell one limb from another. Seconds pass—five, four, three, two—before Sheba shoots up, the sleeping pill finally losing its grip, her thin blond hair tangled against the back of her head. She shouts, panting:

Elise—Where are we?

◆

Elise leans her elbows on the guest house's oak peninsula counter-top, stirring sugar into her coffee with a curved silver teaspoon as she watches Helen and Holly from behind the screen door. Helen is standing in the driveway directly outside the main house with white buds inserted into her ears. She is wearing a neatly pressed shirt and a pair of reading glasses pushed back on her head, hold-ing her hair off her face. She paces a few steps in one direction, a few steps in the other, nodding and looking very stern. Then she stops abruptly and makes a face at Holly, who cocks her hand into a gun shape and holds her index finger to her temple, then drops her arm and keeps walking. Yes. Fine, she says. You've known since yesterday, but if Monday is the best you can do, then what am I supposed to say, Cal? We'll wait until Monday. Holly disap-pears inside the house, then returns with two gray coffee mugs and brings one out to Helen in the driveway. She's wearing a cream cashmere jumpsuit and pink slippers. They sip on their mugs simultaneously, and then Helen says, All right, alrighty, Cal. Goodbye. Goodbye now, and pinches the bud in her right ear.

Is there coffee? Sheba says, descending the guest house stairs, her eyes swollen, dried saliva crusted to the corner of her mouth. She stretches her arms above her head and yawns. I smell coffee.

Elise doesn't respond at first. When Sheba saunters to the kitchen and pours herself a cup from the machine, Elise wonders if somehow she'd made a mistake—switched the dates, missed a text message—about a change of plans around Sheba's return to the United States.

Your moms are outside, Elise says, standing upright. Should I go say hi to them? Helen just got off the phone.

A car door slams, then they hear muffled talking and footsteps tapping against the porch.

No, don't bother, Sheba says, blowing into her mug. They're truly psychos when they return from vacation. Emails, conference calls, hemorrhoids, etcetera.

Really? Elise says, peering outside the window. They won't think that's rude?

They know you're here. They asked whose car was in the driveway and I told them.

Elise looks inquisitively at Sheba, who pulls the glass jug of almond milk from the refrigerator.

I'm serious, Sheba says. They're in a state because their stuff isn't here yet. They don't want to see either of us.

She sits in one of the washed-velvet sofas with her legs folded up and runs her fingers across the fabric. I haven't sat on these couches since I was a teenager, she says.

Elise rests the side of her waist against the counter. They're incredibly nice couches, she says. She keeps watching Helen and Holly, who are crouched on the main house's porch steps speaking intensely to each other.

So, Sheba says, trying to regain Elise's attention. Approximately how many ragers did you throw here without me?

Elise tops off her mug with the remaining coffee in the pot.

I invited all my high school friends over and we smoked gravity bongs in the bathtub.

Sheba places her palms into a prayer. Gramps would be proud.

Elise smiles and tucks her hair behind her ear. Seriously, though, I didn't know you were coming back so soon? she says, not wanting to convey she's upset or disappointed. I texted you yesterday and you didn't say anything about it.

Sheba adjusts her seat. Honestly, I didn't know I was coming back either, she says, hoping to end the conversation there. Elise circles her hand in the air, prompting her to continue. We were supposed to leave London to go to Seville and I was super bummed about it because I met a really hot photographer at Chiltern Firehouse. Then Helen's assistant called and said the yacht club sent an email letting us know that, because my grandfather died, I needed to go through the membership process this summer or else I would no longer be eligible to join the club. Sheba pauses, waiting for Elise to react. It's not something I'm super interested in doing, she continues. I could give two fucks, if I'm being honest. But my moms went completely berserk about it and insisted we come back immediately. They rounded up the troops and got the PJ in less than an hour, saying that if I don't become a member then my hypothetical children cannot become members, and then my hypothetical grandchildren cannot become members, nor can my hypothetical great-grandchildren. So I'm being forced into required activities that start literally today, stupid things like mixers and luncheons that will—she crosses her fingers dramatically—eventually lead to an induction.

Elise covers her neck with her hands. Wow. That's wild. I can't believe you had to cancel your whole vacation for that.

At least you're here, Sheba says after a moment, stroking her mug with her palm. That's the only reason I didn't put up a fight about returning. I chose you over Felix the Photographer.

Elise gazes down at the oak peninsula. I'm sorry your trip was ruined because of some antiquated yacht club initiation.

Yeah, it sucks, Sheba says, shaking her head. And of course this all happened the day after I met the hottest guy. He was wearing a scarf tied around his neck, which I thought was so cute. You know how the Brits do it, folded in half and threaded through. Then, next thing I know, we're in a bathroom stall at Chiltern's together, and he pulls his pants down. I froze and let out a laugh because, believe it or not, I'd never seen an uncircumcised penis before! I clarified I wasn't laughing at him, I was simply stunned. So, to break the awkwardness, I said, You and your penis are wearing matching scarves! Which I found hilarious and he only found somewhat amusing. Anyway, despite all that, we still had sex on the toilet. But now I guess I'm never going to see him again. Thanks very much to the yacht club.

Elise spits a mouthful of coffee back into her mug. She laughs, but she knows this is how Sheba disarms people—by sharing every hyperbolic detail about her life so no one asks any meaningful questions. Even when she and Elise barely knew each other, Sheba confessed she met with a muscular real estate agent who she found on Instagram and gave him head in the parking lot of a movie theater. Elise didn't know how to respond. They were nineteen. She said it sounded dangerous and degrading. Why had she done that? Because she enjoyed giving head, she said, it turned her on, made her feel in control. Elise was curious to understand what Sheba meant by this, but the exchange felt somehow at odds with her burgeoning second-wave feminist identity.

Elise lost her virginity at thirteen years old, which was young enough to cause her to shy away whenever the topic of sex came up. If her friends asked her about her first time, she never revealed her actual age, afraid it indicated something about her self-worth, or how she had been parented, or a hormone imbalance. Sixteen, she fibbed, and even that age seemed too young to some. It had been with her first boyfriend, a fellow thirteen-year-old who was gentle and sincere. They were lying on the cellar door in Elise's backyard, kissing and grasping at each other's crotches, when his skin went hot and clammy and he began to concentrate his breathing at the center of his throat. Elise removed her shorts and underwear and asked if he wanted to lie on top of her. For several minutes, as he moaned continuously, she couldn't quite tell whether or not he had entered her, but when he finished, she felt pleased. Relieved, even. He grasped at her crotch some more until she felt too tender and told him he could stop. Then they went inside and drank grape soda before his mom arrived to pick him up. She didn't regret losing her virginity when she did. What she did regret was that this experience had shaped her understanding of what sex should be, what was deemed appropriate or not, and how much she should share, even with her closest friends.

Last night, when you Ambien-walked over, Elise says, you kept asking me if Harry was here. It was so weird.

Harry? Why would I be asking about Harry?

I don't know. Have you talked to him recently or something?

Of course not, Sheba says, staring wildly at Elise. He was *your* boyfriend.

He wasn't my boyfriend.

Sheba takes a gulp of her coffee and swallows hard. I think you and I have different qualifiers as to what constitutes a boyfriend.

We hardly saw each other, Sheba. He'd pass by me and wave on the way to class. Then he'd show up at my dorm room in the middle of the night when he wanted to get laid.

So? You'd let him in, wouldn't you? A lot of relationships start that way.

Elise clenches her arm. Baseline, we need to spend time with each other sober in the light of day if we're going to commit to each other as boyfriend and girlfriend.

Sheba stands and looks at the clock. I know you're a hopeless romantic, she says, but that's a tad prudish, no? She walks to the mudroom and slides her feet into a pair of sandals by the door.

Are you leaving? Elise asks, following her.

I have to go to tennis lessons at the yacht club, she responds, as if tennis is the dentist. Will you stay here until I get back? Please? It'll only be a couple hours.

Elise stares at her blankly. I need to get home, she says.

Sheba frowns. Pretty please? Don't leave me on my first day back.

I can't, Elise says, her eyes trained on the tile floor. With my mom gone I—she pauses, unsure why she started her sentence that way—I need to be home.

Right, of course, your mom, Sheba says, her tone suddenly soft, and reaches to give Elise a hug. I'm just arguing for argument's sake, by the way, she continues as she steps onto the porch. Harry is a dickwad who doesn't deserve you. Then she shuts the door, heavily, and walks across the stone pathway, back to the main house.

Elise stands still facing the space where Sheba had been, then rotates and glares at the pheasant on the mantel, its feathers glossy with wax coating, its glass eyes reflecting a strip of light across the dark ebony orb. I'm not a hopeless romantic, she says out loud, and grabs the roots of her hair with two fists. She stays like this for a few moments, until her scalp burns, and she unclenches her fingers. Then she puts her and Sheba's mugs in the dishwasher, pours herself a glass of lemonade, and gathers her things to return home.

Outside, the smoke from a controlled burn in the moors carpets the air with the smell of singed earth. Elise hears Sheba's voice reverberating from the main house porch. She watches from her car as Sheba slips into the passenger seat of her moms' Mercedes, wearing a white-and-green tennis outfit. Once they've driven away, Elise turns her key in the ignition and circles around the cul-de-sac.

Behind the gate at the end of the driveway, a large brown van is requesting entrance through the intercom. The iron doors swing open, and she reverses to the front of the guest house to allow them through. The van pulls up beside the main house, blocking the driveway, and three large men hop out. Elise signals for them to go ahead, she can wait, and they unlatch and open the roll-up door in the back, revealing boxes and furniture stacked to the ceiling. They unload a vast array of items: bubble-wrapped chairs, bulk containers of toilet paper, cases of Mountain Valley spring water, artwork and large vases. Helen and Holly must have had them flown in on a private jet, Elise thinks. There's no other way they could have shipped to the island so quickly. Twenty minutes later, the van is empty. The men climb inside and shout their gratitude to Elise for waiting. She follows behind them as they depart Sheba's driveway in a single file, as discreet and unnoticed as when they came.

Elise is standing in the attic when her mother calls, watching several robins poke at the neighbors' lawn, their copper underbellies polka-dotting the green expanse. Hi, Mom, she says, and latches the window shut. Over the past few days, the island's weather has turned tropical—the occasional breeze no longer suffices to cool the balmy air. Elise has been waking up in damp sheets, the crooks of her elbows and the backs of her knees sticky with sweat. She found a small fan in the cellar and placed it on the milk crate between her and Sophie's beds, but it rattles if set on high, and she'd rather endure the heat than the persistent noise. She's considering whether to spend part of her bird-monitoring money on a window AC unit, though that would mean their electricity bill would go up and she would lose the light that streams in during sunset, the geometric patterns that shift across the bedroom.

Filha, you still haven't sent the social security numbers, Gilda says.

Really? Elise says, her stomach sinking. I thought I texted them to you. She puts her on speaker and searches through her text messages.

I have to mail the application today, Gilda says and takes a long drag of a cigarette.

When will we get a response?

No idea. The lawyer says it could be as soon as a few months or as long as a year. Maybe even longer. The sound of a garden hose spraying against tiles transmits through the speaker. I don't want to wait a year, Gilda says. I want to see you girls.

Elise's throat tightens. She coughs to shake it free.

Did my text go through? I sent the social security numbers.

Yes, thank you. I got them. Gilda pauses. Hey—I've been thinking—have you been remembering to lock the doors at night?

Elise opens the bottom of her shirt and holds it over the fan. Gilda has been raising this point a lot lately, about locking the doors, even though they never lock the doors at night; most islanders don't. Yes, I lock the doors, she tells her, wanting to avoid an argument.

Good, Gilda says. I need to make sure you girls are safe.

Elise reassures her that Sophie is sleeping soundly in her bedroom downstairs and that she'll lock the doors again before leaving for work. Then she changes the subject to the weather, a safe topic, says she'll need to bring ice packs and electrolyte drinks to work that morning, that the humidity on Nantucket is probably similar to São Paulo. Gilda adds she should stay in the shade as much as possible, avoid the sun, she doesn't want Elise to get heatstroke.

They end the conversation after a few minutes so Elise can get ready for work. Gilda stamps out her cigarette and gazes up at the mango tree above her. A dead leaf falls off a branch and floats to the mosaic table. She runs her fingers along its brown edges, releases it, and watches it drift and twirl to the tiles, then returns inside.

The day prior, while Elise and Sophie were at work, Aunt

Beth arrived home earlier than normal and found Gilda slumped over her legal paperwork at the kitchen table. A line of empty beer cans was assembled next to the kitchen sink and a pot of water boiled on the stove. Beth turned off the stove, rinsed the cans, then shook Gilda's shoulder, told her to get up, she wanted to go for a drive to town.

What time is it? Gilda responded, glancing at the bird clock on the wall. The second hand clicked between the three P.M. canary and four P.M. parakeet. Why are you home so early?

I finished what I needed to do at work, she said, picking the lint off her sleeve. Gilda observed her sharp navy skirt and flouncy yellow top. Beth usually drove home from her marketing job in São Paulo during rush hour and returned after hours in traffic, the sun already set. I thought we could enjoy the daylight together, Beth added.

Gilda stood, wiping the corners of her mouth, and fixed the splayed immigration forms in front of her. Beth could smell her acetic breath from across the table. I have to review this application one more time, she said. The lawyer files it tomorrow.

Beth swiped the bangs from her face and squinted. I thought we could go to the ice cream shop we liked as kids—do you remember? We'd bring home those wooden spoons and paint faces on them for our puppet shows.

Gilda smiled, her face weary. I think I remember the puppet shows, she said, then shook her head. But I don't remember an ice cream shop.

Come on, let's go, Beth said and checked her wallet for cash. You'll remember when you get there.

Gilda agreed to leave for a little while, only because Beth had taken the time off from work. She splashed water on her face, swished mouthwash, and changed into a fresh pair of underwear. As they drove into Nova Gardênia, passing by the park with its green lake and swan boats, the scent of a dama da noite bush wafting through the window, Gilda could feel the tension in her shoulders and lower back ease. She wasn't ignorant of her sullen mood and fixation on the immigration case—she knew she wasn't adjusting well to this new life, this new state of being. She felt untethered without the structure of her life as she had once known it. Beth parallel parked on a hill and then skipped ahead, waving for her sister to catch up, while Gilda zigzagged under tree canopies several feet behind her, tired from the beer and heavy heat. Beth stopped and waited for Gilda at the entrance of a gelateria with orange plastic chairs and vintage fondue bowls decorating the walls. As soon as they walked in, the owners—a cheerful couple in their seventies—stood from their table and greeted Beth with a kiss on the cheek.

Meu deus do céu, the woman said after Beth explained she'd brought her older sister in to see them. Gilda? She held her hand horizontal above the ground. I remember when you were this tall. You used to do a little dance and stick out your tongue. It was very funny. You always made us laugh.

Gilda sighed and nodded. Yes, yes, I remember, of course, she said, though she still could not retrieve this memory. She felt ashamed that she wasn't able to share in their enthusiasm and told herself the owners must look unfamiliar in their old age, that she had been too young to remember.

You know, Beth said, licking from her chocolate cone. They sat on a bench in the small plaza outside the shop. Days before Mami fell and broke her hip, we came and got ice cream. She always ordered a caramel swirl cup, just like you. And she kept saying how much she wished you were here with us. You know she always wished you were here, right?

Well, not always, Gilda said, stabbing her spoon into the cup. For most of my life she wanted me as far away as possible.

Beth leaned back on the bench and unzipped the top of her skirt. That's not true, Gil. I know it's a shock to be back. But I do think it's good you're finally home.

Gilda hunched forward and placed her ice cream on the brick floor. I don't know if this is my home anymore. Don't you hear how I speak Portuguese now? With an American accent. I have two American daughters living in a country without their mother.

Bring them here, Beth implored, intending to be helpful. They are Brazilian too, aren't they? They can live here with us.

Gilda released a jittery laugh. I'm starting to think it's not good to leave. I moved to another country when I was their age and look what happened to me.

Beth gripped Gilda's shoulder, trying to ease her stress, but Gilda shook her off. I'm worried about you spending all day alone, she said. It's not healthy to keep replaying everything in your head. You have to find a way forward, for your own sake.

As Beth finished her thought, the church bells chimed behind them. Five o'clock. Gilda stood, her body clenched, and collected her ice cream cup. Elise is off work, she said, and I need to review my paperwork. Come, let's get going.

Gilda marched away, and as she did, Beth muttered into the thick air, unable to withhold her frustration: You've reviewed that fucking thing a million times. It's done, minha irmã, over with. Time to move on.

· · ·

As Elise packs for work after her phone call with Gilda, she can't stop thinking about what her mother said about locking the doors and decides to check on Sophie before she leaves. She pushes open Gilda's bedroom door and finds her asleep on top of the covers, one leg crooked over a stack of their mother's sweaters. Sophie, she whispers, but Sophie doesn't stir. She leaves the door ajar, then walks to the front door and pushes the lock in from the inside. FYI—I locked the doors, she texts her from the car. She reaches around the driver's seat to ensure she has a pair of sunglasses and a hat, then sends her mom a string of heart emojis, feeling guilty about her earlier fib.

When she arrives at the beach parking lot, Steve is waiting for her with a hot cup of convenience store coffee, which she spills on her lap as the Jeep ambles over a divot in the sand. She dabs her legs with a wad of napkins that Steve hands her from the glove compartment.

The birds are taking turns brooding the eggs, two pattering by the water to gather food, dipping their beaks into the sand, while the others squat on the nests by the fence. She compiles her daily log—adult count (four), fledgling count (zero), number of eggs (four), evidence of hatching (N/A), weather (miserable)—and then decides to go for a swim to cool the coffee burns across her thighs. She sheds her shorts first, and then her tank top, which she piles discreetly behind her beach chair. The salt water stings as she wades into the estuary. She reclines on the wet sand, the current churning over her legs, and lets the sun blanket her stomach, chest, face, and the tops of her feet, until the heat becomes unbearable, and she submerges herself into the roaring stream.

At the end of the workday, on her way home, she and Steve cross the threshold from no signal to signal about halfway to the beach parking lot. Instantly her phone pings. Seven new voice messages:

1: Filha, call me back, I need to talk to you.
2: Elise, call me. I haven't heard from you all day.
3: I'm starting to worry. Why aren't you answering my calls?
4: Hi, Elise, it's your mom. Please call me back.
5: Static silence, and then the clip of a receiver hanging up.
6: Her aunt is in the background, telling Gilda to stop slamming the counter with her fork.
7: Elise, onde você está?

Elise hides her phone from Steve, who is sensing the commotion.

Everything good? he asks.

Yeah, it's nothing, she replies, digging her fingernail into her palm.

When Elise gets to her car, she waits for Steve to drive off, then she calls Gilda back. The phone rings, rings, but no one answers. She tries again. Ring. Ring. Nothing.

Seriously? she says out loud, staring at a pine tree in the distance.

She unzips her backpack to retrieve her water bottle and takes a long gulp, then exits the parking lot, trying not to invent catastrophic reasons as to why her mother isn't answering. As she approaches the rotary, a call comes in. She pulls to the side, her tires hobbling over the curb, and answers.

Mom? What's wrong?

Where is Sophie? Gilda says, her voice sluggish. She isn't answering my calls.

She's probably still at work. Did something happen?

I was getting worried about you two. You weren't answering my calls.

We talked this morning. I was at work. I don't have service out there, remember?

Oh, her mother says. I forgot you went to work.

Where is Aunt Beth? Elise asks.

She's working too. I'm the only one not working. I'm here with the dogs and they're driving me crazy. Shitting on the patio, barking whenever a leaf blows by.

Maybe you should go for a walk.

No, no. I have things to do, she says, trailing off.

A line of cars passes around Elise, veering into the opposite lane.

You know, I didn't leave Sophie, Gilda says. I asked them to let me call her.

We know you didn't leave Sophie, Mom.

She pulls out onto the road while her mother vents about broken systems and racist presidents, the United States of Wealth and Corruption. By the time she reaches Sheba's house to retrieve a phone charger she left there days ago, a dense fog has enveloped the island. She pauses at the gate and convinces Gilda to slow down, take a cold shower, and drink a glass of water. She's surprised by how quickly Gilda obliges, her sudden turn in demeanor. Yes, yes, OK, honey, she responds and hangs up the phone. Elise rubs her face hard with both hands, then slumps over the steering wheel. She knows her mother sits alone most days, depressed, without structure or companionship, and there's little Elise can do to relieve her pain.

The winter during her sophomore year of high school, when

the restaurant had to lay her mother off for the season, Gilda would leave in the middle of the day for hours at a time, then return to explain, matter-of-factly, that they were being watched. They shouldn't open the blinds anymore. They turned the thermostat down to fifty degrees to preserve heat and slept together with a kerosene space heater in the living room. She piled magazines on top of the slats in the floor, fearing they were bugged, and they ate packaged foods that came in tin cans and polyethylene bags. She began to shower with a bathing suit on, complaining she saw someone spying on her from the backyard. At the time it frightened Elise. Which precautions were necessary, and which were extreme? It was impossible to know. Eventually Elise came to understand that reality had slipped beyond Gilda's grasp for those few months. By the time spring bloomed and she returned to work, she had transformed into her normal self again. But now, through the lens of her mother's deportation, Elise wonders if she had been right about the surveillance, at least in part.

Elise wipes her eyes with her sleeves, her breath jagged, and enters Sheba's birthday into the keypad. She lurches through the driveway, leaning to inspect the road foot by foot in the fog. Close to the cul-de-sac, the outline of a body appears in front of her. She slams on the brakes, her chest bouncing against the horn, causing a small honk. The body materializes from behind the wall of fog. Elise makes out Helen's figure: she is wearing a white silk jumper and a beekeeper hat. She walks around to the driver's side window and pulls back her veil.

Elise, hi, how are you? Are you having a good summer? she says, speaking through the glass.

Elise rolls down the window. Yes, very good, thank you, she

replies and manages a smile. Her mouth suddenly goes dry, and Helen interjects before she can ask in return about her summer.

I'm glad I ran into you, because I was thinking: Holly and I are planning a fundraising dinner, you know, for climate justice, cocktails and small food, that kind of thing, nothing fancy, and we need someone to pass out the hors d'oeuvres, keep the drinks flowing, you know, easy stuff. And we can pay you for it. So you can make a little money on the side and perhaps meet some important people.

Elise notices Helen's jumper has dampened in the fog, revealing two pink nipples.

You want me to work at the dinner? she says, her mind still not recovered from the conversation with her own mother.

Helen pulls her blouse away from her sternum and the fabric peels from her skin. It's up to you, you know, but it's a really great opportunity, because of the important people who will be there. Environmental people. Sheba told me you're very passionate about the environment, and we need some help with the catering, so I thought, win-win, you know. Why not?

Elise puts the car in neutral and cranks the emergency brake. She has no desire to work at this fundraising event, and she's unclear how she's supposed to connect with Helen's guests if she's serving them food, but she doesn't know how to say no to Sheba's mom. Would she be understanding, or would it create a problem for Sheba? Elise does need the money, undoubtedly. Is there something about her that conveys this fact, a frailty, something that Helen has perceived?

OK, sure, yeah, Elise says. I think I can do that.

Helen knocks her knuckles on the car door.

Terrific. It's in a few days. I'll be in touch.

Helen retreats into the fog again. Elise waits until she can hear her on the main house's porch steps, the sound of the front door closing, before she releases the clutch and allows the car to roll forward. Halfway around the cul-de-sac, a deer leaps in front of her. Elise hits the brake again, her breath escaping through her nose. The deer ambles across the driveway, half obscured, its hooves clacking against the stone. It stops and rotates its head, ears long and erect, eyes unblinking, then disappears into the atmosphere.

Elise has never been inside the main house. She's not even completely sure which door is the right door to enter into the kitchen. On the day of the fundraising event, she turns the golden handle on the front entrance and listens for the sounds of pans and glasses clattering, the call-and-response of shouted kitchen instructions. The décor in the foyer is sleek and modern, a blend of off-whites and whites, touches of terra-cotta. She moves down a hallway, through the dining room where the event will be held, and into a sparkling kitchen with marble floors that match the countertops. Three servers sit polishing glasses and silverware at a banquette bench with cream pillows. Cream pillows in a kitchen, Elise observes. She considers the havoc a bowl of red spaghetti sauce would wreak.

When Helen had said the fundraising event would be attended by influential people in environmental science, Elise assumed she'd meant scientists. Or if not scientists, then activists or policy-makers. Leaders from the Sunrise Movement came to mind, co-authors of the Green New Deal, or the Blue New Deal, experts in public health advocacy. But when Helen emailed a guest list the night before (Elise was cc'd with a dozen other people she didn't know), it described a small group of ten people: the CEO of a large, well-known nonprofit that manufactures and distributes water filtration devices in Africa; the president of a Silicon Valley startup developing a rideshare app for electric bicycles; a geologist—the only scientist—who'd lobbied for the fossil fuel industry until a change in administration forced him to pivot to research and development at SpaceX. The rest were spouses and generically wealthy people—the benefactors, the email called them. Elise could already sense the power dynamics at play, the colosseum of money exchange, who would be in the ring brandishing swords, and who would be in the stands drinking from flutes. From this email Elise also learned that Helen had hired a catering company, which Sheba had failed to mention to her as well. She kept referring to the fundraiser as *her moms' stupid dinner thing* and was supremely irritated that Helen asked Elise to help her without consulting Sheba first. Why is she always meddling in my friendships? she kept saying while brushing her hair too vigorously. Why does she think she can do whatever she wants?

Every foreboding talk Elise's mother had given her about the restaurant industry enters her thoughts at once as she stands in the kitchen, aimless with her eyes, trying to figure out who is in charge. Her mother had warned her not to take a restaurant job. It was soul-crushing work, she would never be respected as a woman, and the hours made it impossible to have a family. Elise had avoided hostess and cashier and food-running gigs every summer, even when she saw her friends, including her sister, seductively organizing stacks of bills on their dressers. And yet, because she had never held a restaurant job like her mom and Sophie, they never considered her to be as seasoned or hardworking as them. Whenever Elise complained she was too tired to do something, her mom explained that she was too young to know what it meant to be tired, really tired, tired from years working in a kitchen.

Can I help you? The sous chef looks up from the red, glistening fish she is boning.

I'm here for a job, Elise says. Serving.

She puts down her knife and cocks her head.

Did I hire you?

No, Helen did. She told me you might need help.

The sous gives Elise's black shirt and khakis a once-over.

Helen will pay you directly?

Elise doesn't know the exact answer to this question.

Yes, she says anyway.

OK. Go grab a new shirt from the back.

She slowly wanders the kitchen, trying to discern what *the back* means in Sheba's house, when she hears a scratchy voice call her name. At first she cannot place the woman crossing over to her from the banquette table, with her star-shaped pendant necklace and crackling blue eyes. It's as though the outline of someone she knows intimately has been transposed over a stranger's face. But then her mind adjusts, the outline incorporates, and she recognizes Asia, a friend of hers from high school. The students nicknamed her white Asia because there was a girl from Trinidad who was also called Asia. Elise had been close friends with white Asia in middle school, but in high school Elise began taking advanced placement classes and Asia didn't—in some ways the fizzle in their friendship was as simple as that. Elise became even closer with her longtime friend Amara, whose parents were deported in an ICE raid when they were in high school. She and Amara could lament the struggles of trigonometry and macroeconomics in a way that Asia couldn't.

Are you working this party too? Asia asks, as though they'd

seen each other last week. She is uniformed in khakis and a branded button-down, the dot of a removed piercing above her eyebrow.

Asia, wow, hi, Elise says. I am, but I'm a little lost. Do you know where the extra uniforms are?

Asia brings her to the back—Sheba's backyard—where there is a cardboard box filled with surplus shirts with an embroidered island logo. Assembled by the door are buckets and buckets of flowers: coral and purple snapdragons, pink peonies, peachy gladiolas, chrysanthemums, eucalyptus leaves, and leather ferns.

What are these for? Elise asks, buttoning up her shirt.

We have to arrange them. They're going into the dining room.

Elise nods. Is there anything else I should know? I've never waitressed before.

Asia laughs. Oh, you're serious, she says, stopping herself. I thought you were kidding.

No. I'm not kidding. Elise shrugs.

Shit. Well, this is a small party, so it shouldn't be too difficult. You can follow me. Just don't try to do anything except clear plates and pour water. Don't touch food and don't pour wine. Only carry things that are empty. If a guest asks you to do something, tell me and I'll do it.

I think I can manage that, Elise says, though she feels deeply that she may not. Should I start bringing in the flowers?

Asia picks up a bucket of ranunculus and places it in Elise's arms.

Elise feels more confident arranging flowers than helping with the dining room setup, so she happily sits with Asia and another server, a Bulgarian man named Aleksi, in Sheba's kitchen, cutting the ends off stems and puzzling out length, color combinations, and curvature. As they move the vases into the dining room, Elise notices a small honeybee still clinging to a snapdragon. It flies up, wobbly in its approach, and lands on an adjacent pink snapdragon, following its pattern for the day. Elise opens a window behind her and guides it outside, then watches it fly across the flowerless lawn. They place the flower arrangements on every possible surface: in the center of the long mahogany dining table, on the cocktail bar in the corner, on windowsills and decorative side tables. The air hangs with pollen and sweet perfume. Johnny, a handsome silver-haired sommelier, goes in to greet the guests as they arrive, explains the menu and offers wine pairings, while the rest of the team takes a few minutes to vape out back. Elise doesn't vape, and she's decided to stop cigarettes entirely, but she follows Asia as she'd been instructed and watches her and Aleksi pull deep inhales, pause, then exhale dramatic clouds into the air around them. They discuss, in a slightly competitive way, the other wealthy people they've waited on that week. Asia catered a party at the Johnson & Johnson family's house, she says, and used the bidet. Aleksi was at Bill Belichick's house and he and the other servers took photos of each other in his trophy room during main course. Aleksi points his vape stick at Elise. Where did you come from? he asks.

I'm extra help, she responds. I'll be following Asia.

We went to high school together, Asia adds, smoke streaming from her nose.

So you're a local too? Aleksi says.

Elise nods, feeling slightly judged, then the sous peeks her head through the screen door and calls for them to return inside for first course.

Elise trails Asia into the dining room with a white cloth napkin draped over her left arm. Immediately, she locks eyes with Sheba, who is seated beside Helen wearing a midnight-blue dress, long and sinuous, running her fingers along her wineglass stem. Elise isn't sure if she should say hello to her in front of the guests, or if she should pretend she doesn't notice her wide presence in the room. But then Sheba gives her a small gesture, a defiant raise of her eyebrow, as though they're sharing a secret about her moms' stupid dinner thing. She smiles quickly before shifting away to listen to Helen's speech. Elise adjusts the napkin draped over her forearm, standing without purpose. Asia walks around the table to pour water, then indicates for Elise to follow her back to the kitchen, where the chefs are plating the first course.

The dinner starts with sweet local bay scallops the size of quail eggs skewered on ivory toothpicks, sturgeon caviar, and potato florets. Then there are actual quail eggs, poached on top of burrata with crispy squash blossoms and charred heirloom tomatoes, orange, yellow, and red, to be eaten with a knife and fork. The red snapper, their main course, was caught that morning by an island fisherman, cooked in banana leaves stuffed with thyme, rosemary, and thick slices of lemon, garnished with purple and white flower petals, and topped with yuzu foam. There are also surprises in between, tastings from the chef, that Elise doesn't quite catch—crudo, a single spin of pasta, lamb popsicles. As the food goes from kitchen to table, table to kitchen, Elise feels like a stool placed in the middle of a fine-tuned ballet. Her job is to move to the side or provide a place to rest when Asia tires. Neither Helen, Holly, nor Sheba acknowledges Elise or any of the other servers as they dash in and out of the flowered room. Elise tries to steal a glance at Sheba a few times over the course of the meal, an attempt to break the stiff tension, but Sheba remains dutifully trained on her parents. Elise wonders, as dessert nears, what Helen had in mind when she described this as a networking opportunity. A chance to observe the silent indications the rich make when they want more water? To smell the musty hair spray they leave in the powder room?

The dessert arrives: strawberry rhubarb pie with cardamom ice cream. Elise bends down to pick up a napkin that has fallen next to the table, and when she stands, she finds herself alone in the dining room. That is, without Asia or the other servers. Helen stretches out her arm and places her fingers around Elise's elbow.

Everyone, this is Sheba's friend from college. She's helping me put this little event together.

Helen rests her other hand on Sheba's wrist and Sheba exhales audibly. The geologist leans back and smiles, his mouth rimmed with ice cream.

Elise is from Nantucket, Helen adds.

Oh, really? the geologist remarks. Meaning you live here in the winter?

Yes, Elise says. Even in the winter.

How unusual! the geologist continues. What do your parents do for a living?

Elise opens and then closes her mouth, unsure how to respond.

Helen sits up in her chair. Tragically, she intervenes, Elise's mother was deported earlier this year.

Mom, Sheba interjects and pushes her leg under the table.

A benefactor chuckles, noticing Sheba's chagrin over her mother's comment.

I have three daughters, he says. You can't say anything to please them.

Helen smiles. Elise fiddles with the dirty napkin in her hand.

Elise studied environmental science at Chapel Hill, Sheba says.

Holly chimes in: Oh, environmental science. How apropos.

Where is your mother from again, Elise? Helen says, breaking off a piece of pie crust with her fork.

Brazil, Elise responds.

Brazil—how interesting. So that makes you . . . ?

Brazilian.

A few people chuckle, which makes Elise feel as though she's answered incorrectly.

But your father was, is . . . ?

He's Irish.

Ah, an Irishman, the geologist says with a fake Irish brogue. He takes a sip from a short glass of melted ice and cognac.

Brazilian and Irish. What a terrific combination, Holly says.

Sheba pushes her dessert plate away and stares sharply at the nape of her mother's neck.

Helen takes a bite of pie while Elise continues to stand beside her. A painful flare rises from her stomach, coating her throat, and her vision goes blurry. She announces that she should return to the kitchen and curtsies, regrettably. As she slips through the dining room doors, she hears someone say behind her, lovely girl, and a hum of agreement. She scrambles to the bathroom in the butler's pantry and releases a small amount of vomit into the sink. It's almost over, she tells herself in the mirror, rinsing the vomit from her mouth.

When she comes out, Asia, who doesn't seem to have noticed her absence, tells her they need help washing dishes. Elise dons a pair of rubber gloves and hovers over the sink, scrubbing baking sheets until the party is over, the guests have left, and the catering truck is packed and gone. She pokes her head into the dining room to see if Sheba happens to be there, but the lights are off. Maybe she's still with her parents, Elise thinks. She sends her a text—You around?—and exits the main house from the back.

The night glows with starry clarity, serene but for the June bugs vibrating against the window screens. She's walking down the stone path that connects to the guest house when she notices Asia huddled behind the outdoor shower with three bottles of wine between her legs.

Hey! Asia calls in a whispered yell, signaling for Elise to come over.

Elise stops and gazes longingly at the guest house; she imagines the relief she would feel, staring at the ceiling alone.

Elise! Asia says again.

She turns to acknowledge Asia's calls, then walks over and accepts the wine bottle she holds out in offering. The warm Sancerre awakens her cheeks and throat.

Nice party, right? These people must be loaded. Asia swipes the bottle out of Elise's hands and presses it against her pursed lips, the air suctioning when she tips it down. The best part of catering is there are always leftovers, she says. She opens her purse to reveal several lamb popsicles wrapped in a white cloth napkin. Do you want one?

Elise thanks her but declines. She looks up to try to locate Sheba upstairs in the main house, but the windows are dark and still.

I heard about what happened to your mom, Asia says. So awful.

Thanks, Elise says. And thanks for helping me out tonight. It really means a lot.

Anytime. Asia blows a puff of mint vapor between them.

What have you been up to since high school? Elise asks.

I've been here. Working, mostly. Asia pauses and taps her vape pen against her thigh. I don't know if you heard, but I'm sober now.

Elise hadn't heard. She glances at the bottles on the ground.

I mean, not alcohol. I don't take pills anymore. She turns away as she says this. My parents are still addicts, though. It's sad. Everyone here's addicted to pills. It's the cure for everything. You get rear-ended? Here's some oxy. You have a tick bite? Here's some oxy. You want some oxy? Guess what—here's some oxy.

I'm sorry, Asia, Elise says, thumbing at her pants pocket.

A faint light gleams from the upstairs of the guest house. Elise knows its source—a small stained-glass lamp on a table in the hallway, with a brass pull chain and decorative tulips on the shade. It bathes the staircase in a beautiful caramel color, which is not something she would have ever appreciated before, wasting electricity to luxuriate in lighting, but here she is. She considers if she should tell Asia that the host of the party, Helen, is her best friend's mother, but she decides the gulf between the Elise Asia used to know and the one standing before her is too vast for them to swim across and meet in the middle.

Do you need a ride home? Elise says. I have a car.

That would be amazing. I called for a taxi but they're taking forever.

She takes her phone out of her pocket and checks the black screen. Elise has a feeling a taxi isn't coming. They get in her car and she drives to Asia's parents' house. It's the only house of its kind mid-island, an elaborate two-story structure with shingles cut into intricate patterns and green trim. Her parents inherited the house from Asia's grandparents, who moved to the island from

Fall River in the 1970s and bought the plot of land for $15,000. After they died, the porch turned into a maze of old magazines and canned food for the cats that live in the yard. Kids used to take turns running down the porch as far as possible as a dare, before Asia's dad inevitably stumbled out shirtless and invited them to come inside, which was enough to scare them away.

Elise pulls up next to the picket fence, and Asia invites her to see the shed she built around back. She says it with enthusiasm—You have to come see my shed!—and it feels cruel to say no, so she follows her along the side of the house to the backyard. Welcome to my humble abode, Asia says, unlatching the door. Inside, she has decorated the shed with Christmas lights strung in wide loops on the walls, weaving through photographs she has pinned to lines of twine. The tidy twin bed where she sleeps is cushioned with star-shaped pillows, and on her minifridge, which doubles as a side table, are bubbly letter magnets that spell out words like *love* and *wanderlust*. Asia introduces Elise to her pot plant named Cynthia, whose grow light blankets the room in a purple glow. There is an electric space heater in the center attached to an extension cord, and a metal bucket she only uses in the case of an emergency, when she doesn't want to run across the lawn to the bathroom in her parents' house.

Do you want to stay for some wine? Asia asks, pulling out two stemless glasses from behind a tapestry tacked to a bookcase.

Elise agrees to a small glass, which they drink sitting on Asia's pink shag rug.

This place is really nice, Asia, she says, brushing the rug with her fingers.

It's my oasis, she responds and tips the rest of the wine into her mouth.

Elise returns to the guest house after finishing her glass of wine, expecting Sheba to be inside waiting for her (they had planned for her to stay the night), but the house is dark. She switches on the light and finds an envelope on the kitchen counter with her name scrawled on the front. She peels open the seal. Inside is a stack of one-hundred-dollar bills, and a paperclip holding five business cards. The CEO, the start-up president, and three benefactors have written her notes on their respective cards: *Looking forward to connecting; Hope to speak with you again soon; Thrilled for your bright future.*

Elise flips the envelope over and rests her cheek against the oak peninsula. Not long after, Sheba enters, still wearing her gown. She kicks off her high heels and throws them across the mudroom.

Please tell me you stole some cheese from my mom, she says, bounding toward the refrigerator.

I did not steal cheese. Did you not get enough to eat?

Sheba opens the refrigerator and shifts the contents around.

I'm having a second wind.

She takes out a BLT, half of Elise's lunch, and unwraps the wax paper and tape.

Do you mind?

Go for it, Elise says, and turns her head to rest her other cheek on the counter.

Sheba sniffs the sandwich. I don't know if you noticed, she says. But my mother is a fascist.

Elise picks up her head. What happened now?

What she did to you at that party was uncalled for. I told her she was a fragile liberal with horrible politics and we got in a massive fight about it.

You did? When?

Right after the party. I demanded she apologize to you.

Sheba, why did you say that to her? It only makes it more awkward.

She needs to apologize! She should grovel at your feet.

Elise pushes the envelope across the table. Look at what they left for me.

Sheba takes a bite from the BLT, then places it on the counter. She tips open the envelope with two fingers, its contents slipping into view.

They came in here after the party?

I wasn't here, Elise says. I gave one of the other servers a ride home.

They shouldn't come into the guest house without telling me, Sheba says, almost under her breath. Elise interrupts: Sheba, did you see how much money is in there? It's at least a thousand dollars. I can't accept that.

Sheba opens the flap again, flicking through the hundreds. She puts the envelope down and continues eating the sandwich.

It doesn't matter if she gave you money. She still needs to apologize for how she behaved. You deserve twice as much, frankly, for helping them with that awful party—which I was against from the start, by the way. I told Helen it was weird, but she insisted you wanted to do it.

I think we can call it even.

You're doing her a favor! She gets to tote you around like you're evidence of her goodwill.

If I take the money, then I at least need to write her a thank-you note, Elise says. I can't accept this money and not say anything.

A thank-you note? So now you want to *thank* her? Sheba unzips the side of her dress and lifts the hem. This is truly sick. Am I going crazy? She uses you like a PowerPoint presentation on poverty during her fake fundraising dinner, and you're grateful because she paid you for it? Sheba turns, sandwich still in hand, and walks up the stairs. I'm going to go take a bath, she says over her shoulder.

Sheba, Elise calls after her. She holds her breath, feeling for the stretch in her lungs. After a few moments of silence, she ascends the stairs, deciding she'd rather sleep at home tonight. She's exhausted, drained, humiliated, unable to stay up late untying knots with Sheba. The sound of the running faucet rumbles through the closed bathroom door. She picks up her bag and walks quietly down the stairs.

The light in Helen and Holly's bedroom illuminates the front lawn outside. A figure moves past, casting a shadow across Elise's car. She opens the driver's side door and uses her shirtsleeve to wipe the fog from the inside of her windshield. The flower arrangements have been placed on the ground by the trash shed, still in their vases, apparently to be thrown away. She walks over, picks up one in each hand, carries them to her car, then briskly returns for another, bringing each of the discarded arrangements to the back seat. They will not last much longer, Elise knows this, but for a week, they will make her and Sophie happy. She can put two in the attic, two in Gilda's room, one in the bathroom, and three in the living room. She will care for them, spooning sugar into the vases and trimming the waterlogged stems. She will offer this care until the last arrangement has wilted, and then she will collect the fallen petals, press them inside a heavy book, and wait for them to dehydrate into brittle flesh, so they might live a while longer.

The sun is exactly midway between horizons—if folded in half, a circular burn would mark the center of a cloudless, cerulean sky—when Elise hears Steve's dinghy sawing across the estuary. Her stomach clenches, a tinge of nausea still persisting days after Helen's fundraising event. Steve never shows up to the beach unannounced—only if the weather turns, or if there's an emergency. During her early days on the job, she worried he might, and so she never stepped a foot out of line. But after four summers without a surprise visit, she let go of that anxiety, squatting in the dunes freely, skinny-dipping with pleasure.

Sophie's face flashes between a series of alarming thoughts. Steve idles the boat parallel to shore and shouts:

Get in! It's Sophie!

What's wrong? Elise says, running to him.

My brother called. She was arrested this morning.

Elise pulls herself into the dinghy and they fly across the estuary, the bow bucking against the current, streams of wake cascading at their sides. When they arrive at the parking lot, Elise sits in Steve's Jeep as he dials his brother on his cellphone. There is a pile of balled-up gum wrappers collected on the dashboard and a broken CD on the passenger-side floor.

Elise crosses her arms. Steve is standing outside the door with one hand on the hood.

Randy? he says. Elise can hear the brother's deep timbre through the receiver. I have Sophie's sister, Elise. Can I put her on?

Steve passes the phone to Elise.

Elise, how are ya? Randy says. I hear you're coming to pick up your sister.

A pocket of dry air moves down her throat.

Where is she? Is she OK?

She's here, at the station. She's doing fine. We didn't book her or anything, but we told her someone needed to come pick her up.

Can I ask what happened?

Well. He pauses. Elise hears a crinkling sound on the other end, a bag of chips, maybe. Then he says: She got into an altercation with a construction worker. They said the landlord sent you guys an eviction notice, but I guess when the crew showed up the house wasn't packed up. I understand Sophie got heated and, well, there's no easy way to say this. She kicked him in the testicles.

Elise switches the receiver from one ear to the other. An eviction notice? she repeats back. She looks at Steve, who's outside of earshot, drawing circles with his foot in the sandy lot.

I'll be there in ten minutes, she says and hangs up.

The island's police station used to be an offshoot of the courthouse in town—a small, unassuming building with a waiting room that offered brochures for kayak rentals. Day trippers often wandered in, mistaking it for an information center, and asked for directions to the best bike shop. Locals stopped in to buy beach permits for their cars. But after 9/11, the commission's budget ballooned. They had more money than they could possibly spend in a year. So they bought a fleet of jet skis. Taser guns. Surveillance equipment. They hired twice as many summer cops, who patrolled the island on hybrid bicycles. They shuttered the station in town and built a massive brick building on a large complex mid-island. The new police station resembles a nineteenth-century school for wayward children, with towering white columns that bend as they soar upward, a feat of architectural vertigo. The rooftops are steeply pitched and the waxed floors squeal if walked upon.

Sophie is sitting on a wooden bench out front, her posture unnaturally erect, latching on to the cars that pass by in anticipation of her sister's arrival. When she sees Elise drive up, she stands and rushes to the passenger-side door.

I almost walked, she says as she gets in and buckles her seatbelt.

Elise scans her face for signs of harm, a bruise, a scratch.

What happened? she asks.

I was arrested, Sophie declares flatly.

Elise juts her chin forward.

I can see that. Why was there a construction crew at the house?

Sophie loosens the seat belt strap across her chest.

They told me we have to move out, she says. She's speaking quickly, throwing away the words, and doesn't look at Elise. They said they were there to gut the place. I told them they'd have to physically remove me if they wanted to come in. One of the guys laughed, said it wasn't my house.

Sophie flips down the sun visor mirror as she says this and inspects her skin with her fingers, pulls down her eyelids and pinches her cheeks.

I don't understand, Elise says. Why were they there to gut the house? We've paid rent every month.

Somehow the landlord found out that Mom doesn't live there anymore, and she's the one on the lease.

Elise shakes her head. Steve's brother said they sent an eviction notice. Did you see anything like that in the mail?

No, Sophie says—and then, I don't know. Mom always gets tons of junk mail from credit card companies and stuff.

Jesus, Sophie, Elise mutters. Did you throw away the eviction notice?

I have no idea! Why don't you start going through Mom's mail if you think I'm so neglectful?

Because you hoard it in her bedroom!

Several officers walk outside, their collars starched stiff against their necks, their sun-splotched skin spilling over. They pass a pack of Black & Mild cigars between them. Elise sees her mother, a flower sprouting out of a sidewalk crack, waving her leaves between them as they ash on the petal of her head. She swings the car into reverse and drives too fast over the speed bumps. Sophie grips the armrests. When they reach a stop sign a few blocks away, Elise faces Sophie and says: You know, you're lucky Steve's brother works at the police station. This could have been a whole lot worse. Sophie narrows her gaze out the front window and doesn't respond. Elise regrets the way these words have come out of her mouth; they taste sour, spoiled, the curdled milk of advice.

She drives some more. At the rotary, she turns in to a side road pinched by overgrown hedges. I didn't mean that, she says after a moment. I'm sorry.

Sophie scratches her eyebrow. What are we supposed to do now? I don't think we should go back to the house.

Elise stares at Sophie's knees pressed against the glovebox. They run through possible locations—the beach, the garden outside the church, the library basement, Sheba's house—but none guarantee uninterrupted privacy.

What about the woods? Elise suggests. It was where they would take their bicycles as kids when they didn't want to be found.

Sophie agrees to the woods plan, and they order lunch from her favorite sandwich place, a shop with picnic tables underneath big-leafed trees. Sophie silently picks at the sprouts that have fallen off her sandwich while Elise makes a pit stop at the liquor store. She buys a six-pack of sour beer, walks to the convenience store next door and purchases a bag of marshmallows, then drives with an elbow resting on the window ledge, trying to sort through the past two hours in her head. How long after the incident did the police show up? she thinks, running through an infinite string of questions. Did they ask for a report? Who called them? Did the construction worker try to defend himself? Did the neighbors notice? Did Sophie think of the similarities or differences to what happened when they pulled Gilda over? Or was it only in retrospect that she would draw these connections? Elise wonders how their mother will react when they tell her about Sophie's arrest and the eviction notice. She's sure the news will send her into a panic, like a tiger pacing from behind a chain-link fence, unable to reach her young.

Elise parks at the forest trailhead and lets Sophie know there's a blanket and sleeping bag in the trunk. Some old magazines too, if we want to make a fire. They fill two tote bags Elise finds in the back seat and enter the woods through a passage between bayberry bushes. A wind stirs the fern beds, causing them to ripple like waves, and thin shadows from the tupelo trees bend and sway. They cross a wooden plank that's been laid over a narrow creek and Sophie points at a painted turtle sunbathing on the slick rocks. Finally, they stop at a level clearing and lay the open sleeping bag and blanket around a pit of burnt wood where a fire had been built.

Sophie sits on the blanket and bites into her sandwich, the corners of her mouth smeared with mayonnaise. Elise pops open a beer bottle and takes a long gulp. The carbonation stings at the back of her throat.

Did they put you in a jail cell? she asks.

Sophie shakes her head. They made me sit in an empty interrogation room for a few hours and pretended to decide what to do with me. One officer told me I would spend the night in jail, another told me they might go easy on me because I'm an island kid. Then someone new appeared and said you were coming to pick me up.

Elise rolls her eyes and takes another sip of beer. They really had to torture you like that, huh?

Sophie picks at her shoestring. She asks Elise to hand her a beer.

I'll call Sheba, Elise says, opening the bottle. If we can't get in touch with the landlord right away, we can stay at her guest house until we can go home.

Sophie nods.

She has a nice house, Elise says.

I thought you said it was haunted.

Well, there are dead animals everywhere. But you'd have your own room.

Sophie wraps her arms around her legs and tucks her face between her knees.

We're going to get the house back, Elise says firmly. I'm saying just in case.

OK, Sophie says, not sounding convinced, and stands, brushing off her legs. I'm going to collect some wood to build a fire, she says, and disappears into the brush.

Elise can hear the snap of her footsteps intermixed with a chorus of cicadas. She finishes off the beer and opens another. Sophie returns, arms filled with branches, and drops the bundle by the fire pit. Here, Elise says, handing Sophie the bottle. She takes a swig, then pulls a lighter from her back pocket and sets the corner of a balled-up magazine page on fire. The paper turns blue and purple before fizzling out. After several more tries, they manage to build a large and sustainable fire. Elise wanders tipsily down the trail to find a place to pee. Once she's far enough away, she squats in the brush and watches the flickering firelight cast an orb over the trees.

What if they already began construction? Elise thinks. She had searched the internet for rentals one night, alone in the attic, unable to sleep. A five-hundred-square-foot studio apartment with nothing but empty hooks dangling on the shower rod went for $5,000 a month. They'd be lucky if they could even find an available rental this late in the season. She'd seen in the news that there were workers on the island sleeping in shipping containers because they couldn't find a place to live. Elise knew a driver for a rideshare app who lived in his car for two summers in a row—he would park at the beach at night, lock the doors, recline his seat, then wake in time to pick up passengers from the first arriving flight at the airport. How long would they last, she wonders, living out in the woods? She imagines a version of herself and Sophie as forest-dwellers, strolling into town with twigs in their hair and streaks of ash rubbed underneath their eyes.

I was just thinking, she says to Sophie, returning to the fire.

Someone must have tipped the landlord off. There's no other way he could have known—he doesn't even live on island. We've never seen him before in our lives. How else could he have known about Mom unless someone told him?

Sophie tosses a handful of leaves into the fire. I've been thinking about that too, she says, and stabs a marshmallow onto the end of a long stick. She hovers it above the bonfire and it catches on fire instantly. The Wagners came over once, a while ago, she continues, waving the stick to extinguish the flame. They couldn't find Suzie and wanted to know if I'd seen her. Then Mr. Wagner asked if he could use our bathroom, which I thought was weird, but I let him in, and when he came out he wanted to know how long the bathroom sink had been broken.

What? Elise says. They came into the house?

I didn't think much of it then, Sophie says. But, I don't know, maybe they called the landlord to try to fix the sink. Maybe they thought they were being helpful, ratting us out. Don't all narcs think they're being helpful to someone?

She squeezes the black and bulbous crust on her marshmallow, sliding it off, the cold middle still clinging to the branch.

I roasted it too close to the fire, she says, amused with herself, then eats it happily anyway, licking her fingers clean.

The following morning, a thumb of sunlight presses on Elise's face. Above her, a hazy blanket of morning rays is slung over branches. Sophie is curled in a ball on the other half of the open sleeping bag, one foot hooked around her ankle. The embers from the bonfire have turned to a white ash and scattered in sheets across their belongings.

Elise reaches for her phone. It's seven A.M. She has several texts from Sheba from the night before.

Sheba: Hello? Where are you?

Is everything OK? You never came over.

Elise sits up and wipes her eyes. Fuck, she says, and sends Steve a message: Would it be ok if I take another day off? I'll be back on Monday, I promise, then responds to Sheba: sorry . . . intense day. fell asleep in the woods with soph. will tell you about it in person

She stands and shakes off the ashes that have streaked her clothes. The clamor rouses Sophie. She turns over and murmurs: What time is it?

Early. We fell asleep in the woods.

Sophie stretches out her legs and groans. In the distance, toward the trailhead, they hear a dog bark. Elise notices the top of a purple hat hovering above the brush. We should get going, she says, and gathers the empty beer bottles into a tote bag. Sophie rolls the sleeping bag into a tight bundle and clutches it against her chest.

The purple hat appears from behind a large hickory tree, her dog's nose trained at the ground. Morning! the dog walker says and waves. Elise and Sophie wave back. They wait until she's deep into the woods, her footsteps fading, to pack up the rest of their campsite and head to the car.

When they arrive at their house, they are met with a large pile of splintered wood stacked on the lawn next to a dumpster. Elise pulls into the driveway and sees that the Wyeth print that hangs in Gilda's bedroom is balanced on the wood pile, covered in sawdust. Hanging from the dumpster, like a tongue, is the green carpet that lay between their twin beds in the attic. A pressure swells from behind Elise's rib cage, pushing up against her throat. She looks at Sophie, whose face is immutable.

What the fuck, Elise says. Should we try to go in? she asks, but Sophie's legs are already outside the passenger door.

The front entrance is taped shut with a construction permit, so they use the side door in the kitchen. Elise inhales and swallows a cloud of debris from the drywall that has been shattered with a sledgehammer, leaving a salty chalk taste on her tongue. Overlapping footprints cover the beige carpet and kitchen tiles, trailing the hallway to Gilda's room and up and down the stairs to the attic. Fucking Christ, Elise says. I can't believe this. She reaches for Sophie's arm before she goes too far, fearing that it might be unsafe to walk through, but Sophie ignores her. She announces that she's going to their bedroom and rushes up the stairs, the door slamming behind her. A thought crosses Elise's mind that perhaps the construction crew redirected their anger at Sophie toward the house, which is why the demolition is so chaotic. The kitchen sink has toppled to the floor, the carpet is slashed. They piled the furniture against a wall in the living room and covered it with a tarp. Elise maneuvers down the hallway to her mother's bedroom and turns the doorknob. It stops short, blocked by her bedframe. Through the crack she can see that the walls have been gutted, electrical wiring spilling from the beams. She pushes harder with a sudden desperate need. Come on! she growls, using her shoulder. Open! But the door doesn't budge. Even as her mind struggles to process what her eyes receive, she understands that there is no possible way they will be able to save their house. That much is obvious—the decision has been made for them. I will call Sheba, she thinks quickly, clambering for a safe ledge. I'll convince her to let me and Sophie live in the guest house. But for how long? How long until their roots, planted in soft soil, are washed up by another rainstorm?

Hello? she hears someone call out. Elise, Sophie, are you in here?

Elise wipes the dust off her hands and takes a few steps down the hall. Mrs. Wagner, standing in the kitchen, offers her a meek smile.

A construction worker knocked on my door this morning, she says. He wanted to apologize. He packed up your things and asked if I'd be willing to store them in my basement.

Sophie tramples down the stairs and stops on the final step.

Where is our stuff? she says, breathless.

In my basement. Come, Mrs. Wagner says, waving them on. I'll show you.

Sophie doesn't move from the stairs. She lifts her hand to swipe her hair from her eyes. A stream of blood drips from her fingers, along her metacarpal bones, and stops at her wrist.

Sophie, Elise says. You're bleeding.

Sophie turns her hand and inspects the skin. A red drop falls onto the dust-coated carpet and blooms into an ovular stain. She looks up at Elise and her face retreats, as though she's running over a hill behind her eyes. Before Elise can ask her if she needs help, she says, I think I'm going to faint, then her knees buckle and she plummets to the ground, narrowly missing the corner of the upturned futon.

Mrs. Wagner pulls her sweater over her head and balls it into a pillow as Elise lifts Sophie's head, cupping her warm scalp in her hands. When Sophie regains consciousness a few seconds later, she asks Elise where they are, her gaze circling the ceiling. We're at our house, Elise says, and her chest tightens. She stares at her sister for a beat longer, waiting for a hint of recognition, but she remains unsure if Sophie is comprehending what has happened.

Why don't we go to my house, Mrs. Wagner suggests again. I'll make you both a cup of tea.

Elise assumes that Sophie will resist, but she rolls onto her side and pushes her torso off the ground. Can I have coffee instead? she asks wearily as Elise steadies her arm to help her stand.

They walk Sophie to Mrs. Wagner's living room sofa and she stretches out onto her back. Don't fall asleep, Mrs. Wagner yells from the kitchen. You might have a concussion. Sophie props herself up, her hands resting against her stomach.

Did I faint? she asks.

Elise nods and sits near her feet. Don't look again, but your hand is cut.

Sophie glances down briefly and then tips her head back.

They broke a lamp in our bedroom, she says. I was trying to pick up the pieces.

Mrs. Wagner returns with a tray of sugar cookies and a pot of tea. Chamomile, she says, and arranges the cups on the table. They thank her and she disappears again to fetch a wet towel for Sophie's hand.

How are you feeling? Elise asks.

A little strange, Sophie replies. She takes a small bite of a sugar cookie and leaves it on the corner of the table.

Elise observes her for a moment, wondering if she might bring up the house, but decides to give her time to rest. She pours herself a cup of tea and then excuses herself to the bathroom. On the back of the toilet is an etched-glass bowl filled with potpourri. The toilet lid is fitted with a plush maroon cover that matches the bathmat on the floor. She pulls her pants and underwear to her knees and sits on the toilet seat. Her skin feels cold. She grips her thighs as though they could be attached to a stranger's body.

She wishes she could reverse the times she turned left to drive to Sheba's house after work instead of returning to theirs. She wishes she had tried harder to come home during college. She could have worked longer hours, saved more money. And yet, how could she have known that their life would unfold this way? It's only in retrospect that we can reorganize decisions, invent new motivations, different concerns. Of course it's possible that Mrs. Wagner has been lying to them this whole time, pretending to be a kind and caring neighbor, when in fact she betrayed them as soon as their mother was taken from them. It's possible her kindness toward Sophie is a pendulum swing, rebounding from the guilt she feels for contacting their landlord. Would she let them go on drinking her tea and eating her sugar cookies without telling them the truth?

Elise flushes the toilet and enters the living room. Mrs. Wagner is kneeling on the floor next to Sophie, wiping the dried blood off her hand and wrist. Sophie laughs uneasily as Mrs. Wagner tells her a story about how Mr. Wagner came home one day with a fishing hook caught through his thumb. He didn't want to go to the hospital, she says. I had to use a bolt cutter to pry off the barbs, then push it all the way through.

Elise clears her throat. Where are those boxes again? she asks. With our stuff.

Let me show you, Mrs. Wagner says, handing Sophie the rag. She leads Elise into the basement and points to a corner where five cardboard boxes are stacked. That's it? she wants to say. She had imagined that the entire basement would be filled with their life, but seeing it now, she realizes how little they actually own, how little they need to live. In a way, it feels liberating. She finds a duffel bag balled up in one of the boxes, inexplicably sticky and covered in cobwebs, and packs clothing, shoes, and toiletries for her and Sophie, as well as a gold braided necklace that belonged to her grandmother, and the box of photographs Sophie had arranged on the dresser. She carries the bag up the back steps, across the flattened sedge grass path, and to the trunk of her car. When she returns to the Wagners', she finds Sophie alone, her eyelids languid.

How are you feeling? Elise asks loudly, intending to rouse her.

Good, she responds, her voice delicate, and rolls onto her side.

I think we should go to Sheba's, Soph. You're starting to fall asleep.

They say goodbye to Mrs. Wagner, who tells them they can use her basement as storage for as long they need, that Mr. Wagner is the only one who goes down there anyway. Before Elise pulls out, they idle in front of their house for a moment, its rubble spilled out, the cloying smell of sawdust hanging in the air. Finally, Sophie says: Can we go? I don't feel like being here anymore. Elise drives, checking the rearview mirror as she exits their road. She sees Mrs. Wagner standing in her lawn, a yellow robe pulled around her. Initially Elise thinks she's facing them, watching them leave, but then she realizes she's turned in the other direction, toward their house. She stands for several seconds, clutching the robe close to her neck, then she bends over to pick up the newspaper and returns inside.

Driving down Milestone Road, Elise keeps one hand steadied on top of the steering wheel and three fingers pressed against her lips. When should we tell Mom? she says, looking at Sophie.

I don't know, Sophie says and pulls her sweatshirt hood over her eyes. Not now. Later. I can't handle that now.

Elise slows to turn onto Polpis Road. She has the inappropriate urge to tell Sophie that, when they get to Sheba's, she shouldn't point out how expensive the washer and dryer are, and that, generally speaking, rich people don't like to be reminded of their wealth.

Be nice when you meet Sheba, she says instead. She's my closest friend, but she's very particular.

Thanks for the reminder, Sophie says. Usually I maul people when I meet them.

Elise laughs jerkily.

Seriously, though, Sophie continues. You always make her sound like a sociopath.

Elise frowns. I just want you two to get along.

When they pull up to the gate and Elise enters the code, Sophie sits up and pushes her hood back. She rotates her head, making note of the evenly clipped lawn, gables that resemble perpetually raised eyebrows, balconies that overlook pristine island land.

It's huge, Elise says, trying to sound dismissive and complimentary at the same time.

Uh, yeah, I can see that, Sophie says, leaning closer to the dashboard. They park in front of the guest house and Sophie rolls down her window.

This is for real where Sheba lives?

Sort of. It's their vacation house. She pauses, searching for a qualifier. I know. It's unbelievable.

They carry the duffel bag into the house and Sophie immediately darts to the taxidermy animals, which she rearranges according to their position on the food chain. Elise dumps out the old coffee and begins to scoop new grounds into a filter. Sophie plops onto one of the washed-velvet sofas and declares: I'm sleeping here.

You can if you want, Elise says. But there's an actual room upstairs you can sleep in.

She pours water into the back of the coffee machine and flips the red switch.

I'll be back, she says. I'm going to make sure the beds have sheets.

She ascends the stairs and searches for indications of Sheba sleeping in one of the rooms—a toe peeking from behind the corner, discarded clothes on the floor—but she isn't there. The second bedroom is freshly made up, new towels folded on the bed. In the room where Elise has stayed, the sheets are pulled firm, disturbed only by a book dropped on the mattress. She sits on the edge of the bed and falls back, drawing out her arms and feeling for a pillow. What will happen, she wonders, if Sophie and Sheba are home alone together? Sophie prefers silence, detests mornings; Sheba is a geyser of chatter, a twenty-four-hour clock. How long will the volcano of their combined personalities remain dormant?

Her eyes fall shut; they're too dry and sting as the lids close. She thinks about her mom, how devastated she will be, how she will blame herself. How will they even tell her, after everything she's been through? Maybe she will be comforted to know her daughters are still together, living in the guest house, only a wall separating them, just like her and Aunt Beth. Or would she be angry with Elise for not being more diligent, for not calling her immediately?

Elise thinks about a time, as kids, when Sophie decided she

wanted to run away from home. Snow had been falling for hours and the night was quiet, alarming in its serenity. Elise thought, She won't do it, she won't run away. She was only five years old. There's no way. And then, when Sophie opened the front door, a knapsack filled with gel pens and socks flung over her shoulder, she thought, Mom won't let her do it. But then Gilda did let her do it. She stood in the kitchen fluffing a pot of rice, refusing to acknowledge what she called Sophie's rebellious tantrum. Elise watched her baby sister, knee-deep in snow, trudge across the lawn—wearing only a wool sweater, no hat, gloves, or coat— beyond the perimeter of light and into the dark.

Elise cried. Between her and Sophie, she was the one who always cried. She wondered if she lacked an important instinct Sophie possessed resolutely: the ability to know when to leave, to detach, to start over.

I hate you! Elise yelled at her mother.

You don't hate me, Gilda said, picking at the dried calluses on her palms. Go to your room.

Elise hid underneath her bed for twenty minutes before Sophie returned. She spied from the top of the attic stairs as Sophie hugged Gilda's legs, burying her face in her thigh, and Gilda stroked her head. But then, on a flip, Gilda told Sophie she was grounded. She needed to stay in her room with Elise and not to come out until morning.

Where did you go? Elise asked while Sophie unpacked her bag, her cheeks and nose bright and glistening.

I found a new tree, she recalls Sophie telling her. We can go there tomorrow if you want.

.   .   .

Elise rolls over in the guest house bed and rubs her throbbing, stiff jaw. How long had she been asleep? She hears Sheba's voice chiming through, loud and eager. Elise can sense she's already embraced Sophie, her arms pinning down her sister's sides. Sophie doesn't like to be hugged, especially by people she doesn't know. Elise stands up from the bed and hurries downstairs. But when she reaches the kitchen, she finds they've already gone outside. Elise opens the screen door and steps out onto the porch. Sheba and Sophie are sitting cross-legged and barefoot on the lawn. Sophie is hunched over, her hands in her lap, and Sheba is rubbing her back. When she hears the swing of the screen door, Sophie looks up and wipes her red, puffy eyes.

Is everything all right? Elise asks. A crow lands on the guest house drainpipe, startling her. She steps a few feet closer.

Elise, Sheba says, and places a hand over Sophie's foot. Why didn't you tell me you and your sister need a place to live? Of course you can stay with me.

✦

Elise wakes to the sound of nothing, and then she listens a little closer. Two gray mourning doves are perched on the windowsill, their breasts ballooned and opalescent in front of the rising sun. At times life can be so still, she thinks, if she waits between its moments. Then she hoists herself off the bed, washes with a bar of charcoal soap, and descends to the kitchen to drink a glass of grapefruit juice before work.

Downstairs in the guest house, every light has been left on: the recessed lights above the fireplace, the floodlights outside the mudroom door, the hood light on the stove. A pizza box is open on the oak peninsula with two half-bitten slices inside. She turns the corner to the living room and finds Sophie asleep on one sofa and Sheba asleep on the other. *Earth Girls Are Easy* is paused on the small flat-screen television in the corner. Elise went to bed early, at ten, because she had to work in the morning. Sophie had told her she would follow shortly after. Elise takes a blanket from a chest near the door and tosses it over her. Then she pours herself the grapefruit juice, drinks it slowly, puts away the pizza and wipes the crumbs from the counter, shuts off the lights, and rushes out the door.

The ocean is a metallic slick today, lumbering up the shore and then retreating in a single gulp. A flock of oystercatchers glides above the coarse sea waves, their wings sharp and steady against the wind. Elise writes in her composition notebook: adult count (four), fledgling count (zero), number of eggs (four), evidence of hatching (N/A), weather (cloudy), and then adds: Elise (tired). This makes her chuckle. She checks on the eggs one more time through her binoculars and finds them resting among dried sea-weed and skate casings. She slips her notebook and binoculars into her backpack and decides to go for a stroll.

She and Sophie have been living at Sheba's for a week. They have not told Gilda what happened to Sophie or the house. Elise attempted to call the landlord—she at least wanted the opportu-nity to explain that their mother hadn't voluntarily broken the lease agreement—but the phone number she found was discon-nected. They haven't been back since they first encountered the demolition, but Elise assumes the house is gone, its dust floating around the corners of her consciousness, not yet settled. She worries that this fact might break her mother's hope for return-ing. She's not even sure what she would say to Gilda, what words would come out, how she would explain, because she doesn't quite understand it herself. What does it mean that when they envision their home, the image that comes to mind no longer exists?

Elise is standing at the shore skipping flat, smooth stones across the estuary. Her defenses are down, contemplating tranquil wa-ters, the daylight slanted across these tender clouds, when she hears the strong flap of a wing, a string of cries. A prickle runs over the surface of her skin. She notices a bird flailing by the shore, feigning a broken wing. Elise glances over her shoulder and sees a great black-backed gull in a flash, stabbing its beak into the soft, speckled shells. Before she can even react, it flies away, leaving the eggs shattered and strewn on the sand.

The tide rushes forth, wets the hem of her pants. She faces the horizon, presses her fists into her stomach, and screams across the ocean.

When Steve arrives to pick her up, she does not meet him at the shoreline as usual. Elise! he calls out. She remains huddled on the sand next to her beach chair. He pulls the dinghy out of the water and walks toward her.

What's wrong? he asks.

They're dead, she says stoically.

He looks around, as if he doesn't know who she's talking about. The birds?

Elise nods. The eggs. A seagull killed them while I was on a walk. This was my one job and I fucked it up.

Steve puts his hands on his hips and squints up at the sky.

Oh, kid. It had nothing to do with you. This happens, it's life. They'll brood again.

She squeezes her knees closer to her chest. She'd only lost one other brood, during her final summer before she left for college. An investment banker drove up to the beach in his Land Rover on a Friday, flashing a cooler filled with rosé and blanco tequila, a small bag of cocaine tucked into his shirt pocket. I'll call the fucking cops, he said to her when she told him he had to leave, perhaps not understanding that she was a government employee. He smashed the eggs in the middle of the night, allowing the beach to reopen the following week.

You don't know if they'll brood again, Elise says to Steve. This could have been their only shot.

She can tell Steve is uncomfortable. He bows his head and kicks at the sand.

Come on, he says, reaching out his hand. You've been through a lot this year. Get up, brush yourself off. You'll feel better in the morning.

She concedes, and when he drops her off at her car, he gives her a quick hug. I'm sorry, he says. I know it's tough. And then he rolls away in his Jeep, an eighties rock station blaring from the speakers.

As Elise pulls up to the gate at Sheba's house, a rabbit darts in front of her right tire and jukes to the side of the road. She heels into the brake, the seat belt catching between her breasts. Down the driveway, Sophie and Sheba are sitting together on the guest house porch. She considers waiting in the car until her emotions pass. Her eyes are visibly raw and burning. But she knows they'll notice her eventually. She drives forward, and they wave as she approaches. She parks, unbuckles her seatbelt, wipes her cheeks, and dries her palms on her shorts.

Sheba is sitting on the porch railing, skirt hiked up to her hips, swinging her legs. Sophie is on the Adirondack chair across from her.

You know she's only eighteen, right, Sheba? Elise says, pointing at the gin and tonics they're drinking.

Yes, and we were angels at that age.

What's wrong? Sophie asks. Have you been crying?

Elise digs her fingertips into her cheekbones and shakes her head. Nothing, she says, and then bursts into tears again. Sheba and Sophie stand and embrace her. She feels embarrassed for disrupting the mood—she can tell they were enjoying each other's company, the two of them without her there. Can I have one of those? Elise says after a few even breaths and gestures at Sophie's cocktail.

Sheba goes inside and returns with a drink for Elise, a sprig of mint dangling off the rim. Elise takes a gulp, then explains what happened step by step, how she was by the shore, her back to the nests, gazing out at the water, when a large seagull swooped in and killed all the eggs. It happened in a matter of seconds. Elise heard the parents crying, trying to lure the predator away. That was my one job, she says again, to protect the eggs, and I fucked it up.

Sheba hops off the railing and sits on the side table between Elise and Sophie. You're the best egg protector I know, she says.

It's not your fault, Sophie says. You couldn't have stopped the seagull—it probably stalked the nests for hours, waiting for the perfect moment. You know how seagulls are.

Do you think they'll lay more eggs? Sheba asks. Like, if all your children were murdered by a seagull, would you even want to have another round?

Elise drops her chin into her hands. I hate the idea of them dying and the parents never having chicks again. They have to at least try.

What about you? Sheba says, looking at Sophie. Would you lay more eggs?

Sophie shrugs. It's different for me. If I have children, my girl-friend and I, or wife or whatever, would have to adopt or find a sperm donor. I don't know if the agency would let me have more children if my first round were murdered?

Wait a sec, Sheba says, suddenly elated. Sophie, you're gay? You never told me that!

She barely talks to me about it, Elise says into her drink. And I'm her sister.

It's weird to talk to your sister about that stuff, Sophie says.

Sheba places a hand on her sternum.

I'm bisexual.

Sheba, come on . . . You made out with a couple of girls in college, Elise interjects. I don't know if that's the same thing.

Whoa, Sheba says. I think I can handle my own queer assessment, thank you.

Sophie holds her hands up in surrender. I'm staying out of this one.

Anyway! Sheba says, flicking her hair over her shoulder. I think it's better being raised by two moms. Men complicate everything. I'm so grateful the three of us get to wake up with each other every day. Sheba takes hold of each of their hands. We're like sister wives without the creepy Mormon man ruining the dynamic.

Elise shakes her hand free, grossed out by the suggestion that she's in a throuple with her sister. She glances at Sheba's other hand, which is still clasping Sophie's. I'm going to get the gin, she says, and deposits the rest of her drink into her mouth, the liquid running over her molars.

An hour later they've finished the bottle, so Sheba runs to the main house and brings back two very expensive bottles of chenin blanc that they demolish over one round of Up the River, Down the River, a card game Sophie teaches them. The night air turns chilly, so they venture inside and stand around the oak peninsula, littering it with popcorn shrapnel and rings of condensation. Sheba announces with her finger in the air that she has to use the ladies' room and climbs the stairs on her hands and knees. Fifteen minutes pass and she doesn't return, so Elise leaves to check on her and finds her splayed across the bed, palms postured to the ceiling. Downstairs, Sophie climbs onto the couch, muttering she's too tired to brush her teeth, and falls asleep.

Elise tries to lie next to Sheba, but the insides of her eyelids are spinning, so she takes her phone into the bathroom and closes the door. She sits on the floor against the wall, welcoming the cold tiles against her legs. In the corner behind the door is Sheba's underwear, inverted and twisted into a ball. An empty Acqua Panna bottle has rolled next to the toilet. She unlocks her phone and begins scrolling through old photos on her social media, stopping on a photo she took of Harry in her dorm room. He's wearing a pair of her silk pajama shorts and posing like Rodin's *The Thinker,* his impeccable abdominals on display. The post has 104 likes, one of the highest counts she's ever gotten. She smirks and zooms in on the pointed fold on the seam near his crotch. She closes the app and searches for their last text message conversation, forgetting she deleted their text history soon after she returned to the island. She opens up a fresh message.

Elise: Hiiiii. It's me.

She finds it strange to see Harry's name at the top of a blank messaging space. She places her cell face down on the tile floor and slides it toward the toilet. It hits the Acqua Panna bottle with a clank. She places her hands flat on the floor to stand herself up, then looks in the mirror at her drooping eyes and mouth. Her phone vibrates. He responded immediately, she thinks, feeling satisfied. She likes that she can still contact Harry whenever she wants, and in this way, he is still hers.

Harry: I'm at a party. What's up?

Elise: ooh. cool. cool cool

mr. party

like its 1999

She looks in the mirror again and fixes her hair. She's imagining the kinds of friends he has made in New York: women with thick chain-link bracelets and dental work, men with combed side parts and monogrammed socks.

Elise: you're at a party and im not invited?

Harry: haha. are you in the city?

Elise: lol. no. sorry. had a rough day and then got drunk accidentally

kinda wish I didn't.

Harry doesn't say anything in reply. Elise begins to wonder if he only answered so quickly because he thinks she's vulnerable in a way he isn't. This sensation overwhelms her, a desire to dispel his perception of her as a victim. He needs to remember how attractive he thinks she is, how, one time at breakfast in the dining hall, he'd rested his head on her shoulder, inching closer to her, and her friends thought he was being so sweet, that maybe he would finally ask her to be his girlfriend. He moved his hand up her pleated skirt, subtly, and pushed her underwear aside. She inched her legs open, laughing and nodding at whatever they said across the table, and he slipped his finger inside her. They kept talking, she'd take a drink from her orange juice, her face tingling and warm, and he fingered her until she couldn't disguise it anymore, and she had to take him by the wrist and pull him away.

She removes her shirt and bra. Her breasts are as drunk as her face. She braces them with one arm and opens her mouth, then clicks a photograph of herself in the mirror. It's blurry, focused on a bottle of mouthwash on the counter, but she hits Send anyway.

His text bubble fills and pops, fills and pops, for what feels like an eternity, until the reply floats into thin air.

Harry: Haha. I remember those ☺

Elise stares at the response. Her eyes try to jumble the letters into something erotic, or if not erotic, then decent. She places her phone in the sink and walks downstairs, pours a large glass of water, and sits outside in an Adirondack chair.

It's raining. She feels a mist blow from the curtain of water running off the shingles. How enlivening it would feel, she thinks, to stand on the railing and dive in, to hover above the ground. She imagines gliding through the downpour, and with each pass of her cupped hands, the raindrops part into the stars. She swims down the stone driveway, past the hyacinth bushes and swamp milkweed, through the cranberry bogs. But before she reaches the spot where she and Sophie used to pick blueberries, the rain stops, and she falls, deep down, down-down-down, to a place where no one can reach her.

PART III

The Main House

✦

A stream of cars feeds into a set of four gas station pumps across the street from the island's main supermarket entrance. Two attendants are managing the line: an elderly Black man and a white teenager. The elderly man is wearing a flat cap and squeegees the car windshields with a bucket of murky water, biding his time until he hears the click of the gas nozzle. The teenager runs back and forth in camo-print sneakers to deliver change and receipts for drivers. Across the street is an empty self-service gas station with a much larger lot, but no one relinquishes their position at the full-service station.

Elise stretches her legs into the brake and clutch, realizing the mistake she'd made by taking the most direct route home from work. Cars disappear and replicate in front of her: one car finishes getting gas and is replaced by a new car, but the total number of cars never seems to shrink. If no original cars remain, she thinks, is it still the same traffic line, the same Ship of Theseus? She finds a packet of M&M's in her car door and sucks on one until her tongue turns green and sweet milk chocolate coats her mouth.

After half an hour of stopping and going, she approaches the rotary where the traffic has cleared, but when she turns onto Polpis Road, she finds herself stuck behind a family on low-rider bicycles wearing matching polka-dot bathing suits and tiny leather backpacks. As she drives by them, veering around to give them ample space, they wave to thank her. She waves back, and as she returns to her lane, the family shrinking in her rearview mirror, she feels a teardrop drip off her chin and onto her lap, a stroll of emotion loitering inside her.

She and Sophie have been living in the guest house for nearly a month. The ocean connecting them with Gilda has formed a mass in their minds, a volume of distance. Elise knows they have been distracted by their jobs and living with Sheba, but Gilda has become preoccupied by her life in Brazil too. She hasn't been spending as much time waiting around the house for a phone call from them.

Elise parks, steps onto the guest house porch, and nearly trips over a cardboard box taped shut and covered in postage stamps. She picks it up and reads a Brazilian address with no name on the sender's line. The departure stamp is from over a month ago. The box has collected stamps through the north of Brazil and two separate customs checks, through Florida, Virginia, and Western Massachusetts. It was originally sent to their house, but someone (Mrs. Wagner, most likely) crossed out the address in black Sharpie and redirected it here. It's probably a copy of Mom's waiver application, Elise thinks. She asked her to send one weeks ago, but Gilda had been unable to find an affordable place to make a scan. Elise carries the box inside the guest house, and when she places it on the oak peninsula, she feels a heavy weight shift from one side to the other.

Hi, Sheba says, reclined on the sofa, her hand skimming the floor.

I didn't see you there, Elise says, and slides the box toward the coffee maker.

They left, Sheba says, sitting up. They went back to New York.

Who? Elise says. Helen and Holly?

Sheba nods. They said they had to leave for work, but I think they just don't want to see me anymore.

Elise walks around the oak peninsula and sits beside her on the sofa. Sheba's cheek is creased from where she had been lying.

Why wouldn't they want to see you?

Why do you think? She grabs a pillow and tucks it into her lap, fidgeting with its braided corners. The yacht club. I got rejected.

No way, Elise says in genuine disbelief. That Sheba wouldn't be accepted hadn't seemed possible. How do you feel about it? she asks.

Sheba sighs and collapses over the pillow. I didn't even want to be a member! I wanted to stay in London, remember? But now that I didn't get in, I'm, like, paranoid about why they rejected me. Was it something I did? Was it something I said? I probably said dick or titty in front of a senior member and didn't even realize it. My mouth is a liability.

You should be able to say dick or titty without retaliation, Sheb. Seriously, fuck that place. It's much more interesting not to be a part of the yacht club.

Can you say that loud enough so that my moms can hear? They're probably at Teterboro already.

Fuck the yacht club! Elise yells. Sheba laughs and rests the side of her head on Elise's shoulder.

We're parentless now, she says. No supervision needed.

Elise rubs the back of Sheba's hand, massaging her soft skin and thin bones.

Your parents will be back, she says, not directly to Sheba but to the taxidermy animals on the mantel, who resemble a jury, or perhaps a promenade of angels. I don't know if my mom will ever be able to come back.

Sorry, Sheba says. I shouldn't have equated the two.

We'll be OK, Elise says after a moment and lets go of her hand.

The sofa begins to vibrate, and Sheba searches with her hands beneath their seat. Elise fishes the phone out of the crack in the cushions and sees that it's her mom. They look at the phone, then at each other. Elise feels a pang of guilt for knowing she needs to leave Sheba to answer. I should take this, she says finally. I haven't talked to her in a few days.

Sheba groans and rolls into a ball on the sofa, her face obscured, as Elise carries the phone outside. She sits on the bottom porch step, rubbing the soles of her feet against the grass.

Oi, filha, Gilda says. Where are you?

Why? Elise answers instinctively, afraid the question might be foreboding.

No reason, Gilda says. I tried to call earlier but you didn't answer.

Oh, Elise says, scratching her forehead. It took me forever to get home from work. Traffic was terrible.

I don't miss that summer traffic, Gilda says. The way she says *that traffic* makes Elise think maybe it is the same traffic, even with different cars. You sound a little blue, honey, she adds.

I'm just tired. I haven't been sleeping well.

Hey, Gilda says, trying to sound upbeat. I called because I want to tell you some good news. I got a job. I'm doing bookkeeping for a kitchen-supply store in town.

You did? Elise says and stands. You're not cooking anymore?

I cook, just not for work. I can't be on my feet twelve hours a day, filha. My back is killing me.

I thought you said getting a job would hurt your case, Elise says. You told me you didn't want to show you were planting roots.

Yes, I know, but the lawyer said it will take time to hear back.

Elise leans against the still-warm hood of her car. I didn't even know you were looking for a job.

I want to help your aunt with the bills, and I need something to do during the day.

Sophie and I can send you money, Elise replies. We've been saving.

Her mother's voice goes thin. Oh, Elise, she says and releases a slow breath. Don't waste your money on me. I'll be fine.

Elise glances up at a cloud passing overhead. So, how did you find this job?

Well, Gilda says, and laughs a little. It happened really because Beth is terrible about buying fruits and vegetables. I mean, she goes to the grocery store and comes home with butter, cheese, bread, and ice cream. So I decided to walk to the open-air market that's in town on Saturdays. I have to send you pictures—they sell the most beautiful, red, delicious strawberries, nothing like the flavorless strawberries in the U.S. I finished my shopping and then I thought, Since I'm here, I'll go to the internet café and send you girls an email.

Did you get my email, by the way? she says as an aside.

Yes, Elise says, I got it. It was an email about Elise's future, musings on what Gilda thinks she could do as a career. Elise hadn't written her back yet, overwhelmed by her candor. As I was writing you all of these thoughts, Gilda says, I began to list in my head all the jobs I've had in my life. I'm in my forties now and I've been working since I was a teenager—can you believe that? So I thought, Maybe it's a good idea to write everything down. Because, you know, I was starting to tell myself this story that all I've ever done is cook, and so all I'll ever be able to do is cook. But as I was listing each of these jobs, I remembered that as a sous I did all of the product ordering for the kitchen, every week. And I calculated plate cost every time we changed the menu. I have experience expediting tickets and negotiating with vendors. It was actually really cool to lay it out on the screen, because—she pauses, her voice wavers—I was beginning to think I hadn't accomplished anything in my life. That I had worked all these years and had nothing to show for it.

That isn't true, Elise says. You have done so much.

I know, I know, filha. But it's easy to start thinking that way after what happened. They threw me out of the country like I was a nothing. Like I was nothing more than a little flea. And I began to think that maybe it was true. But as I wrote down everything I've done, to record it, like a résumé, I realized it wasn't true. I have accomplished a lot. I have skills, and I have things to offer. So I printed out ten copies, and I walked to the stores in town and handed them out, said that if they needed someone to help with sales or ordering or bookkeeping, that I have the experience. And then—you won't believe it, Elise—the next day I got a phone call. Only one day later. If my grandmother was alive, she would say it was an act of God. I was so nervous. I haven't gone for an interview since, I don't even remember when. I told Beth and she said she would help me prepare. She put on a pair of reading glasses and pretended to be an interviewer, and—Gilda laughs—Beth was much harder on me than the actual interviewer was. Actually, the owner was really impressed with my experience and seemed to like me. She didn't mind that I hadn't worked in Brazil for so long. And then, at the end, she told me I got the job. Beth was waiting outside in the car, and when I came out, I ran to her screaming! I couldn't help it. We were both dressed up, had makeup on and everything, so we went straight to a restaurant to celebrate, ordered a big steak and a bottle of champagne.

Gilda stops, realizing Elise is silent on the other end of the line, and waits for her to say something.

Hello? she says. Are you still there?

I'm here, Mom, Elise says and returns to the porch steps. Sorry, I'm just taking it all in.

Gilda slows down. I just finished my third day, and I really like it there, she continues. The owners are nice people. They said I can leave early if I need to, for errands or appointments. And they gave me my own desk by a window. There's a hibiscus bush outside.

Elise taps her fingers against the wooden railing. I'm happy for you—really. It sounds perfect, she says, trying to sound upbeat.

Are you sure you're not sad? Gilda says.

I'm sure. I'm just tired.

You should take a nap. Make some chamomile tea, she says. Give your sister a big kiss from me. I love you.

I will. Love you too.

Elise hangs up and leans her torso over her knees, pressing the air out of her lungs and stomach. When she feels her face expand, turn hot and red, she sits up and gasps for air, dark clouds blooming in her vision. I guess that's all it is, she thinks as her breath steadies. My mom has a job. She has a new job, a sister, and a life in Atibaia. She stands, stretches her calves against a step. I think I need to go for a long walk, she says to the open air, and looks through the window at Sheba, who is standing at the oak peninsula, rotating the package in her hands.

Is this from your mom? Sheba asks as Elise walks inside. Let's open it.

I don't know. I think so, Elise says. I should wait for Sophie to get home from work to open it.

Did you ask your mom what's inside?

No, I forgot, Elise says, shaking her head. It's probably just legal paperwork.

How do you always put off opening packages? Sheba says and pushes it toward Elise. I open everything the second it arrives.

Elise shrugs, ignoring the box. I'm going to go for a walk, she says instead. Do you want to join? It's beautiful outside. She figures Sheba will probably decline, but to her surprise she agrees. She dons a straw hat and a pair of tennis shoes, and suggests they walk on a trail at the back of the house that leads to a series of kettle ponds. They hop over a split rail fence behind the garbage shed, then follow a sandy path lined with dense arrowwood and hazelnut bushes. Sheba points whenever she thinks she hears a bird, likely for Elise's amusement—towhees and catbirds squawking in the brush. Elise can tell she's trying hard to lighten the mood, but her mind is still swirling about her conversation with Gilda, how she said she felt like she hadn't accomplished anything in her life. The thought makes Elise's heart hurt. The truth is, she's had the same thought before too, about herself and about Gilda. As a teenager, she resented her mother for not accomplishing more, for not striving further, for not being like other moms who seemed to work in an office and cook dinner every night and clean the house, the motherly tasks Gilda didn't do. Elise? Sheba says. Are you listening? Yes, sorry, she replies. Her thighs are slipping against each other with sweat. She feels bad for having these thoughts, but she's hurt that Gilda has moved on, that she—subconsciously or not—is building a life in Brazil without her and Sophie, even if it's the only option Gilda has. Elise stops in the middle of the fire path, the sun dipping below the tupelo trees. An indiscernible amount of time has passed, and it's unclear to Elise how far they've walked.

Where are we? Elise says. Sheba mutters something to herself and turns around. When they return to the guest house twenty minutes later, Elise stays behind on the porch to shake out the sand from her sneakers. I am happy for her, she thinks, knocking her heels against the ledge. Maybe this is the version of my mother I've always wanted.

She walks into the guest house barefoot, carrying her shoes and socks. As soon as she enters, Sheba retrieves the package from the oak peninsula and presents it to Elise.

Open it, she says. I can tell you want to.

I'm hungry, Elise responds, dropping her sneakers by the door, and pumps sanitizing lotion from above the kitchen sink into her palm. I'll open it later, when Sophie's here. Sheba relents, and they put two frozen cheese pizzas in the oven and turn on a nature documentary. When the loop of advertisements begins to stream, Elise glances at Sheba, whose eyes are fluttering and slowing to a close.

Do you want to go to bed? Elise says and moves Sheba's plate off her lap and onto the coffee table. Sheba's head wags up and down. Elise walks with her up the stairs, knowing she won't sleep if she thinks Elise might stay up later. After a few silent minutes, she returns to the kitchen downstairs. A text from Sophie nearly causes her phone to rattle off the counter.

Sophie: Mom got a job—did she tell you?

Elise stares at the message.

Elise: Yeah. I talked to her a few hours ago.

I'm not sure how I feel about it.

Several minutes pass and Sophie texts back.

I think it's good. She was starting to go stir crazy. She needs to keep busy.

Elise: I get it. I just think it's weird she's just like, moving on.

She places the phone down and then picks it back up.

Elise: A package came from Brazil. I'm assuming it's from Mom but there's no name

Sophie: Did you open it?

Elise: No not yet. I was waiting for you.

Sophie: Open it! You always wait to open packages

Elise: I thought you might want to be here

Sophie: I'm not going to get home until late. Open it and text me a photo

Elise searches the kitchen drawers for a pair of scissors, then gives up and uses a chef's knife to slice the packing tape. She lifts

the flaps. At the top is a note from Gilda, written in perfect cur-
sive:

Share with your sister.

I love you.

Mãe

Elise folds the note into a small square and slips it back inside
the box. She crumples up the yellow tissue paper underneath, the
smell of roses and cinnamon wafting from within. The first gift
she removes is a miniature statue of a tree made of wires and
purple amethyst pebbles. Elise carefully bends the pliable branches
back into tree shape. The next gift is a decorative string of plush
felt stars with a plastic ring at the end for hanging. She drapes the
stars over the wire branches and stone petals. The final present—
three making it impossible to share evenly with Sophie, but such
is her mother's logic—is a refrigerator magnet of a bushel of red
chili peppers, symbolizing good luck.

Elise lines them up against the coffee maker and texts a photo
to Sophie and Gilda.

Elise: Love them so so so so much. Thank you

She sits on the velvet sofa for a bit longer, fussing with the
objects and inhaling the tissue paper scent. She imagines the store
where her mother bought them, its particular musk and creaky
floors, how the shopkeepers would have been excited to learn
Gilda would be sending these presents to her daughters in another
country. When she retires upstairs to brush her teeth, she places

each object on her bedside table. Sheba's face is buried in her pillow on the other side of Elise's bed, her breath muffled. She clicks off the lamp and lies on top of the covers, clutching the string of stars. As she falls asleep, her phone blinks with light.

Gilda: I love you too, filha. I hope you get some rest.

Sheba texts the group chat early in the day saying she wants to cook Elise and Sophie dinner at the main house, because the sound system is better than in the guest house, and the couches are cozier, and there is a wider selection of food in the pantry. Sophie opens the text while at work and responds several hours later saying she'll be there, that she doesn't have to go in for the dinner shift. Because Elise doesn't have service on the beach, she receives the text on her way home. She arrives at the guest house and finds Sheba and Sophie have already gone to the main house. Sheba is in the kitchen, obscured by the steam rising from a pot of boiling water, and Sophie is grating a block of parmesan cheese next to her. I'm making cacio e pepe, Sheba announces as Elise enters. She and Sophie are in matching pinstripe aprons.

Pasta? Elise replies. She knows Sheba only makes pasta when she plans to drink her body weight in alcohol.

Do you want a glass of Beaujolais? Sheba asks while pouring the bottle.

Elise walks around the kitchen counter to give Sophie a hug. Sophie takes a pinch of cheese and drops it into her mouth.

Sheba stirs parmesan into the pasta with loads of black pepper and piles the cacio e pepe into a large serving platter, then sets it at the center of the banquette with cream pillows where Elise had arranged flowers for the fundraiser. She turns on the stereo system and upbeat jazz resounds around them. This feels very adult, Elise remarks. They're using cloth napkins and a gravy boat for salad dressing.

I think we should go to a bar tonight, Sheba says, biting into a cascade of pasta.

Elise gestures at Sophie, who is helping herself to more wine. She can't. She's not old enough.

I have a fake she can use, Sheba says. Sophie mixes her pasta nonsensically and doesn't react, which makes Elise believe they discussed this plan without her.

You look nothing alike, Elise says. And everyone knows who Sophie is.

I know the person who works the door at the Chicken Box, Sophie interjects.

Oh yeah? Elise says. Who?

Sandy. We work together at the Lunch Counter and I cover their shifts all the time. They owe me one.

Sheba takes a big gulp of wine, her teeth tinged purple.

Remember how much fun we had going to bars when we were Sophie's age? she says. Illegally, I might add.

A guilt trip isn't going to work on me, Elise says, twirling her fork.

Whatever. I don't have to go, Sophie says. I'll text Sandy and tell them my sister won't let me leave the house.

Why would you say that? Elise says. This doesn't have to do with me.

You're the only one who doesn't want to go, Sophie retorts.

You're not old enough. That's not my fault.

Sheba snaps a hair tie on her wrist.

We can have fun here, Elise says. Where no one will be arrested.

I'm sick of hanging out at home, Sophie says. I need to do
something different. I'll use Sheba's fake. And I can wear different
clothes—a disguise.

Sheba, emboldened by Sophie's plea, chimes in: I have a wig
she can wear.

Sophie stares at her older sister, a slight tremble in her bottom
lip. Sheba eyes Elise too, their looks reminding her of all the times
Sheba and Elise had gone out dancing together, Elise borrowing
Sheba's clothes—hours and hours spent on the dance floor—
while Sophie solved trigonometry proofs alone in their bedroom,
and their mother pressed her sixteenth hanger steak into a pan.

Fine, Elise says and finishes the last of her glass of wine. This
wig better be good.

It's a lace-front, Sheba says and blows Elise a kiss between the
candlesticks. Let's go upstairs and try it on.

Sheba leads them to the walk-in closet in her bedroom, which,
she explains, was an office that was never used, so they tore the
wall down to convert it into her closet. It has a royal-blue sofa in
the center and a mechanical roller system that pulls out hidden
layers of clothes. Elise tries not to appear mesmerized, but she is;
she runs her hands across a section of silk blouses and clenches her
teeth.

Damn, Sheba, Sophie says. I'm guessing you don't have to
wash all of this laundry yourself?

Sheba shrugs. Sometimes I soak my underwear in the sink if
my period bleeds through.

Good to know you bleed like the rest of us, Elise mutters, and Sophie covers her mouth to prevent herself from spitting wine all over the rug.

Sheba flips through hanger after hanger, a slow reveal of her clothes, figuratively twirling her nipple tassels as she assesses the correct outfit for Sophie. Sophie sits on the floor, her wineglass balanced between her legs, while Sheba holds out various garments for her opinion. Sophie inspects each item, listing narrow preferences Elise did not know she had. I don't like orange, chiffon makes me sweat, I love sequins, no halter tops, I won't wear animal, do you have anything with zippers? Once they've whittled down several choices, Sheba stops abruptly and declares that they should have a fashion show. She instructs Elise to sit outside while Sophie gets dressed.

Why can't I stay here? Elise asks.

Because you're the judge, Sheba says, handing Sophie a faux-leather dress.

It won't take long, Sophie says to the side. I already know which one I like.

Elise obliges and sequesters herself on Sheba's bed. Sheba has slept in the guest house for so long, her main house bed is hardly touched. The bedside table is arranged with a Diptyque candle that has never been burned, a skinny gold lamp, and a pearl bracelet snaked across a poetry collection. Elise pushes the bracelet aside and runs her fingers across the embossed lettering. Yeats. She picks up the book, its soft, loose spine hanging by cobwebs of glue.

Through the narrow gap in the closet door, she sees Sheba lifting Sophie's shirt over her head. Elise can't see Sophie, but the shadows of her raised arms are cast over Sheba's face. The T-shirt flies; they laugh. Sheba wraps a dress around Sophie and zips it up the front, then they move to a space where Elise can no longer see either of them. She remembers a time in college when she, Sheba, and Harry were pregaming in her dorm room and Sheba leaned over and bit Elise's earlobe. She wanted to rile Harry up, to see him sweat. Harry unplugged Sheba's music from the aux cord and suggested they leave. Later, he told Elise he thought Sheba was in love with her. Elise responded, So what? We're in love with each other. If you show her you're jealous she'll fall in love even harder.

The closet door slides open and Sophie lets out a hard laugh.

I look like I'm thirty, she says.

Sheba presents Sophie to Elise.

Voilà.

The wig looks exactly like Sheba's ideal hair, when she flat-irons, curls, sprays, then brushes it. She's wearing platform shoes with bows tied around the ankles, and the dress is partly unzipped to expose a hint of cleavage. Sheba's drawn cat eyes on Sophie's lids that make her look cross-eyed in a tender, submissive way, and her skin has been dusted with a pale powder that flattens its natural honey depth.

You look like Sheba, Elise says and tilts her head.

Sheba seems pleased by this. She goes to her underwear drawer and pulls out the fake ID from the back. The picture is of an eighteen-year-old Sheba wearing flicked eyeliner and smooth curls. She hands it to Sophie.

Right. I look like a Latina version of Sheba, Sophie says.

Do you like it? Elise says.

Sophie pauses, inspects the dress. I kind of do, she says.

You look amazing, Sheba says, ushering Sophie out the door. Elise and I need to get dressed, then let's take a shot and I'll call a taxi.

I hope the music isn't terrible, Sophie says and tosses her new hair over her shoulder.

When they arrive at the Chicken Box, Sophie realizes there's been a misunderstanding. Sandy isn't working the door, they're bar-backing tonight. She learns this halfway through the line, which causes her to obsesses over the order in which they should stand. Maybe I should go last, Sophie offers without any apparent reasoning, and leaves the line to stand behind Sheba. A group of men ahead of them are singing their college anthem, and Sheba groans that the fraternal nationalism is stressing her out. She asks the women behind her if she can pay them five dollars for a Marlboro Red.

Don't worry, Sheba says, thumbing their lighter. The end of her cigarette sparks and she inhales a long drag. This ID has never failed me.

Sheba will go first, you go second, and I'll go last, Elise says to Sophie and takes her by the arm. If something happens, I'll be there to back you up. Sophie agrees to this plan and waits quietly, cupping the ID in her hand and glancing at it every few seconds. Under the dark whisper of island night, nothing but atmosphere and ocean around them, she resembles a sheepish teenager in wolf's clothing. It's going to be fine, Elise adds. Worst case scenario, we leave.

At the door, the man on the stool barely examines Sophie's face. He has an assembly line process: take the ID, scan it, move on to the next. Sophie trains her eyes on his hairline. When he returns the ID unfazed, she is so excited she yells, I made it! and stumbles in Sheba's platform heels. They hurry her away from the door and find an open foot of space behind the mass of people vying for the bartender's attention. Elise inspects the crowd for someone who might recognize them—a former schoolteacher, an older sibling—but there's nothing but slim women in chunky necklaces stretched against the pool table and men in lobster shorts organized in towering packs. Sheba tries to push forward to the front, but the crowd is stalwart. One woman who has a wet beer stain down her dress snarls at her to wait her turn.

This is impossible, Sheba says, retreating to Sophie and Elise. Why did we leave the house again?

Sophie tugs on the hem of Elise's shirt.

Hey—isn't that Rahul? she says, and points up at the bartender, who's standing on an elevated platform.

You're right. That is Rahul, Elise says, recognizing the skinny, acne-riddled boy from her childhood, who had a straight mop of black hair that he constantly brushed from his eyes. He and Elise took advanced mathematics classes together and Rahul once went to Elise's house to study for an exam. When he left, Gilda commented that he would grow up to be a very handsome young man. At the time Elise was mortified by this thought—she couldn't believe Gilda had remarked on the future attractiveness of her friend. But now she sees her mother was absolutely right. She's stunned by how different he looks, how appealing, with his muscular arms scooping ice and lifting kegs, his hair buzzed on the sides and tousled on top.

Wait a minute, Sheba says. You know that hot bartender?

We went to school together, Elise says.

Well, go on. Sheba nudges Elise forward. Get his attention.

She walks up to the back of the crowd and, unsure of what to do, raises her hand. Rahul continues sliding vodka sodas and beer bottles across the bar, plucking through the crowd person by person. Rahul! she says, her voice drowning in the bar noise. Rahul!

she tries again. Remarkably, they make eye contact, and at first he doesn't register who she is, but then he smiles, revealing his gently crooked teeth, a quirk that only adds to his handsomeness. Elise! he says and puts down the cranberry juice he's pouring. He lifts the bar door and steps down, the crowd begrudgingly parting for him.

He's coming over, Elise says and moves behind Sheba.

Elise, I can't believe it, after all these years, Rahul says, approaching and bending over to embrace her. She stands on her tiptoes to hug him back. Are you here for the summer?

I am, she says. She notices that several people from the crowd are watching them talk. What about you? Do you live on island?

Oh, fuck no, he says. I'm at MIT. Just here for the summer money.

Mathematician by day, bartender by night.

You get it, he says, and winks at her. Hey—do you need a drink?

Sheba nods exaggeratedly.

Beer OK? he says. Sheba doesn't usually drink beer, but everything is beer in here, the floorboards are sticky with it, the air recapitulates it. Beer is great, Elise says, and he returns to the bar, uncaps three bottles, pours four shots of well tequila, and returns to them with a tray balanced on his shoulder.

This round's on me, he says, and takes a shot with them. They drink them down in unison, one tip to the mouth, and Elise swallows multiple times to tame her stomach. After the alcohol settles, she grins at him. It's so good to see you, she says, and he hugs her again. Sheba grabs on to Elise's shoulder as he walks away.

First of all, that was so sexy, she says. Second of all, I didn't know you were so popular.

Elise rolls her eyes, brushing the comment off, but inside she delights. Sophie stands beside them, smiling and bobbing to the music. A song plays that Elise loves—she can't remember the name but it used to be her favorite, she says. She takes Sheba and Sophie by the wrists and squeezes them through to the dance floor. Elise closes her eyes and swings her hair around. Sophie spindles her arms and twists her legs, mouthing along to the lyrics. This is so much fun! she shouts. Occasionally a man attempts to crowd their circle, but Sheba and Elise bat them away. When a Shania Twain song comes on, Sheba leans over to Elise.

I need another beer! Can you ask your boyfriend Rahul for another round?

Sure! But he's not my boyfriend!

What? Sheba shouts.

I said he's not my boyfriend!

I'm drenched in sweat! Sophie yells. Her face is flushed and shiny.

Don't take the wig off! Elise says. I'll get you a water!

Sheba twirls Sophie around by the hand. We'll wait for you here!

Elise maneuvers her way back to the bar, swimming through damp backs and jutting elbows. A large, immobile group on the periphery of the dance floor blocks her from being able to pass. Every time she tries to walk around them, one moves, not seeing her, and obstructs her way. Finally she taps a tall man on the shoulder. Excuse me, she says. He turns around and looks down at her.

Elise, holy shit! the man says, and Elise realizes she's standing face-to-face with Harry. He's sunburnt and worn, the back of his neck slashed with uneven red stripes. He puts his beer on the ledge behind him.

What are you doing here? Elise says.

Harry grabs on to the shoulder of a purple polo shirt facing away from them.

My buddy Tim from Morgan Stanley has a house on Nantucket.

Tim turns and looks down at Elise's shoes, then at her forehead.

Are you Stephanie?

No, Elise says. I'm not Stephanie.

Harry doesn't bother to explain how she and he know each other. Tim tips his bottle at Harry and then swivels his head back around.

Should we go to the bar? Harry asks. I'll buy you a shot.

Elise knows she doesn't need another shot, but she agrees. Harry leads the way, finding no trouble navigating through the dense crowd. He even manages to find a free bar space and flags down Rahul.

What kind of shot do you want? he asks Elise as Rahul makes his way over. Harry thinks Rahul is coming for him and begins to ask for two shots of Fireball, but Rahul interrupts: Elise, what can I get you?

A tequila. Thanks, Rahul. She glances back at Harry. Oh, and a shot of Fireball for him.

Rahul pours the two shots in front of them. Elise tries to drop a twenty-dollar bill on the bar, but Harry stops her.

I've got it, he says and unfurls a fifty from his shirt pocket.

Her shot is on me, Rahul says, and snatches Harry's fifty.

You can keep the change, Harry says and turns his back to Rahul, who tosses the remaining forty dollars into a tip bucket.

Cheers to your fifty-dollar shot, Elise says, and drinks the tequila. She feels the room shift, the alcohol buzz on her tongue.

So, she says. How long have you been on island?

A few days, he says. I've been beaching, paddleboarding, drinking mudslides on the wharf. It's been amazing. He purses his lips and tells her he loves the island so much—yesterday he met a surfer on the beach and they sat for hours, he and this surfer, talking about how Nantucket was formed by a glacier thousands of years ago. Who was the surfer? Elise interjects. I probably went to high school with him. Harry can't remember his name, but he says their conversation was life-affirming. As he speaks, she can't help but think about how large he is, physically, how his one hand covers the small of her back, how his jawline tenses when he speaks. If she needed him to, he could bend his spine and form a pocket with his stomach so she could fit underneath him. She wonders what she would do if he tried to kiss her. Would she let him? Would she care if Rahul saw? Did you know, he continues, there's still a dent at the bottom of the Atlantic Ocean from where the moon was formed? A meteor jolted it free. She licks her front teeth. You know I majored in environmental science, right? she says. But he keeps going, keeps relaying to her the connection between moon and tides. Of course I know about planetary formation, Harry. I know how life, in its earliest bacterial form, evolved from water. I know why humans are mystified by the ocean, in the way every living thing is drawn back to its home.

I sent you a nude photo of me, she says. And you replied with a *ha ha*.

I did? Harry says and narrows his eyebrows.

Yes. And then you never texted me back.

I'm sorry. I was in the middle of a party.

He leans over so he can speak directly into her ear. She's reminded again of his curvature. He puts his mouth against her cheek and he smells familiar. Salt, vanilla, pine needles.

I feel like I really know you now, he says, talking into her. Why didn't you ever bring me here?

For a moment the baritone in his voice, the low rumble of it, enters her bones, and she's reminded of how she'd reach up for him, begging for a kiss, and he'd lift her up higher by slipping two cupped hands into her jean pockets, their mouths smashing together. His whisper-breath travels from her ear to the edge of her lips. Were you trying to keep it a secret? he says. His tongue juts out, breeching her teeth, and enters her mouth. She can taste the difference in temperature between her saliva and his as he moves his tongue across her gums.

No, she says, pushing him back by the shoulders. You have to delete the picture, Harry. It embarrasses me to think you have it.

Harry pauses, still leaned over. She waits for him to acknowledge what happened, but he returns upright without speaking, his head helmeted with bar noise, searching the crowd for his friends. He's not going to delete the photograph, she thinks. He crashed into her long ago and she crumbled off, absorbed into him, and the part of her that's with him will continue to sway her, one way or another.

I have to go, she says. I was supposed to bring my sister a cup of water. Harry mumbles something about a beach clambake and leaves to find his friends.

Elise waves down Rahul, hoping he didn't see Harry kiss her. He seems hurried, a bit miffed, but he doesn't mention anything. He brings her a big cup of water and she goes to find Sophie and Sheba. The crowd has morphed—there are more people massed at the end of the bar, and she has to shuffle through them to access the dance floor. When she reaches the other side, she sees Sheba and Sophie entwined on each other's shoulders toward the back corner, their nearly identical heads swaying to the music. Sheba raises her chin off Sophie's shoulder and whispers something close to Sophie's mouth, then moves to her ear. They are so close, Elise cannot discern where Sheba's hair ends and the wig on Sophie's head begins. She rushes toward them and grabs Sheba by the arm.

Hey, she says. What are you doing?

Sheba's eyes widen at the sight of Elise. Where have you been? she says. I've sent you like a hundred texts, then she mouths the words *Sophie's wasted*.

Wonderful, Elise says and tries to scoop Sophie from Sheba's arms.

Go away, Sophie says, resisting Elise. We're dancing the hiccups gone.

You won't believe who I just saw, Elise says to Sheba. Harry's here.

What? Where? Sheba searches over Elise. Ew. I see him. He's very . . . red.

Sophie, drink this, Elise says, and hands her the cup of water. You're very drunk and underage, so we need to bring you home.

Sophie hiccups and nods. Sheba passes her right arm to Elise and they guide her to the exit. Should we say bye-bye to Harry? Sheba jokes as they walk outside. They grab a red minivan taxi with a disco ball hanging from the rearview mirror. Sophie sits on the floor between their seats with her head on Elise's lap, and they make soothing noises, soft promises that they'll be home soon, until the taxi pulls up to the main house and they hoist her inside.

Sheba prepares a spread of saltine crackers, soda water with sliced ginger, and aspirin while Elise brings Sophie upstairs to

Sheba's bedroom. They prop her up on pillows and convince her to chew several saltines and drink a cup of water before going to sleep.

Sophie mumbles: What are you two going to do if I go to sleep?

We'll be right here, Elise says and watches Sophie until she dozes off a few minutes later.

It's uncanny, Sheba says, leaning against the doorjamb, and points at the crooked wig still pinned to Sophie's head. She looks exactly like me.

Elise swipes a strand of blond wig hair away from Sophie's mouth.

I don't think she does.

Oh, come on—the bouncer didn't even flinch.

She's wearing your wig and your clothes, so of course she looks like you. But not actually, not without this costume.

Sheba crosses her arms, grinning.

Why won't you admit it? Does it bother you there's a resemblance?

Elise can feel the tequila stirring in her stomach. She takes a saltine from the tray and breaks it off into her mouth.

Admit you're a teeny bit jealous, Sheba says, holding the doorjamb as she kicks off her heels.

Oh, I see now, Elise says. You're trying to bait me.

Sheba places her wrists against the sides of her head, then flops her fingers like two rabbit ears. Dangle a carrot for me, she says, hopping in place. Bait me back!

Elise rolls her eyes and faces Sophie. I'm going to stay here and make sure she's OK.

Sheba returns her hands to her waist.

Just say it, Elise. Why don't you think Sophie and I are alike?

Elise picks up a glass perfume bottle from Sheba's nightstand, smells it, then dots her wrists.

I don't know, Sheba. Let me think. You're the heir to the Play-Doh fortune. She pauses, waving her wrists to dry. That's the first difference that comes to mind.

Sheba stands still for a moment, her mouth slightly open, then moves toward Elise.

If we're so different, she says, her voice firm, why are you even friends with me?

Elise raises her eyebrows, sensing Sheba is more offended than she should be, and tells her not to be dramatic. Sheba reaches for Elise's shoulders and presses their foreheads together. Elise can feel Sheba's skull rubbing against hers.

Promise you love me for more than my house? Sheba says.

Elise tries to pull away, but Sheba giggles and presses harder.

Stop it, Elise says, and Sheba releases her grip. Do you really think I'd put up with this just to stay in your house?

Sheba frowns. Why won't you say it out loud? Say it. I'm like Sophie, and you love me for more than my house.

Elise lays a palm over her forehead. The skin where their heads were pressed is pulsing with heat. Elise had contemplated a few times whether she would still be friends with Sheba if Sheba were poor, the subtle difference being that Sheba's money doesn't make their friendship—it makes Sheba, the other half of their friendship. Trying to imagine Sheba without her wealth is like imagining a life in the United States without capitalism. Would they have the capacity for a longer, more trusting, abundant, and overall healthier relationship? Yes. But Sheba's generational wealth is so intertwined with her preferences and boundaries, her humor, her belief systems, her phenotype, the way she holds her shoulders when she walks—in other words, who she is—imagining her without it would mean imagining a different person.

You're being insane! Elise shouts. I didn't even know about your house for most of our friendship, OK? And I'm not going to say you look like my sister just because you want me to.

Sheba yawns and stretches her arms above her head. Elise realizes she's made a mistake losing her cool, that Sheba has declared a victory. She glances at Sophie, who is still propped up and snoring softly.

This is stupid, Sheba says and walks to the door. You're cranky because your ex–boy toy Harry didn't tell you he was on Nantucket.

And you're upset you weren't there to flirt with him, so now you're torturing me.

Sheba rolls her eyes. I'm going to sleep in my moms' room. You're welcome to come if you want. She laughs, then says: We can play *Sleeping with the Enemy*. I'll let you be Julia Roberts.

How fun, Elise says and closes her eyes. After Sheba walks away, Elise leans over and carefully unpins the wig from Sophie's head. She places it on the dresser, then rests the back of her hand against Sophie's cheek, trying to assess her temperature, though she has no idea how to tell if she's too hot. Sophie murmurs and stretches her limbs into a star shape. Elise eyes the sofa in Sheba's room, considering if she should curl up there or investigate the downstairs for a spare bed.

Ultimately, she decides it would be best to join Sheba in her moms' room, call it a truce. Elise enters Helen and Holly's bedroom and Sheba gets up, without saying anything, to retrieve for Elise a pair of silk trousers with scalloped hems, then switches on the gas fireplace. They watch the flames in silence until Sheba says, You're the most important person in my life, and offers her a hand underneath the sheets. Elise gives Sheba's hand a squeeze, but quickly releases as soon as Sheba's breath deepens into sleep. She reaches to click off the bedside lamp and sees her phone light up from the charger. She almost doesn't reach to check who it is—she knows it's Harry—but she can't resist the compulsion.

Maybe Rahul: Hey—Just got off work. Is this still Elise's number?

She smiles with relief at the sight of Rahul's maybe name and types back, Yes, hi, it's me. She's aware of the loud blue light radiating from her phone. Sheba stirs, rolls toward her, and she minimizes the brightness. He writes back, It was nice to run into you ☺. Elise presses the phone into her chest and smiles. Let's do it again soon? she writes, and waits for him to say yes, really soon, before she powers off her phone. She falls asleep facing Sheba, so close that when they exhale, their breaths meet midway, a little bit of the other intermixed with each following inhale.

They don't make the decision to move into the main house; it happens as a matter of physics, like spilled water spreading across a granite countertop. After their night out at the Chicken Box, they wake and stagger to the kitchen, where they eat leftover cacio e pepe and scrambled eggs. The fridge contains neat rows of sparkling Perrier. Sheba opens a bottle and pours it into three tall glasses filled with crushed ice and halved lemons. They spend the day underneath braided cashmere throws, the air-conditioning blasted and the sunshades drawn, watching *Eternal Sunshine of the Spotless Mind*. The film makes Elise emotional in a cathartic way, especially the scenes on Montauk's snow-covered beaches.

Thus begins the transition. By the end of July, Sophie and Elise stop returning to the guest house after work, instead inhabiting the upstairs of the main house. One morning Elise passes by Sheba's bedroom door and sees a sliver of Sophie seated at the vanity, applying a glossy balm to her lips. It occurs to her that Sophie has had to share a bedroom for her entire life—even when Elise was in college, her empty bed occupied half the space where Sophie lived year-round. In the guest house, Sophie rotated between the second bedroom and the couch downstairs depending on where Sheba decided to fall asleep.

Elise and Sheba are enjoying the accomplishment of Helen and Holly's room, with its layers of silk sheets and cushioned drawers filled with jewelry. There are other bedrooms downstairs, but they feel too impersonal, too far away from each other. Elise loves that Helen's bathtub looks like half an eggshell and faces banks of rolling moors that collect pools of fog early in the morning. At night, before bed, Sheba brings them two cups of raspberry tea and a box of powdered donuts, and they wear thick robes and sit at the edge of the tub to soak their feet. In the main house, the fridge is always organized, pristine, and stocked. The laundry is folded in stacks, even their underwear; the toilet never has a rust-colored ring that must be swished around with a brush; and the toaster oven is emptied of burnt cheesy drips that would other-wise catch on fire. This isn't magic, of course. Elise assumes the housekeepers must come while she is at work, because she has never seen their cars parked in the driveway, nor has she crossed paths with them as they come and go. She asked Sheba, once, if she had ever met the people who clean her home. Sheba seemed trapped by the question, as if it were placed only to make her feel bad.

I don't think they want to interact with me! she said and flipped to another television channel.

It's the beginning of August, the month the billionaires arrive on island. They enter through clandestine back-door channels, docking their yachts in private ports, helicoptering onto rooftop pads, chartering luxury jets from the Cayman Islands. The bil-lionaires don't want to pay for anything—meals are comped by restaurant owners, island-branded T-shirts and hats are gifted in swag bags, and gratuities shrink to the single digits. Six days a week, Sophie caters to the billionaires who venture out for a ca-sual lunch or dinner at the Lunch Counter. Her arms are perpetually bruised, her clothing stained with smears of coffee and ketchup. Some days she is so tired, she hobbles upstairs as soon as she returns home and Sheba and Elise bring her leftovers that she eats with her fingers in bed. It disturbs Sheba, how overworked Sophie is. She's never seen someone so tired from having to stand for fourteen hours a day, smiling through complaints about everything from table placement to the temperature of complimentary bread.

Because of the persistence of their work schedules, and the exhaustion that comes in the final stretch of summer, and for reasons that are not as clear or straightforward—why they each feel burdened, not lifted, by the communication—they have fallen out of their routine phone calls with Gilda. Last week, they only spoke once, on Wednesday, and it's been several days since either has sent a text checking in.

Gilda thinks about her daughters on impulse, like checking a clock, but she has been busy with her new job and a recent family reunion with their cousins from Piracicaba. For the first time since she started her life in Brazil, Gilda wasn't conscious of the passing hours: she and her family listened to Gal Costa, ate grilled pineapple with ice cream, and passed around black-and-white photographs printed on thick cardstock.

It was around the day of the reunion that Gilda received a phone call from her father. The call wasn't entirely unexpected— Beth had arranged for him to come to the reunion to meet Gilda for the first time since she returned to Brazil. They thought that having a crowd might alleviate some of the pressure; they could mingle in the beginning, and then find a quiet corner if the opportunity felt right. A few days before the party, however, Manuel called to suggest it might be better for them to meet privately. He wasn't sure how he would react, if he would be overcome with emotion, and he didn't want an audience in case he started to cry. Gilda had had the same hesitation, she told him, but hadn't fully identified it until his phone call. He explained that he lives in Joanópolis, so they made plans to meet at a park there, where the Rio de Piracicaba begins.

Gilda riffled through Beth's dresser drawers searching for clothes to wear. How should one look when they're going to meet their estranged father? She tried to imagine what Elise would tell her to do—brush your hair down, Mom, you don't have to stick it inside a chef's hat now. Wear something that makes you feel comfortable and beautiful. She missed her daughters so much, she worried that if she brought them up to Manuel, she may become inconsolable. Would he know what to say to her to alleviate the misery of saudade? She pressed her hands into her stomach, then pulled a floral shirt from the top drawer and held it against her chest. It reminded her of Elise. The vibrancy and the colors. She swiped a matching pink lipstick from the bathroom and dotted some on her cheeks, then drove Beth's car to the park an hour away.

Gilda arrived before Manuel, so she decided to secure a table at the little outdoor restaurant that overlooked the river. She hadn't remembered this park when they first spoke on the phone, but as she walked through the entrance gate, the memories returned: six years old, swimming in the small waterfall at the end of the trail, the skinny, lush trees circling her overhead. Manuel had suggested it because he hoped it would conjure positive times from their earlier years together. At this stage in his life, he explained to her on the phone, he only wanted to dwell on the good memories. He couldn't afford to relive the sad. Gilda understood what he meant. Though she hadn't lived as long as he had, she felt that the years she'd spent on earth had accumulated the sorrow of a hundred lifetimes, and she worried that if she thought about it too much, her future would be erased by the suffering of the past. She wanted to move forward, she assured her father. She had no desire to rehash that which had already happened.

A family next to her ordered a basket of coxinha that smelled delicious, and she decided she'd order some too. Since she left Brazil at eighteen years old, her taste for Brazilian cuisine had frozen in time. She wondered if her father loved coxinha as much as she still did. But when the basket arrived at the table, she couldn't stir up an appetite to eat one. I'll have a beer, she told the waiter. Um chope, to calm her nerves. She took a long gulp, her mouth puckering at the taste of bitter hops, and glanced toward the parking lot. An older man wearing a fedora and a button-down shirt was leaning against the gate. She stood to get a better look at him. He approached a woman walking up the path, and Gilda questioned whether it could be her father, since the man had seemingly found who he was meeting. He and the woman chatted for a moment, then he shook his head and returned to his spot on the gate.

Pai! she shouted, now certain it was him. Estou aqui!

He swung around and, seeing her, grinned and threw his arms into the air. He was very handsome, she thought, and had clearly dressed well for their meeting. There were aspects of him she recognized instantly—the slope of his shoulders, the way his mouth crooked to one side. He still exuded a youthfulness, even though he now used a cane and occasionally reached down to squeeze his right thigh as he walked toward her. She had imagined they would go for a stroll to the spot at the waterfall where she had swum as a child, but seeing his gait, she suggested they sit and talk at the restaurant for a while.

I ordered us coxinha, she said, and nudged the basket toward him.

Oh, wonderful, he replied, though he did not take one to eat. I think I'll have one of those, he said, pointing at her beer. Gilda gestured to the waiter for another chope. I thought it would help calm my nerves, she said, laughing a little, and they made a toast when his beer arrived. For old time's sake, he said, clinking their glasses together.

They settled in on neutral topics, mainly having to do with the river, about which Manuel had many facts. It is 115 kilometers long, he told her, and the Tupi call it the place where fish stop by. Gilda asked him if he still played music and he showed her photographs on his phone of his small jazz band. That's me on the conga drums, he said, pointing to himself on the screen wearing the same hat. Gilda smiled and admired each of the photos, though thoughts about Sophie and Elise pushed against her attention. She had so many things she wanted to tell him about them. Manuel didn't even know that she had children—Beth hadn't told him about her deportation, or that she was intending to return to the United States to reunite with her daughters. She pressed the bow of her thumbnail against her lip, searching for the sentence that might begin to explain.

You know, Gilda, Manuel said as he tucked his phone into his shirt pocket. He coughed, reviving his voice. I want you to know I didn't leave you and your mother. I hope you believe me. He paused, his jaw quivering, and allowed space for Gilda to respond. She blinked silently and took a sip of her beer. I don't want to excavate the past, he continued. These things are buried, and there is no sense in dragging up that which is already done and gone. But I need you to know that it wasn't my choice, he said, rubbing the skin above his eyebrow.

Gilda rested a hand on his shoulder and leaned forward to embrace him. I know, she said. Pai, don't worry. I understand how complicated life can be.

True to their agreement, they didn't linger much longer on these difficult subjects. They spent the following hours talking about Caetano Veloso and Alfred Hitchcock and Jorge Luis Borges, relishing in the tastes they shared. Gilda drove back to Beth's house after arranging to meet with Manuel a second time, lunch together the following week. As she pulled into the driveway, however, a sense of regret lodged in her throat, making it difficult for her to breathe. Not about meeting her father, of course. That had been a gift, a new reason to keep living. She left with the regret of not having told him about Elise and Sophie. There were several moments when her desire to let him into her life nearly overwhelmed her fear, but then the topic changed, and her mind switched, the moment passed. Meeting her father forced her to examine why she had stayed in the United States all those years, why she hadn't left after Sophie was born and Peter abandoned them. Even if she had spent her life working in Brazilian kitchens instead of American kitchens, at least they would have had a family to come home to. Sophie and Elise could have had a grandmother and grandfather, she thought, and an aunt, second cousins, even third cousins. Admitting to her father she'd had two daughters in another country would mean admitting she'd decided to raise a family apart. The reality, she knew, was not as straightforward as the allure of possibility—she had been miserable when she left Brazil, and there was not one part of her that wanted to return to living in Frieda's apartment. The United

States was a place she could call her own (or so she thought), a country that she knew in a way the rest of her family did not.

Days pass, and Gilda decides she needs to tell her daughters about their grandfather's existence before she can tell her father about Sophie's and Elise's existence. Or maybe it's vice versa? The interdependent logic makes it impossible for her to break free. She hasn't learned yet that she cannot sort through which aspects of her past to erase and which to keep; every experience, joyful and not, will be severed and will remain attached, simultaneous and forever, the quantum entanglement of life.

Elise returns to the main house from work, removes her baseball cap, and shakes out a heap of sand from her hair. Days at the beach have been slow and brutally hot. She's begun to question whether her presence is necessary anymore without the eggs to guard. Who cares if she spends hours on end keeping watch over animals that will or will not procreate with or without her?

Sheba hurries downstairs and stops her before she can move past the foyer. Sophie's exhausted, she says. I don't think she should go to work tonight. Elise steps outside onto the porch to brush off the sand from underneath her bra strap and inside her pockets. This is typical in August, she says. I'm tired too. We just need to get through the next few weeks.

They sit beside each other on the porch steps. The days are already shrinking—the sun skims the tops of the backlit birch trees, and pastel clouds swirl through the sky.

I want to give Sophie some money, Sheba says. Elise looks at her sideways but doesn't respond. Whatever she'd make. I can give it to her so she doesn't have to work for the rest of the summer.

Sheba. Elise shakes her head. That's too much.

How can I sit here, with more money than I could possibly spend in a lifetime, and watch her toil away in a restaurant? At a certain point it's immoral.

You can't pay her to not work, Elise says.

Why not? Sheba replies.

Elise isn't exactly sure of the answer to this question, but the first thought that comes to mind is their mother. Wouldn't it be a betrayal of her? How could Sophie accept Sheba's money when their mother worked seventy-hour weeks to support them and it still wasn't enough?

Giving your inheritance to Sophie won't solve income inequality, Elise says, and stands. They hear the sounds of Sophie's footsteps plodding down the stairs. She stops, noticing Elise's and Sheba's silhouettes outside the window, and opens the screen door.

I have to go to work soon, Sophie says, her voice raspy.

OK. I'll come hang for a bit, Elise says. Sheba crosses and uncrosses her legs, intending to stay outside on the porch, but once she hears the door close behind her, she decides otherwise, stands, and follows them inside.

◆

I heard back from the government, Gilda says to Elise, who is seated in the driver's seat of her car in the beach parking lot. It is the Schrödinger's cat of sentences, both alive and dead. A whistling wind blows through the crack between the car's door and roof, making it difficult for Gilda to hear Elise's response. Steve glances over, trying to assess why she hasn't gotten out and walked over.

Is it good news or bad news? Elise asks, wiping the sweat on her upper lip.

It's not good and it's not bad, Gilda responds. They say they need more information.

She explains that the request is about Sophie. Because Elise is twenty-two years old, she does not count as Gilda's child anymore, not in the eyes of the United States Citizenship and Immigration Services. Only Sophie is still considered her dependent, because she's eighteen. We need to prove it's too much of a burden for Sophie to be kept away from her mother, Gilda says, trying to remain matter-of-fact, though Elise can hear her heartbeat tripping up her tongue. Sophie, the defiantly independent daughter, who has spent her teenage years trying to prove she doesn't need anyone's help, must now demonstrate her dependency on Gilda. A sudden gust kicks up a sheet of sand and sprays it across the windshield. Elise instinctively presses her palm against the inside of the glass to prevent it from cracking.

How does a mother prove her child needs her? Gilda continues. Isn't that the definition of a child? A child isn't a child without a mother.

Elise considers this for a moment. What does the lawyer say we should do?

He said we need a letter from someone who isn't a family member. Someone who can explain why Sophie needs me. She laughs, incredulous. If you could help me with this, Elise, I would really appreciate it.

Maybe I could write the letter, Elise says. Since I'm not your daughter, technically speaking. She buries this last part under her breath and then asks: Have you told Sophie?

Gilda clears her throat. No, not yet. I haven't heard from Sophie in days.

Steve taps on his horn to get Elise's attention. They make eye contact, and she points to her phone. *So sorry, one more minute,* she mouths from behind the window.

Mom, Elise says. A mood has stricken her, the need to come clean. She digs her knuckles under her chin, searching for the right way. I need to tell you something important, she says, and inhales a long breath. Sophie and I aren't living in the house anymore.

The speaker clanks and Elise realizes her mom has dropped the phone. Did you hear me? she asks.

Where are you living? Gilda says.

At Sheba's. The landlord evicted us because we aren't on the lease. He's renovating the house and will probably sell it for twice what he paid for it.

Gilda is silent for a long moment and Elise waits for her to respond.

Who is Sheba? she says finally, which is not the question Elise expected her to ask. My friend from college, remember? Elise says. She has a summer house on island.

How long has it been?

I don't know, Elise says, and grips the door handle. A couple weeks?

You should have told me sooner, Elise. I am your mother— I need to know where you are living.

Steve interrupts by knocking on the window loud enough that Gilda can hear through the receiver. What was that? she asks as Elise pulls the phone away from her ear. She rolls down the window and a strong rush of wind pushes inside the car. Sorry to interrupt, Steve says, but I have to drop you off and get back to the office. I can't wait any longer.

Mom, Elise says into the phone. I'm sorry, I have to go to work. Can we talk more later?

Gilda mutters something in Portuguese and tells Elise she needs to call her back as soon as possible.

Elise huddles on the beach with her legs tucked inside her hoodie, observing two of the birds as they stand braced against the wind like a pair of calcified rocks. One squints, and the wind blows back its feathers, forming a rippling collar around its neck. Elise imagines the self-immolating monk who remained motionless while his body burned in protest of the Vietnam War, and how his heart, remarkably, remained intact. No one will disrupt the birds in this weather, she thinks, not even the seagulls. But if she went home, then Steve would have no reason to pay her. This is how she makes a living: by suffering through sand pelting against her skin. She checks her phone, futilely, to see if she has a bar of service to call her mom back. Gilda is in the middle of her work-day, and by the time Steve retrieves Elise and brings her to the parking lot, Gilda says she can't answer Elise's call and that they will have to speak later that night.

Elise drives home frightened, her fingers numb, feeling she's made a terrible mistake telling her mother about the house. Now she, not Sophie, will receive the brunt of Gilda's disappointment.

She retires upstairs when she arrives at the main house. As she passes by Sheba's bedroom, she notices her sitting at the vanity, brushing out her hair with a wide-toothed comb.

You're in your room, she says, standing in the open door. Where's Sophie?

Sheba turns around, her arm draped across the back of the chair, and Elise realizes she's made a mistake—it's not Sheba, it's Sophie. She's wearing the wig Sheba lent her the night at the Chicken Box.

Oh, Elise says, embarrassed. I thought you were Sheba. Why are you wearing that wig?

Sheba gave it to me, Sophie says, and swings back around, the loose curls flopping against her shoulders. She said she doesn't need it anymore.

Elise tightens the hoodie tied around her waist.

Well, why do *you* need it?

Sophie peels the wig from her forehead, a red line impressed on her skin, and places it on the vanity table. Her hair is in a mat-ted bun at the base of her head.

You're in a bad mood today, she says.

Elise crosses her arms and leans against the door. That wig is probably several hundred dollars. I don't understand why Sheba would give it to you on a whim.

Sheba gives you lots of expensive things on a whim. She's rich, she doesn't care.

You've only known her for a couple months, Elise says. She and I have been friends for a long time.

Why does that matter? Sheba and I are friends too.

Elise lets out a forceful laugh. They're still standing at a distance from each other, a pair of Sophie's work pants crumpled on the floor between them. Elise steps into the room and sits on the edge of Sheba's bed.

I talked to Mom this morning. She says she hasn't heard from you in days.

I've tried to call her, Sophie says and pulls a bobby pin from her bun. I can't talk to her while I'm at work.

Every time we speak she asks where you are, how you're doing, if I'm taking care of you. I can barely have a conversation with her without her worrying over you.

That's not my fault. I don't ask you to talk about me with Mom.

Elise tucks her hands into her armpits and raises her shoulders. I told her that we're not living at the house anymore.

You did? Sophie says and faces Elise. I thought we were going to tell her together.

She needs to know where we're living. She got a letter from the government asking for more information on her case, and I couldn't go on pretending like we were still living at the house.

Sophie shakes out the wig and places it in her lap. Why are you acting like this is somehow my fault? Sorry I can't call Mom while

I'm at work, but don't forget you're the one who was gone for four years.

Elise presses her lips together. I was in college, she says firmly. Earning a degree.

Oh, please. You were out partying with Sheba, your rich friend, who gave me a *wig*! It's only a fucking wig!

Yeah? And you're going to be stuck working takeout at the Lunch Counter if you don't get your shit together.

I'm eighteen, Sophie says, no longer sounding angry, but imploring. All you do is sit on a beach all day.

Elise stands, walks toward the door, and shouts over her shoulder, closing in: Just give me a heads-up first if you're going to start fucking my best friend, she says, and leaves the room. When she reaches Helen's bedroom, she feels Sophie's heaving breaths echo inside her.

The summer after Sophie turned eleven, the phosphorescence drifted to the island's waters several months early. Elise was in town ordering a ham-and-cheese sandwich when she overheard two teenagers recounting their weekend, how they drank coconut rum at the harbor docks and went skinny-dipping under a sliver of moon, the water turned inky in the barely illuminated night. As they waded with arms and legs churning, they noticed that their movement caused a subaquatic strobe of green lights.

Phosphorescent jellyfish, the taller, gap-toothed one said, and ordered a tuna melt from another teenager behind the counter, who confirmed their sighting. I saw them with my family on the South Shore last week, she said, tapping their total into a calculator. My brother said they're never on the South Shore and they're never this early.

Elise clung to the words in her mind, *phosphorescent jellyfish,* and when she got home, she repeated the story to Sophie. They turned on Gilda's desktop computer, opened up a browser window, and typed in the search term: *Foss four essent jellyfish.*

The internet suggested back to them: *Phosphorescent jellyfish?*

They clicked on the suggestion and discovered more suggestions: Bioluminescence. Dinoflagellates. Comb jellies or Cte-nophora. Hermaphroditic organisms that are not jellyfish at all but transparent, brainless sea walnuts with ciliated ribs that glow green when agitated. A video compilation of various biolumines-cent creatures auto-played in the center of an article. Fungi, click beetles, fireflies, deep-sea anglerfish, luminous and pulsating, a negative of a filmstrip, greens, blues, and purples encased in black.

These really exist in the ocean? Sophie said and refreshed the video.

That's what the teenagers in line were saying, said Elise, who regarded intel from older teenagers as sacred text. They devised a plan to investigate the phenomena themselves and set an alarm for one A.M., when they estimated Gilda would have fallen asleep after work. Minutes before the clock sounded, Sophie whispered: Elise? Are you awake?

Elise shuffled under her sheets.

No, not yet.

I heard Mom go into her room an hour ago.

Sophie stood and pulled Elise's covers off the bed.

Let's sneak out before you fall asleep again.

They slinked down the attic steps and clicked open the cellar door, still wearing Gilda's hand-me-down cotton nightgowns that hung to their shins. Elise pushed the bulkhead door above her head, allowed Sophie to slip through, and carefully lowered it shut. They waited, inhaling shallow breaths, watching for a hint of movement from Gilda's bedroom window, a sign she'd heard the metal latch rattle. Their skin shivered with goosebumps and the cold grass stung against their bare feet. When they felt a tacit opening, a freedom, they ran across the front yard and to the end of their road. The moon's slight eye cut through the sky, revealing empty pavement, quiet yards, unlit windows. They encountered a family of deer feeding on a hawthorn bush on the way to the beach; otherwise, they were the only ones traversing the island roads that night.

I can't see anything, Sophie said as they approached the beach sand. It's too dark.

Look out at the horizon, Elise told her and pointed to the thin, rippling razors of light on the ocean's surface. Your eyes will adjust.

They linked arms to cross the beach, kicking clumps of seaweed and skate casings, until they felt the rush of water washing around their ankles.

Why isn't it glowing? Sophie said, looking down.

Elise bent over and stirred the tide with her hand.

I think we have to go in deeper, she said after a moment. Sophie took a step backwards, onto dry sand. Recently, she had developed an aversion to opaque water after a crab pinched her heel while she was swimming on the North Shore. She'd dunked her head and opened her eyes in the salty current to try to locate the source of the pinch to quell her fear. Of course, she couldn't find it, the crab had vanished, and so its danger transformed into a ubiquitous presence—barracuda teeth, piranhas, sea snakes, bull sharks, and more.

It will be fine, Elise said and reached for her hand. The tide is low. We can run out quickly if anything happens.

Elise pulled her nightgown over her head and tossed it onto a bed of tangled dry seaweed. Her tan lines appeared as two white flashes in the dark. Sophie undressed too, and they counted backwards from three, palms clasped, and darted into the current. Contrasted against the cold night air, the ocean felt warm on their skin. Sophie cupped her hands and poured water over her chest. A green light momentarily glimmered in the inner crook of her elbow.

I saw one! she shrieked.

Where? Elise shouted back. How do you know?

Sophie, no longer afraid of the unseeable bottom, advised that they walk out even farther, until they were chin deep in water. They swam out, stretching their toes to anchor on the soft sand. An invisible swell lifted them off the ocean floor and lowered them down again.

Try now, Elise said and swiveled, whipping the water around her. The viridescent glow from dozens of comb jellies glided around her body. I want to stay here forever, she called to Sophie, who floated onto her back and made a neon snow angel in the sea. Let's never leave. Let's invent a way to breathe underwater.

They were only in the ocean for a few minutes when they heard an unmistakable call from the shore: Elise! Sophie! Get out of the water, this minute!

They rubbed their eyes and could see the outline of their mother standing in her thin terry cloth robe, nothing but bare skin underneath, her toes hanging over her house sandals.

Get out or you'll drown! she shouted, both a warning and a threat.

Sophie and Elise trudged out of the water, the phosphorescence sparkling at their thighs. They hadn't accounted for the nights when Gilda woke from a panic in her gut and ascended the attic stairs to check on her daughters. Usually they were fast asleep—this was the first time her internal alarm had proven her correct. Gilda reached out and snatched their arms, dragging them onto land.

What are you doing? It's the middle of the night.

Sophie gestured behind them, back at the ocean.

We came to see the comb jellies, she said.

Phosphorescence, Elise explained, as if that would clarify things for Gilda.

Children die swimming at night without telling their mother, Gilda said.

A wave ran over the sand and Sophie dragged her toe through the water, lighting up a green jelly.

There! Did you see it, Mom? she asked.

Come look, Elise said, tugging at her mother's wrist. It's the most amazing thing you'll ever see. Gilda didn't respond, though she had caught a quick glimpse of the mysterious illumination at Sophie's feet. Holding tight to Elise, she took a few steps forward. They continued this game, testing Gilda's willingness to venture deeper into the water. Gilda reprimanded the girls for their recklessness, but she continued to follow them in, the water skimming at their knees.

See? Sophie said, wiggling her feet. It's like ocean stars.

Gilda marveled, whispering to herself, incrível, nossa, incrível. They bent at their waists and passed their hands through the water. Elise suggested they go in even deeper, to where they'd been before—it was better out there, she pleaded, floating over the swells. A wave rolled forward, knocking Gilda off balance, and her sense of wonder snapped in two. She grabbed her daughters by the elbows. It's time to go home. You girls nearly gave me a heart attack, sneaking out in the middle of the night like that.

For weeks Elise and Sophie dreamt about the phosphorescence, an emerald trail swirling in their wake. They were ravenous for sleep, a chance to dream about a luminescent world, until even dreams couldn't sustain their desire for more. They woke again at one A.M. and snuck downstairs, crept through the cellar, and lifted the bulkhead door. They ran all the way to the ocean, stripping off their nightgowns and dropping them on the sand without waiting for their eyes to adjust in the darkness.

I don't see them, Sophie said, splashing with her limbs to no avail.

Keep trying, Elise responded.

They continued for nearly an hour, their lips pale, their fingers and toes shriveled. It was too late—the phosphorescence had already come and gone. The ocean turned familiar again, a sway of dark water under a navy-blue sky.

Elise is sitting on the sand under her umbrella, arms wrapped around shins, logbook pages flapping in the wind. A flock of sanderlings are switchbacking over the ocean, moving as one tumbling sheet. She's remembering the night she and Sophie first discovered the phosphorescence. Their mother was so upset with them at the time, but Elise is happy she and Sophie have the memory. She searches with her binoculars across the sand and notices two eggs placed against each other, shell to shell, in the same scratched indent where the other eggs had been shattered. Are they eggs, she thinks, or an optical illusion, curves and shadows mimicking an egg shape? She stands, walks closer, and peers again. They really are eggs: twin casings, salt-and-pepper freckled, that contain brand-new developing embryos. The birds are near the shore, tossing white crustaceans into the air with their beaks. She retrieves her logbook and marks a new note:

Number of eggs (two)

The corners of her mouth lift into a smile. Her smile turns into a laugh. The phosphorescence arrived that summer months earlier than normal, by way of a warming jet stream and rising sea levels. Their stay was ephemeral. Sophie and Elise had left the beach in tears, thinking they'd never witness real-life magic as they had that night. Except, now, Elise does.

Elise is at the grocery store for the first time in over a month, just to remember what it's like—the cold, still air and dewy bundles of lettuce, the towering rows of cereal boxes, the mechanical chirp from the checkout scanner. She didn't even go to the big supermarket; she's at the market connected to the local farm, where they sell island-grown corn, rhubarb pie, homemade chicken salad, and salami-and-butter baguettes. Her plan is to buy a bottle of kombucha and a bag of salt-and-vinegar chips, wander around the farm, maybe visit the cows and horses, maybe find a sunflower to pick. Instead, she's been aimlessly walking the aisles, trying to expand time, even though the sun will set no matter how long she delays going back to Sheba's, no matter how long she avoids the possibility of seeing Sophie, whom she hasn't spoken to in days, since their argument.

She picks up a bag of chips, noting the ways kelp has been repurposed into edible additives, when she hears her name being called from the refrigerated section.

Elise? Mrs. Wagner says. Her hair is brushed out and parted down the middle, and she's carrying a roll of paper towels underneath her right arm. For a quick moment Elise contemplates ignoring her and hurrying toward the exit, but Mrs. Wagner moves closer, rendering the escape impossible. After a choppy pause, in which they each try to speak but interrupt to allow the other to speak first, Elise asks her how Suzie is doing. She doesn't know why she asks about the dog first, but she senses this is the question Mrs. Wagner wants to be asked. Mrs. Wagner tips her head down, as if recalling a fond story, but when her chin lifts Elise sees that tears are trapped in her eyelashes.

We found out yesterday she has cancer, she says and then covers her mouth. God, it feels too real when I say it out loud.

Elise hugs the salt-and-vinegar chips in her arms, the bag crinkling loudly as she presses into it. I'm sorry, she says. How old is she?

Fifteen, Mrs. Wagner says. Which is eighty-three in human years.

Really, Elise says and scratches her elbow. How do they make that calculation?

Mrs. Wagner shakes her head. I'm not sure, actually. I read it online.

They pause, searching for the next thing to say, when Mrs. Wagner asks about Gilda. The question feels as odd as Elise asking about Suzie.

She's good, Elise says. Working a lot. She filed her waiver application, but the government asked for more information. So we're working on submitting that.

Mrs. Wagner narrows her eyes in a gentle way, to convey sadness or empathy. Elise notices that the hair on the crown of her head is thinning—her exposed scalp is dotted with small red moles. Usually, Mrs. Wagner wears her hair pulled into a tight, fluffy ponytail, like a wisp of cotton candy protruding from a caramel apple.

I didn't know your mother very well, Mrs. Wagner says. But she was a good person. She doesn't deserve what happened to her.

Yeah. Thanks, Elise says.

Has our country forgotten what the Statue of Liberty says? Give me your tired, your poor, your huddled masses? She paid taxes, I'm assuming. She worked and contributed to society. Elise's face remains placid. Mrs. Wagner repositions the paper-towel roll to the other arm.

Anyway, she continues, I'm preaching to the choir.

Elise shrugs and sings a choral note, *fa la la,* and feigns a chuckle.

I have to ask you something that's been on my mind, Elise says after a moment, straightening her stance. Do you know how our landlord found out that our mother was gone?

Mrs. Wagner asks Elise to repeat herself. I'm sorry, she says, what did you say?

The landlord knew that my mom wasn't living in the house anymore, she says, firmer this time. That's why he kicked us out.

Mrs. Wagner lets out a guttural breath.

You have to understand, Elise . . . Mark and my husband have known each other since they were teenagers. And he sometimes calls us to ask how things are at the house. His house.

Elise tilts her head. Mark? Is that the landlord's name?

Yes, Mark, Mrs. Wagner says, sounding confused by Elise's confusion. He and Tom played football together in high school. That's why Mark bought the house—Tom advised him to, as an investment.

Mr. Wagner is friends with our landlord? Elise says.

Yes, exactly. He's a friend, and it was the kind of question he asks all the time—how are things at the house? Because he lives in California and can't see for himself. And so we told him about what's been going on . . . innocently! Just catching up, as usual. But as we discussed it, it made sense that it wasn't right for you two to be living in the house alone like that. Not without your mother.

I'm twenty-two years old, Mrs. Wagner. I can make that decision myself.

Mrs. Wagner nods. Well, maybe. But it *is* Mark's property. I don't know, it's so complicated. I was only trying to do what's right. You have to believe me. I pray for you and Sophie every night—

Mrs. Wagner is startled midsentence by Elise popping open the bag of chips. She pinches one chip between her fingers and places it in her mouth, and then eats three more. Mrs. Wagner mutters a few more pleading phrases, her eyes shifting around the aisle.

Complicated, right, Elise says and licks the salt off her lips. It's funny how people make bad decisions very quickly and then call them complicated afterwards. She pauses, takes another bite of a chip. Like what you're doing to your dog. An old dog like Suzie shouldn't have to suffer through chemotherapy, but I'm guessing you'll put her through it. Not because it's right for the dog, but because it's what will make you feel better. Because you don't want to be sad. So she'll have diarrhea all over the house and you'll follow her around with a paper towel. She points to the roll under her arm.

Mrs. Wagner's face closes into a line of wrinkles. I don't know what we'll do about Suzie, she says. We haven't made the decision. And you and Sophie are still welcome over whenever you want. OK? I'll store your belongings for as long as you need.

Oh, you'll store our belongings? What a lifesaver, thank you. Elise laughs harshly and Mrs. Wagner shifts nervously from side to side, unsure which way to turn, then places the paper-towel roll on the shelf and walks out of the store.

Elise circles the aisles for another hour, replaying the conversation in her head. Did Mrs. Wagner always have the Statue of Liberty plaque memorized, or did she learn it in case she saw Elise again? She folds the empty chip bag and tucks it into a stack of avocados. There is a relief in knowing the truth about what happened, even if she has to bear the knowledge that Mrs. Wagner, a person who spends most of her spare time watching home-shopping networks, has had an outsized influence on the trajectory of her life. She leaves, ready to never speak with her again, sucking her fingers clean as the automatic doors close behind her.

The following morning, Elise lies awake in bed listening to Sheba's breath sway like a deserted tree swing. Sophie has already left for work—the front door closing wrested Elise from sleep. She's been listening to airplanes hum across the sky, the garbage truck collecting garbage, a lawn mower's vibrato traveling across the moors. Elise is swallowed by a sense of loneliness, which happens sometimes; sometimes solitude persists like hunger or fatigue, even after she's eaten or slept, even when she's in Sheba's company. She slips out from underneath the covers, careful not to rouse her, and gets dressed in the walk-in closet. She goes downstairs, retrieves her car keys from the gold bowl by the door, and decides she's going to visit Sophie at work.

A potential rain forecast has redirected every tourist into town for restaurant meals and shopping instead of a day at the beach. They circle the cobblestone roads in SUVs, congregate into indistinguishable masses of salmon pink and madras on the narrow brick sidewalks, nannies pushing strollers, children shouting at hostesses and cashiers, prep school graduates drinking Dark and Stormies from red plastic cups. Elise finds a rare parking spot on Centre Street and walks toward the Lunch Counter. On her way she texts Sophie to ask if she's too busy for her to visit.

Sophie: Come on over. I'm at the takeout counter

Elise squeezes past the line of people extending from Sophie at the register, out the door, and alongside the shingled building to the corner. Elise manages to make eye contact with her sister, who is working alone, chipping away at customers by ringing up orders on the point-of-sale machine, preparing drinks, slinging vats of ice, and dragging trash bags caked with pounds of wet coffee grounds. Elise sits at the bar beside the register and Sophie passes her an iced coffee, then returns to her station. The line of pastel shirts multiplies—a man with a tight, glossy face wants five lime rickeys, no sugar, so Sophie must squeeze fresh citrus while the other customers grumble with impatience. A couple severs off from the back of the line and leaves, no longer willing to wait. When Sophie finishes, the man asks to split the lime rickeys between multiple credit cards. Elise winces, sure Sophie will tell him to fuck off with his credit cards, and a part of her hopes for it, but she doesn't. She calmly presses a sequence of buttons on the screen, processes the credit cards, tells him to have a good day, and moves on to the next. She reaches the final customer in line forty-five minutes later, a mother of three who places her toddler on the counter, his seersucker legs kicking against the wooden panels. He grabs at a basket of individually wrapped biscotti next to the register.

No, no, Sophie says, moving the basket away from his grasp.

The mother orders three steamed vanilla almond milks for the children and an oat-milk triple iced latte with an extra shot for herself. When Sophie passes her the drinks in a carrier tray, she throws in a biscotti on the house.

Thank you, the mother says, her smile grateful, and drops a ten-dollar bill into the tip jar. The toddler chews on the biscotti through the plastic wrapper.

You're so good at this job, Elise says as Sophie walks over to her, wiping her hands on her apron. Sophie pulls out a transparent to-go container filled with water and sips through a metal straw.

It's not rocket science, she says with a shrug.

You're right, Elise says. Rocket scientists sit in ergonomic chairs while they work.

This makes Sophie laugh.

Rocket scientists are notoriously lazy, she says.

Elise twirls the melting ice in her cup. I feel like I haven't seen you in forever, she says. You doing OK?

Sophie's gaze splinters off to a string of mopeds wobbling over the cobblestone street.

Yeah, I'm OK, she says. The strangest thing happened to me this morning. A woman walked in before we opened and started reading the menu posted on the hostess stand. She had short curly hair pushed back with a bandana, and she was hunched over as she read. I told her we opened at nine, and when she looked at me, I thought it was Mom. Like, I really thought it was. You know that spiky feeling you get in your stomach when something feels so real? I even called out to her, but when she looked up a second time, I realized it wasn't her. So I ducked behind the counter and pretended to stock the fridge until she left.

Imagine, Elise says. If Mom somehow found a way back and waltzed in like that without telling us.

They laugh, probably too hard, but it feels good to shake out the ghosts.

I'm sorry about the other day, Elise says after a moment. I've been feeling awful about it.

Sophie bites the end of her straw. You were really upset about that wig.

It wasn't the wig. It's everything. The house, Mom. Work. Sheba's been getting on my nerves. I shouldn't take it out on you.

Sophie shrugs, pretending to be less hurt than she is. We're sisters. We fight sometimes.

True, Elise says. Still. I don't want to fight with you.

Sophie takes Elise's coffee cup for a refill. Elise is already buzzing with caffeine, but she doesn't object to Sophie's care. She wipes the counter as she lifts the cup, moves to the exact position where the coffee vat is, and returns it to Elise with a new paper straw. Through the open door, Elise sees the family from earlier sitting on a wooden bench, sipping their almond milks under the hazy clouds, the youngest chewing on the biscotti Sophie gave him.

The other day, Elise says, Sheba offered to pay for you to quit your job. She's noticed how exhausted you are. She said she'd cover whatever you'd make for the rest of the summer. Honestly, she'd probably pay you more.

Sophie presses her hip against the counter ledge and crosses her arms.

How much more are we talking?

I'm not sure, exactly. We didn't talk about it for long. I think she's worried you're working too much.

Of course she is, Sophie says. An hour of work is too much for Sheba.

There's no shame if you decide to take it, Elise says. Money is money.

Sophie picks at the coffee grounds stuck underneath her fingernails.

Do you really believe that? she says. There's no shame in taking Sheba's oil money?

Play-Doh money, Elise corrects.

Whatever. Play-Doh money.

If it means you'll have a cushion to start a new life without having to work fifty hours a week, then I think you should take it. As the words leave Elise's mouth, she realizes she's not being generous—she means it. She wants Sophie to take advantage where she can.

A group of teenagers approaches the counter, three boys and a girl, the boys shirtless and dusted with sand, the girl in a crop top and dangling star-shaped earrings.

I'll think about it, Sophie says and taps the counter, even though she'll never think about it again, not as a legitimate offer. She will work the rest of the summer, until her hands are raw and peeling and every white T-shirt she owns is ruined. Elise reaches over the counter, her arms outstretched, and they embrace, hips creased over the thick lacquered wood, chins hooked over shoulders.

I'll see you at home? Elise says.

See you at home, Sophie says, and returns to the register to take another round of orders.

.   .   .

That night, Elise sits up in Helen's bed, legs crooked under the silk duvet, her computer rested on her lap, while Sheba listens to a podcast in the shower. Elise twists her hair into a bun on the top of her head, opens up an internet browser, and navigates to her email. In her drafts is a letter she wrote to Mrs. Wagner on her phone a few hours prior. She clicks on it, skims the contents, and deletes *Sent from my iPhone* from the bottom of the page. She hits Send, then unsends when the option pops up a second later. Dear Mrs. Wagner, the email begins. I know it was tense the last time we saw each other, but my family needs a favor for this waiver application. She imagines Mrs. Wagner at her computer on the other end, the subject line appearing in her inbox—Immigration Letter for My Mom. She takes a deep breath and releases the air slowly through her nostrils, then presses Send again. This time, she closes her laptop afterwards and places it on the bedside table. She slouches into bed, facing the left wall, and tries to listen beyond the podcast's political volley emanating from Sheba's phone in the bathroom. She tries to parse the sound, to listen only for the patter of water falling.

◆

Through a set of arched French doors leading to the backyard, centered on the main house's fastidious Kentucky bluegrass lawn, is a slick infinity pool with a flirtatious inflatable swan drifting across its surface. Helen doesn't usually allow the swan to stay in the pool, but Helen isn't home anymore, so Sheba lets the swan graze and bounce against the stone-and-concrete ledge, its eyelashes perpetually poised. On Tuesdays and Fridays, a man in a navy polo shirt and matching Crocs checks the pool's chlorine levels and temperature-control system. He uses a green net attached to a long pole to skim the clumped-up goldenrod petals that blow in from the wild, so that by the time Sheba wakes to swim laps in the morning, the water is perfect. She wears a silicone cap and an athletic one-piece to optimize her strokes up and down the topaz water. Afterwards, she has an iced cashew-milk latte and an apple Danish on the chaise lounge, the teak wood underneath her darkening wherever she drips.

This is why they never go to the beach anymore. Why go to the beach when there's a pool with a floating swan, steps away from heated toilet seats and an outdoor shower, where rainbows of light pour in while you deep-condition your chlorinated hair?

Sheba and Elise are sitting on the edge of the pool with their feet dangling in the water, Sheba's apple Danish half bitten on a plate between them. Sophie opens the French doors with a yellow towel rolled underneath her arm, and shouts, I want to go to the beach today. We never go to the beach anymore.

They shield their eyes and gaze at her. Elise speaks first. It's true, she says. We haven't been to the beach in ages.

Sheba twists her mouth and lowers herself into the pool, her arms bent like a cormorant, hopping around to acclimate to the cold.

But there's sand at the beach, she says.

Yes, exactly, Sophie says. There's sand, and seagulls, and crabs, and other people.

Are you sick of me and your big sister already? Sheba says, expecting Elise to respond. I like the pool, Sheba continues. Saltwater makes my skin sticky. And I hate when seaweed gets trapped in your bathing suit and dries against your nipples.

I'm going to the beach, Sophie says, mostly addressing Elise. You can come if you want to.

I'll come, Elise says and walks toward Sophie, her wet footsteps evaporating in the hot sun. Sheba waits for them to cross the threshold into the main house before she calls out, Fine, I'm coming too, and hurries to catch up to them. Elise and Sophie agree to wait while Sheba takes a shower—she says she needs to wash her hair or else her highlights will turn green—and packs a large tote bag with magazines, lemon water, and various pretzel snacks. Elise drives to her and Sophie's secret beach spot: an uninhabited stretch of sand between two of the island's most popular beaches. To find this beach requires knowledge of an inconspicuous right turn, marked only by a weathered black mailbox covered in poison ivy, and a willingness to drive through deep mud puddles and narrow brush.

What if I have to use the restroom? Sheba asks from the back seat, trying her hardest to sound polite even though her manifesto, "In Defense of the Pool," lengthens with each passing minute.

You have two options, Sophie answers. The ocean or the dunes.

For both number one and number two?

Sophie turns around to gauge Sheba's seriousness.

Oh, in that case, you cup your hands like this. Sophie joins her hands together in demonstration. Sheba lowers her sunglasses in horror.

I'm kidding, Sheba. We'll bring you to a toilet if you need to take a doo-doo. Sophie faces forward, smirking. We're not monsters.

Elise parks against a picket fence and they gather their things from the trunk, then walk through a valley between the sand dunes, pink beach plum bushes and bending sprays of grass hugging their sides. Other beachgoers pile their flip-flops at the top of the path, but Sheba keeps hers on, remarking that she had a pedicure and the sand is too hot on her exfoliated feet. The path opens to a blurry horizon, one that continues unobstructed for miles and does not stop until it reaches Europe. Years from now, Elise will peer across the port in Lisbon and remember it is a continuation of her own horizon, and her gaze, at a certain point, will meet itself in the middle of the Atlantic.

How much farther? Sheba asks, trailing them with her beach chair and tote bag.

Sophie and Elise stop at a spot not too far from the water, but far enough that the rising tide won't reach them. They unfurl their towels perpendicular to the shoreline and Elise buries her face in the cotton threads, the sand underneath molding to her cheekbones. Sophie strips down to her bikini, declares she's going to dive into the water no matter how cold it is, and runs off. Sheba presses open her beach chair and immediately hides her face behind a magazine. They hear a splash and Sophie emerges from the dark, glassy water like a glittering torpedo, a caterpillar in a chrysalis.

Sheba drops her magazine in her lap, interrupting the lull of waves and salty breeze.

You could have backed me up, she says. At the house.

Elise glances up, squinting her eyes.

About what?

The pool. Objectively speaking, it's more convenient than the beach.

Elise lays her head back down.

Enjoy yourself, Sheba. It's a beautiful day.

I'm just saying—she picks up the magazine and snaps through the pages—you could have backed me up.

Elise doesn't say anything in return. She props herself up on her elbows and watches the edge of the water. Sophie is taking long strides out of the break, wringing her hair. She stops to talk to two passersby who cross in front of her as she reaches the shore. By the looks of Sophie's friendly demeanor, Elise guesses they must be from the island, but she can't make out who it is. The one closest to Sophie stands with her legs firmly apart and one hand akimbo. The other has an infant strapped across her chest in a lavender cotton wrap. She rubs the baby bulge with her palm.

Who is Sophie talking to? Sheba asks, leaning forward to get a better look.

I'm not sure, Elise responds, though she's begun to wonder if it could be their childhood friends Jacqueline and Amara. The possibility forces her to sit upright. She hasn't spoken to them since junior year of high school. After ICE raided the grocery store where their parents worked and they were deported to Jamaica, Amara dropped out of school and took a job as a housekeeper to support herself and her sister. The island's Jamaican community set them up in the basement of the Methodist church until Amara saved enough money to rent a room from a Guatemalan woman who ran a hair salon out of her kitchen.

As the three of them approach, Elise notices the small details that remind her of Amara: her midfielder legs and the keloid scars that run across her biceps (she tricked their classmates into believing she got them battling a tiger in Jamaica). She hears Jacqueline's raucous laugh bursting between sentences, her long, beaded braids clacking against her arms. When Amara sees Elise, who jumps up to greet them, her mouth breaks into a wide grin.

My God, Elise, how long has it been?

Elise hugs her, the baby cushioned between their sternums.

Too long, Elise says, and turns to hug Jacqueline.

Sheba clears her throat and retrieves the pretzels from her tote bag.

This is my friend from college, Sheba, Elise says, extending an arm. Sheba, this is Amara and Jacqueline. We grew up together.

Sheba offers a wave. They say hello and she picks up her magazine again.

Amara, is this your baby? Elise pushes the cotton fabric back to reveal her son's soft, round face, pursed in the sunlight. His name is Imran, Amara says. He's three months.

He's beautiful, Elise says, and touches the space between the baby's brows.

Sheba remains crouched in her beach chair, watching. Are you two sisters? she asks finally, pointing at Jacqueline, who is cast in silhouette from Sheba's vantage, the sun haloing around her. Jacqueline, Amara, Elise, and Sophie all respond in unison and then erupt into bright giggles.

I don't think you've ever told me about these friends, Sheba says to Elise.

Haven't I? Elise responds, detecting the sharpness in Sheba's question.

We haven't seen each other in years, Amara says. I've been meaning to ask where you've been.

College, Sheba answers for her. In Chapel Hill.

Amara pats Elise on the back. Good for you, Elise. You were always one of the smartest in our class.

A rash of heat rises to Elise's cheeks. You were way smarter, she responds.

Sheba lowers the brim of her hat and gazes toward the ocean to ruminate on Elise's body language, how she leans forward onto her toes every time Amara speaks, how easy Amara's face is when Elise offers a compliment. Sophie, meanwhile, has lost the ability to say anything. Her attention is tacked to Jacqueline, eagerly awaiting her every move.

Sophie touches Jacqueline's pocket, admiring the embroidery on the hem.

I like your pants, she says.

Jacqueline leans toward Sophie, unleashing the sun on Sheba.

Thanks. I got them in Oakland.

Is that where you live now? Sophie asks, observing her floral parachute pants and knit top with *San Francisco* scrawled in whimsical lettering. Jacqueline nods. Normally that kind of demonstrative coolness would make Sophie's eyes roll to the back of her head, but she's transfixed by her old friend Jacqueline, who pinches the end of Sophie's pinky finger and swings her arm.

I heard through the grapevine that you were hassled by the cops, Jacqueline says. Because of some gentrification bullshit. Is it true you got arrested?

Not really, Sophie says, and digs her foot into the sand.

I think it's pretty admirable, Jacqueline says.

Jacky, Amara steps in. You can't just come out and ask if someone was arrested.

Sophie's lips tense into a smile. It's all right. It was really nothing.

So, Elise says to Jacqueline, helping Sophie change the subject. Are you on island all summer?

I wish. Jacqueline reaches out her palm and cups Imran's head. I came to see my new baby nephew. I'm heading back West in a couple weeks.

Sophie's face drops. She rubs the corner of her eye.

Maybe we can get together again before you leave? Elise suggests.

I would love that, Jacqueline says and smiles at Sophie.

Amara motions down the beach to where their friend group is sitting. Her boyfriend, Bryan, is playing guitar, his back broad and tan, his hair a mass of salty blond frizz, and a couple of people are balancing on a slack line they hammered into the sand. They chat for a while longer about how much the island has changed since they were young, and how they hardly want to go anywhere anymore because of the crowds. Jacqueline says she hasn't been back to the island since she graduated from high school last year. Elise confesses it had been four years since she had been home, which she regrets, but she hadn't anticipated how strange it would feel to

see wealthy tourists on vacation every day, especially after what
happened to their mom. Sometimes she's not even sure how
much longer they'll be able to call Nantucket their home, she
says. Elise, this will always be your home, Amara replies, rocking
the baby. We can't let them buy up the land from under our feet.
Sheba looks up and turns a page in her magazine, her legs a bright
hue of pink. She's never heard Elise say anything remotely like
this before, about not being able to call the island her home. The
entire cadence of how she's talking to Jacqueline and Amara
sounds unfamiliar.

Elise and Sophie embrace their friends as they prepare to leave.
Sheba leans back in her beach chair. It was nice meeting you
both, she says and waves a stiff goodbye.

After Jacqueline and Amara depart, Elise announces she's going
for a swim.

Does anyone want to come?

Sophie and Sheba decline, so she walks to the water alone, eyeing Amara's and Jacqueline's silhouettes moving closer to the horizon. She wants to ask Amara about her relationship with her
parents, how she manages to connect with them in Jamaica when
the distance feels impossible. She wants to know if Amara is afraid
to mother a child in this world. Not the world generally, but their
world specifically—the world they share. She wants to hear Bryan
play guitar, songs he's written especially for Amara, and thank
him for always protecting her friend. She longs to follow them,
but she is weighted in place, waiting for an appropriate time, too
cautious, perhaps.

She wades out past the small ledge in the sea floor until she's
submerged to the top of her neck. The ocean swells around her,
pregnant with water. She relaxes, letting her lungs buoy her onto
the surface. As she floats, her arms out, her eyes mirroring the

shifting clouds, she hears the sound of the geologist's fake Irish accent, Helen prodding her about her mother's birthplace, and now, You could have backed me up. Back me up. Back up. She pulls herself underneath the water and attempts to exhale, but a wave passes through and the ocean fills her mouth. She scrambles to the surface and swims to shore.

When she returns, Sophie is asleep and Sheba has taken off her sunglasses, tipping her face to the sun. They sit in silence—punctuated only by Elise identifying a passing bird—until hunger sets in and they decide to go home. In the car, Sophie is absorbed by her cellphone in the back seat and Sheba quietly balances her head against the passenger's side window. After a few minutes, she glances at Sophie behind her.

You were so obsessed with that girl Jacqueline, she says.

Sophie lifts her eyes from her phone. What's that supposed to mean?

You were like a puppy dog when she arrived. It's obvious you have a crush on her.

Elise glances at Sophie in the rearview mirror.

Sheba, you literally don't know what you're talking about, Sophie says.

Jacky and Sophie have known each other for a long time, Elise says, trying to temper the exchange. They were excited to see each other.

So you're saying you *don't* have a crush? Sheba says, twisting to face Sophie.

Sophie throws her phone onto the seat beside her.

Let me live my life, Sheba. You don't have to be an emotional terrorist just because we didn't hang out at your pool.

They pull up to the main house and Sheba hurries to exit the car first. She's been irritable all day, Elise says to Sophie, watching

Sheba ascend the porch steps. They wait for her to enter the house before they step out and hang their damp towels over the porch banister. Sheba retreats to her bedroom, her original bedroom, Sophie's room, and shuts the door.

I should go talk to her, Elise says.

Sophie sighs, still focused on her phone. I would let her sulk. She'll get bored and snap out of it.

They hear a door open upstairs. Sheba crosses the hallway to her mothers' bedroom and the door slams. Maybe you're right. I should wait, Elise says, smelling a container of bluefish pâté from the back of the fridge. Sophie remains affixed to her phone. Are you scrolling social media? Elise asks.

Jacqueline texted me, Sophie says, allowing a smile to escape. She still has the same number from middle school.

Elise spreads a dollop of pâté onto a gluten-free cracker made mostly of seeds. The fish tastes briny and tart. She watches Sophie edit and reedit her reply texts to Jacqueline for several minutes, then closes the lid on the bluefish and returns it to the fridge.

All right. I'm going to see how she's doing, she says, and leaves Sophie in the kitchen.

Upstairs, Elise finds Sheba in her moms' room with a towel wrapped around her, vacuuming the silk duvet with a DustBuster.

There's sand everywhere now, she shouts over the loud suctioning noise.

Are you OK? Elise says. You seem testy.

How would you know? You barely spoke to me today.

She shuts off the vacuum and throws it on top of a pile of shoes in the closet.

What do you mean? Elise says, stepping closer to her. We talked.

You acted like you barely knew me. *She's my friend from college.*

Wow, really? And I don't understand why you wouldn't agree with me about the pool. You know I don't like the beach, but you'll do whatever your sister wants.

I wanted to go to the beach too! We're always here, at the house, with the pool. We swim in your pool all the time, Sheba.

Sheba spins her hair into a tight twist over her shoulder.

If you hate my pool so much, then maybe you should leave, she says.

What? Elise shifts from one foot to the other. What do you mean by leave?

If this place is so awful, and I'm some kind of *emotional terrorist,* maybe you shouldn't live here anymore.

Sheba—are you actually asking us to move out?

Sheba grunts and throws her fists against her thighs.

Why is everything about you and your sister! she yells, and erupts into tears. Her towel shifts and falls to the floor, revealing her porcelain body, a pinched belly button, and a narrow wisp of pubic hair. Elise bends down to collect the towel.

I don't want it, Sheba says as Elise tries to hand it to her. She throws herself facedown onto the bed. Elise opens the towel and covers her.

You know, maybe it's not exactly the same, but I lost my moms too, Sheba says. They refuse to talk to me. This yacht club drama really took a toll on my mental health. But I feel like I can't talk to you about it because so many horrible things have happened to you. And, like, I'm sorry I can't relate to you like Amara can, but, you know, you're not the only one who saved Sophie from jail. I had a part in it too. And then she calls me an emotional terrorist? I offered her a place to live after she was arrested!

Elise can feel the tips of her ears burning. She doesn't understand Sheba's persistence with Sophie. Does she want credit for her sister's well-being?

Sophie can be cutting with her words sometimes, she says, trying to find a middle ground. You can understand that, right? Saying harsh things you don't actually mean?

Sheba rolls over, facing Elise. I know this is probably the wrong thing to say, she whimpers. But I feel like, because your life is so tragic, I'm not allowed to feel bad about the things that happen in my life.

Elise rubs her chin. I wouldn't use the word *tragic,* she says finally.

Sheba, perhaps realizing she crossed a boundary, reaches for Elise and says: But you're a much better sister than I could ever be. You're the best. I wish in another life you'd be resurrected as my older sister.

Elise takes a deep breath, her lungs stuck. I have a lot going on in my life, she says, but that doesn't mean you can't tell me about your life, Sheb.

Sheba tucks herself into the fetal position and clutches the towel underneath her chin.

There was a moment, on the beach, she says, when I thought you were going to leave me for Amara. You went for a swim and I thought for sure you were going to follow them down the shore.

Elise swallows the saliva caught on the back of her tongue.

But I didn't, she says, before Sheba closes her eyes.

✦

At dawn, the hatchlings knock against the insides of their thinning shells and crack open the hard outer case, that which has protected them, allowed them to grow. They emerge, slick and chirping, and begin a creaky balance on dainty limbs. Elise arrives and discovers the eggs broken and abandoned, which alarms her initially, until she locates the hatchlings nestled in dried pearls of seaweed, prodding a broken quahog shell, grasping at pebbles with their newly unfurled feet.

Elise drops her logbook when she sees them, the pages cutting into the sand. She watches through raised binoculars until her hands go numb, their bodies a puff of white feathers, their stubby beaks chattering. When Steve arrives to retrieve her in the afternoon, she waves one hand in the air, gesturing for him to hurry over. He anchors the boat and jogs to the fence.

I told you they'd breed again, he says, nudging her with his elbow.

Don't try and take credit, she says. This one's all me.

He drags over a large piece of driftwood that the tide has carried ashore and offers for them to sit for a while. I downloaded a meditation app, he tells her. They say it's important to be present during moments of joy. He retrieves a bag of sunflower seeds from his back pocket and pours a handful into Elise's palm.

When I was little, Elise says, spitting a hull into her other hand, we used to go to that beach over there. She points east, over the estuary, to a coast carpeted with shells. My sister, Sophie, and I would pretend the waves were stampedes of animals. If it was a big wave we'd say, Oh no, here comes a herd of tigers! Or if it was a small one we'd say, Don't worry, it's just a bunch of sheep.

You know tigers don't stampede in herds right? Steve says with a cheek full of seeds.

Yes, I know that, Elise says. This is when we were kids.

If you're going to be my endangered species monitor, you need to know basic animal hunting facts.

Elise laughs. You've clearly never seen a tiger-stampede wave.

I sure have, he says. That's my favorite fishing spot over there.

They pass the binoculars back and forth, watching the chicks dig and nestle under their parent's soft underbelly, already scurrying and plucking at crustaceans. Eventually Steve asks Elise if she would consider working through the end of September or maybe mid-October, to help him in the office. Elise is relieved by the offer. She was hoping for more time to decide how she'd make money over the winter. She tells him she can work for as long as he needs. On the drive home, Elise smiles as she cruises on the open road, a conveyor of lavender sky above her. She picks up her phone and dials Gilda, who answers from her desk at work.

Mom? she says, pressing on the brake to allow a stray cat to pass. Guess what? The eggs hatched. There are two new chicks.

You're kidding! Gilda says, matching Elise's enthusiasm. That is incredible news.

I know, Elise says, accelerating again. I'm happy.

When she arrives at the main house and ascends the porch steps, a text message from Rahul vibrates on her phone. Her thumb wanders to their conversation thread as she opens the front door. They have been chatting on and off since they reunited at the Chicken Box, not about anything of substance, but with a twittering playfulness. He wishes her good morning and good night with silly GIFs and sends her stupid articles, like one about a pet koala bear that dresses up like a panda bear on Halloween. Sheba is curled up on a sofa in the living room and Sophie is reclined on the sofa beside her, each staring at their respective phones. A triangle of sky peeks between a gap in the curtains. Elise assumes Sophie is talking to Jacqueline, with whom she is engaged in a prolonged text affair; they write to each other from the moment they wake until they fall asleep with phones still in hand. Elise doesn't know who Sheba is talking to. It's possible she's scrolling so as not to seem like the only one without phone obligations.

The chicks hatched today! Elise announces as she enters the room.

Hey, that's awesome, Sophie says, momentarily glancing up from her phone.

Yay, chicks, Sheba says and drops her phone against her stomach. Who are you texting?

No one, Elise says and tucks her phone into her jeans pocket.

It's Rahul, isn't it? Sheba says. You're sexting with the hot bartender.

Sophie makes a gagging motion with her finger. Elise slumps onto the sofa.

I knew it! Sheba says. You're so obvious. She grabs a pillow from behind her and tosses it at Elise.

For real, Elise? Sophie says. Rahul? Mom will be so proud.

Cool it, OK? Elise says, smoothing over her mouth. Nothing is going on between me and Rahul.

A reply from Rahul lights up her screen: There's a bonfire party in the woods tomorrow. You going?

Is that him again? Sheba says, practically unzipping herself with glee.

He invited us to a party tomorrow, Elise says and buries her face into the pillow Sheba threw at her.

Is it the bonfire party in the woods? Sophie says. Jacqueline invited me too. I think I want to go.

Oh my God, you're both nauseatingly in love, Sheba says. What are we going to wear?

Sophie furrows her eyebrows. Have you ever been to a bonfire party?

No, Sheba says. They didn't have bonfires at the Gramercy Park Hotel when I was growing up.

I wouldn't wear your finest silks, Sophie says.

Sheba crosses her arms. I don't care if there's a bonfire. Your sister needs to look hot for her new boyfriend.

Elise ignores them and opens up her conversation with Rahul.

Elise: Will you be there?

Rahul: I'll be there ☺

Elise: See you tomorrow night then

It's after one A.M. and Elise tells Sheba she's going to take a bath in the eggshell tub. My bones are cold, she says. I need to warm up. Sheba retires with a book in hand and falls asleep before opening the first page. Elise runs the tap, steps into the hot water, and submerges her ankles, knees, thighs, and belly button, slowly inching the steaming water up her body. When she's acclimated, she pinches her nose and dunks her head under. Her breasts float, breaching the surface. She's hoping the bath will relieve her anxiety about seeing Rahul at the party. She can't stop assessing what time they should leave—she would prefer if Rahul was already there when they arrive, since she's not sure who else will be at the party. She plans on wearing a black dress—something short but casual—strappy sandals, and a zip-up sweatshirt tied around her waist, in case the temperature drops. She hopes Rahul wears a loose button-down shirt partially undone. She loves his chest hair, the playful black ribbons, a field ready to be trampled. Had he been serious when he said he wanted to visit her at work and see the birds for himself? She had told him about how she lost the first brood but the second successfully hatched this morning. She imagines them sitting together on a thick woven blanket, their legs touching slightly, sticky in the heat, as they watch crowds of sanderlings butt and juke against the tide. She lets her hands buoy in the bathwater, one moving to his imaginary thigh. She can feel the muted pulse of her heartbeat under the water, her hand reaching deeper into his swim trunks, the warm humidity inside, the dense prickle of his pubic hair. Can I? she imagines he would ask her while scanning her breasts. She'd nod and he'd bite her nipple over her bikini top. She laughs and sighs slowly, her hand still searching. He tongues his way down her rib cage and gazes up at her. Yes, do it, please, she tells him. He places his open mouth against her bathing suit fabric and exhales, the warmth of his breath expanding against her pubic bone. He takes the end of her bikini string in his teeth and unties her. She tilts her head back, cheeks aflame, a flock of seagulls flapping overhead.

They drive into the woods on sandy dirt roads that thunk against the bottom of Elise's car. There are no streetlights or road signs, only a series of intuitive lefts and rights that end with a line of cars parked diagonally against the bushy thicket. They hear a dull clamor of voices coming from a glow in the trees, at once close and distant, like the sonic whirl inside a conch shell. Sheba has an open prosecco bottle wedged between her thighs from which she's been stealing swigs as Elise drives. Sophie is in the back seat with a six-pack of warm hard cider she found in the pantry. As soon as Elise cranks the emergency brake, Sophie cracks open a can and the cider fizzes onto her jeans.

Now my hands are sticky, she says, licking her palms.

Sheba steps out of the car, drinks the last of the prosecco, and tosses the empty bottle into the back seat.

Let's go find your boyfriend, Rahul, she says, swinging the door shut.

Elise steps out on the driver's side.

Not my boyfriend, she says for the fifth time that night, and checks her mascara in the side-view mirror.

They walk down the grassy hump in the middle of the road,

careful with each step in the darkness. The woods smell of over-ripe mushrooms and straw. A pop breaks through the black lattice of trees—wet wood catching the flame, or an empty beer bottle bursting—lighting up the rough, craggy scales on the surrounding pine trees.

I can't believe this is what locals do for fun, Sheba says, and asks for a sip of Sophie's cider.

They enter the clearing, and Elise recognizes people she had almost forgotten about—boys with shaggy haircuts puncturing the sides of beer cans, girls in fleece jackets sitting on the ends of open truck beds, all clustered into predictable groups around the bonfire. The boys suction their mouths to the punctures and open the cans from the top, gulping the beer down in a few seamless breaths. Above them, smoke spirals into an open space between the treetops.

There he is! Sheba whisper-yells and hugs onto Elise's arm. She gestures her chin toward Rahul, who is veiled by wavy fumes drifting off the fire. Elise stops walking, pretends to look in the opposite direction. Sophie announces she's going to say hi to Jacqueline and vanishes before Elise can ask where. Let's go over there, Sheba says and drags Elise by the hand through the party. As they pass by, several people wave, recognizing Elise, but Sheba doesn't allow for a pause to say hello. Rahul notices them approaching and stops his conversation.

You're here, he says, and leans over to give Elise a kiss on the cheek, but lands on the corner of her mouth. I wasn't sure if you were still coming, he says. You never texted me back.

Sheba swipes at Elise's arm. She's so bad at texting, she says. Elise takes in his appearance: his loose, unbuttoned shirt covered in a palm-frond print, chest hair visible, a slight beard darkening his jawline. Even through his adult attractiveness—statuesque, symmetrical, yet not overly perfect, slightly disheveled—she can still see the echoes of his younger self in subtle mannerisms, the way he places his hands on his hips when making a point, how his gums show when he laughs too hard.

Have you been here long? Elise asks, touching her bottom lip.

An hour or so, he replies and brushes off a mosquito that lands on his nose. I kept hoping you'd come and save me from some awkward conversations. Elise smiles and tucks a strand of hair behind her ear. Sheba clears her throat. Hey, bartender, she says, pointing to a case of beer behind Rahul, can I have one of those? Of course, Rahul says, and hands a can to Sheba and one to Elise.

I'm driving, Elise says, declining the drink.

How responsible, he responds, which Elise isn't sure how to interpret.

Asia trudges out of the bushes from behind Rahul, zipping up her fly. What the fuck—Elise! When did you get here? she says. She's wearing liquid eyeliner drawn nearly to her eyebrows. You should have texted me! I could have given you a ride. I have my dad's truck.

Elise introduces Asia to Sheba, who doesn't acknowledge her and reaches for Rahul's shirt collar. Is this a silk blend? Sheba asks him, rubbing the fabric between her fingers. Asia extends her phone out with her arm and clicks a selfie of her, Elise, and Sheba, then presents the photo to Elise. Asia is leaning her head on Elise's shoulder, her eyes mid blink, and Sheba is holding on to Rahul's shirt.

Come with me to say hi to Blake, Asia says to Elise, and reminds her that Elise and Blake performed a flute duet together in the seventh grade. I'll be right back, Elise says to Rahul, who warns her that the party is teeming with old friends who want to catch up. Blake is standing alone in black pants adorned with button pins. She seems pleased to see Elise, and they try in earnest to recall specific aspects of their time in band together. Across the fire, Elise watches Rahul and Sheba take swigs from a clear bottle. She attempts to break off from the conversation and join them, but she is stopped again by an ex-girlfriend of Sophie's, who tells her she makes her own dolls and sells them on the internet. Elise excuses herself, says she needs to find her college friend who isn't from the island, and searches for Sheba and Rahul.

You're like the prom queen tonight, Rahul tells her as she approaches.

It's because I've been away for so long, she says. It wasn't like this in high school.

Rahul insists that isn't true. You were always the one everyone liked, he says, smiling, then leaves to take a piss behind a tree. While he's gone, she is intercepted by Rahul's younger brother, who is very drunk and confesses that Rahul was madly in love with Elise in middle school. He says: Rahul had a folder on his desktop of his favorite photos of you from social media. Isn't that creepy?

Elise spits out her water. She tries to elicit more recent details, but Rahul's brother stumbles off and they do not speak again.

By this point, the party has dwindled to its last drunk stragglers, and Elise, who is sober, is beginning to find it unbearable. I think it's time for us to head out, she says to Sophie, who is still sitting with Jacqueline on a stack of pallets and singing Alanis Morissette songs from memory. She glances around to say goodbye to Rahul, resigned that this won't be the night for their romantic connection after all, but he's nowhere in sight. Sophie leans against Jacqueline and frowns. I don't want to leave yet, she says. Asia and Sheba appear from behind them.

The mosquitos are eating me alive, Asia says, slapping at her bare thighs.

Sheba drapes her arm around Elise's waist. She smells sharply of vodka.

After-party at our place, she says. Rahul's riding with us.

Elise removes Sheba's arm. We can't host a party. If your moms find out we'll be dead.

Don't be a drag. They'll never know, Sheba says, walking away with Asia in tow.

Elise looks at Sophie, who is tipsy and amused. You want to come? she offers to Jacqueline. Sheba has a massive house. Elise grumbles, but is ultimately convinced by the possibility of having more time with Rahul, and exits with them through a part in the trees.

As Elise tunnels through the night—her headlights carving into darkness—she glances in the rearview mirror at Asia's truck trailing them. The sky is moonless, so Elise drives hunched over the steering wheel, poised for animals that might dart under her tires. Asia's truck only has one working headlight, a cyclops barreling down the center of the road. Sheba is in the passenger's seat adjusting the radio. Rahul is sitting in the back seat with Jacqueline and Sophie. When Elise checks the rearview mirror, she sees half of Rahul's face reflected. He's trading glances between his phone and the passing road between the front seats.

I saw your brother at the bonfire, Elise says to him. Is he coming over?

God, no. He was wasted. He got a ride home with his friend Julian.

We chatted for a while, she says. He told me all of your secrets.

Rahul catches Elise's eyes in the mirror.

Oh yeah? What did he say?

Elise scrunches up her nose.

I promised I wouldn't tell.

She returns her eyes to the road and briefly imagines what it would be like to tell her mother that she and Rahul have reconnected. Gilda would revel in her foresight. She'd say things like, He was always such a sweet boy, and, You two will make very beautiful children. Sheba turns up the volume on the radio and leans toward Elise. You are such a fucking flirt, she whispers, and sings along to the lyrics.

Elise turns in to Sheba's driveway and Asia pulls up to her rear, the single headlight glaring into her car. Elise enters Sheba's birthday into the keypad and Asia follows her through the gate. They pull up to the main house and Sheba and Sophie leap out of the car and head straight to the kitchen with Jacqueline and Rahul. Elise hangs back and pauses in the unlit dining room, a mausoleum of stiff high-backed chairs and candelabras, the site where she had once followed Asia around awaiting her instruction. Asia is the first to walk in from the other car, with a six-pack of beer gripped in each hand. Elise wonders if maybe she doesn't remember having been here before. Maybe all the summer houses she's catered loop together seamlessly in her mind. But then Elise sees the transformation in her face as it goes slack with recognition. She observes the details of this particular summer house: walls the color of unpasteurized milk, layers of throw pillows creased down the middle, the abstract landscape paintings, and the French doors that reveal Sheba's silvery pool and gliding swan. Elise balances a hand against the dining room entranceway. Asia places the six-packs on the floor, grabs her friend by the shoulder, and says: I've been here before. The friend seems impressed, wants to know how, when, why, and Elise feels a complicated sense of pride wringing inside her, as though this were her house, as though she had something to claim here. She steps outside the dining room and Rahul spots her from the kitchen. He creeps behind her, his arms outstretched, and when his hands grab on to her sides like a pair of tongs, she shrieks. He laughs. She places a hand on his chest and exhales with relief.

Elise, do you remember this house? Asia says, walking toward her. We worked a party here together! It was for that stuck-up group of environmentalists. And I stole the wine!

Hang on— Rahul says, calculating. I thought you said you lived here?

I'm staying here, yeah, Elise responds.

You live here? Asia's friend says, and Asia parrots her: Yeah— You live here?

Elise bites down on her bottom lip. It's my friend Sheba's house. She's letting me and Sophie live here for a while.

Asia still looks confused. Do you work for her? she asks.

Elise forces a laugh. She feels embarrassed to admit she's living with a wealthy summer person. Asia's face barely flickers, awaiting an explanation.

No, no. I don't work for Sheba. She's a friend from college. I didn't live here when her mom Helen threw that fundraising party, but Sophie and I were kicked out of our house, so Sheba's letting us stay here.

Each set of eyes blinks at her simultaneously, a slow pat of eyelashes. Rahul wraps his arm around Elise's shoulders, leaning into her.

This is so fancy, he says. Don't forget about us when you're rich and famous.

Elise slides out from underneath his weight.

I need a drink, she says. Let's go to the kitchen.

I remember how to get there, Asia says and walks ahead.

Sophie and Sheba are behind the marble island making a large pitcher of rum punch. Sheba dumps an entire jar of maraschino cherries into the opaque orange liquid, pressing them down with her fingers as they bob to the surface. Drink, anyone? she says, and everyone raises their hands. She takes out ten crystal glasses from the cabinet and passes them out like carnival prizes, sloshing the rum onto the stovetop. Elise suggests maybe disposable cups might be a better option, but Sheba brushes her off. These are more environmentally friendly! she says, lighting a long white candle. She circles the kitchen with a box of matches, melting candlewax onto bread plates and gluing candlesticks to them until there are more lit flames than people in the room.

Elise finishes her drink and pours another.

I told her this wasn't a good idea, she says to Sophie, who is cozied up with Jacqueline in the banquette seats. Word's going to get out about an after-party and this is going to be a nightmare.

Sophie shrugs. I'm not sure what to do at this point.

We live here, Elise says. Don't we get a vote?

By Elise's third drink, a chain of text messages passing along Sheba's address and gate code has expanded beyond the parameters of Elise's and Sophie's social circles. Year-rounders who didn't grow up on island have congregated on the porch and are smoking American Spirits and dropping the butts into empty beer cans.

Locals who Elise never overlapped with in high school are bouncing ping-pong balls into beer cups on the dining room table. Aleksi and Asia's catering co-workers are dosing ketamine and dancing to synthpop in the living room.

Elise has given up trying to convince Sheba she should shut the party down, tell everyone to go home, and change the gate code, even though summer parties like this have the potential for disaster: an unsuspecting summer person combined with the pent-up resentment of local residents, bricks thrown through windows, stolen artwork, flat-screens flung from balconies. She doesn't even know where Sheba is, and Sophie has escaped to her bedroom with Jacqueline. The insides of Elise's cheeks are raw from the rum punch. Where's Rahul? Asia asks Elise. Elise checks her phone. I don't know, she says. I think he may have left. They're standing with a group in the kitchen reminiscing about cartoons they watched as children—a conversation Elise heard play out in college so many times it's lost its nostalgia—when a man with a red, patchy beard walks into the kitchen.

Is Asia here? he says, barely moving his jaw. He's wearing a long-sleeved T-shirt with barbed wire designs snaked up the sleeves. Asia runs over to him and leaps into his arms. Elise recalls that his name is Drew. He was a few grades above them and, rumor had it, he French-kissed a substitute teacher in the auditorium bathroom and, at her request, pressed his hand against her throat until she lost consciousness. Everyone in high school learned the term *erotic asphyxiation* that year.

Asia seems very proud he's turned up to Sheba's crystal-glass-and-candle party with a six-pack of homemade IPA. She takes him by the hand and offers him a mushroom cap she has floating around at the bottom of her purse. As she does, her hair swings around and slices through the candle burning on the counter. The flame moves gently to the side, then stands erect again. Asia's hair erupts into a buzz of flame that eats loose flyaways from end to scalp. Elise, in a delayed reaction, dowses her with a glass of punch.

What the fuck? Asia says, looking down at her red-stained shirt.

You were on fire, Elise explains.

Drew laughs. That was awesome, he says, and opens a bottle with his teeth.

Asia pats at her crisp, wet hair. Her eyes sink toward Drew and shoot back at Elise.

My shirt is soaked, she says. Hello? Aren't you going to find me something new to wear, since you supposedly live here?

It's not my house, Elise says, and puts the glass down. But sure. I'll find you a shirt.

She goes upstairs and thumbs through the stacks of clothing piled against the wall in Helen's room. A strip of light shines from the bottom of Sheba's closed bedroom door, through which Elise can hear the soft beat of Sophie's and Jacqueline's laughter. Elise knows that whatever shirt she lends Asia she probably won't ever see again. She chastises herself for not being more like Sheba, who willingly parts with her wigs, her houses, her zippered dresses, who doesn't mind if strangers litter her deck with cigarettes and crushed jelly beans. Everything, to her, is replaceable.

Elise decides to check the guest house to see if there's clothing over there she'd be willing to give away. She walks downstairs, through the crowd on the porch, and across the stone pathway. The back door is already cracked open, the foggy night air having permeated the guest house living room. Elise drags her finger across the moisture on the fireplace mantel, the taxidermy animals glistening with dew. She ascends the stairs and opens the door to her old bedroom (her, the possessive, in a fragile state), and finds Rahul seated on the end of her (her?) bed. Sheba's bent knees are saddled around his hips, her fingers clutching his shoulder blades. Her hair swings onto his back, the wet strands stuck to his skin in untethered swirls.

Sheba opens her eyes, the whites staggering in the dim light.

Elise—wait. She unravels from Rahul's waist.

Wow, really? Elise says, her chest tightening. Did you seriously have to do this here?

Rahul slouches over, covering his crotch and avoiding Elise's eye contact.

I'm sorry, Elise, he says. I'm really sorry—this was a stupid mistake.

Please don't be upset, Sheba interrupts. She drops to the floor in front of Elise, prostrating, her lips rubbed red, her mascaraed eyelashes imprinted on her cheekbones and lids. He's right, this was a stupid mistake! I'll do anything. Please forgive me!

Elise steadies her hands on the tops of her thighs and bends over.

Sheba, stop it. This is embarrassing, she says, trying to pull her up. Rahul takes his balled-up jeans into the bathroom.

Elise, you hate me, don't you? You think I'm awful, I'm the worst friend. Sheba's slurring her words, and her face is puffy from alcohol. Elise considers telling her, yes, she hates her, if only to disrupt the melodrama she's been lured into, and yet she knows how quickly Sheba's desperation could flip into anger, and so she simply says, You're a fucking idiot, Sheba. Stand up—what's wrong with you? Get up off the floor.

Rahul appears from the bathroom with his pants on and tries to shuffle past them. Elise waits to see if Sheba will try to stop him, but she doesn't register him. She presses her mouth against Elise's kneecap, her breasts grazing Elise's shins.

You're going to leave me, aren't you? she cries, grabbing on to Elise's ankles. You're going to move out!

I'm going to sleep, Elise says, steely. Don't forget I said all of this—she circles her arms wide through the air, and it's unclear if she means the party, the island, their living arrangement, or a much bigger, more intangible issue—was a terrible idea.

Elise shakes Sheba from her ankles and exits the room. Sheba doesn't move; she remains hunched on the floor, her rib cage expanding. Elise doesn't look back, though she wants to. Sheba is being loud and visceral (Don't leave me, she keeps repeating, I love you) and every molecule in Elise's body wants to magnetize to Sheba's demands. It's a chemical reaction, but Elise fights the urge. She marches to the main house, where Asia is kissing Drew against the French doors, the flickering pool reflections sheathed across their faces. Drew's hand moves toward Asia's neck. Elise retreats to Helen and Holly's room and closes the door.

In the morning, the house smells like ash and punch. Elise is asleep in Helen and Holly's bed, alone, and Sophie and Jacqueline are in Sheba's room. Sheba fell asleep on the guest house floor shortly after Elise left her. Because of this reversal in the sleeping order, Helen doesn't find Sheba on an initial inspection. She arrives in her rented Mercedes-Benz and first notices the front door propped open with a cement block. The wind rattles a single beer can against the porch railing. When she enters the house, she restrains herself from calling out for Sheba—her house, she thinks, is as dirty and worn as the underside of a work boot. Is her daughter really arrogant enough to think her mothers won't find out about what she does when they aren't around? No, she doesn't want to give Sheba a warning shot. She slips off her satin ballet flats, carrying them in one hand, and tiptoes up the stairs, her low-cut socks slipping against the wooden floors. She doesn't make a sound. She opens up her bedroom door and finds not her daughter but a stranger sleeping in her bed.

At ten A.M., the temperature is already scrambling toward a hundred degrees. The only birds that are out are the grackles, their black feathers pearlescent in the sun, tearing out insects from the lawn. The housekeepers, in less than twenty-four hours, have returned the main house to its normal state. Helen is outside, reclined in a chaise lounge underneath an umbrella with yellow fringe tassels, applying various tinctures to her face. Her choice of location is unspecific; it's as though she took a dozen steps from her house to the middle of the lawn and, *veni, vidi, vici,* she unfolded her chair. She rubs zinc onto her arms and legs, plastering her skin with a chalky, alabaster tint, and texts Sheba, requesting that Elise and she come speak with her in the yard.

I don't need to explain the shock one feels in finding a stranger in one's bed, Helen says to the two of them, clenching her teeth, as if to convey that she could yell if she wanted to, that she was doing them a favor by sparing them her wrath.

Am I a stranger? Elise asks, almost pleadingly. She and Sheba didn't bring chairs, so they're standing outside the umbrella, crouched and peering through the fringe to make eye contact with Helen.

You could have been anyone, she says, dabbing the perspiration above her lip.

I understand, Elise responds after a moment.

You and your sister can stay in the guest house until the end of summer, but then I think our arrangement needs to change, Helen says. If I do have guests, they'll need a place to stay. This was never a permanent solution.

I understand, Elise says again, silently counting the days until the end of summer. Sheba watches a plane soar across the sky, leaving a cut of smoke in its path.

You're a loyal friend, and Sheba needs that in her life, Helen says. Elise adjusts her stance, pressing her right foot firmer into the soft lawn. She regrets not having put on shoes before rushing out to meet Helen; there's something more demeaning about being scolded while barefoot. Sheba is wearing a pair of rubber slippers. Her mouth twists into a knot, wordless. Why is it that she and Sophie are the ones being punished and not Sheba? Elise wonders. Sheba was the one who insisted on having the party. If only Elise could have a chance to explain . . .

As much as she drives me crazy, Helen says, as if she knows what Elise is thinking, Sheba is my daughter. She sips a glass of iced water that has gone limp in the sun. Of course. Sheba is her daughter—how could Elise argue with that? This isn't the first time and won't be the last that she's cast aside for the priority of someone else's daughter.

Don't worry. Sophie and I will be gone soon, she says. A grackle jabs at the grass behind them, expertly unearthing a hidden grasshopper. Elise feels obligated to thank her, and so she does. Thank you, Helen, she says. As she begins to walk to the guest house, Sheba makes a sound to speak, but Elise cannot bear to make eye contact with her. She continues walking while Sheba remains planted by her mother's side.

Elise and Sophie move their possessions back into the guest house later that day while Helen and Sheba are out to lunch in town. I guess we shouldn't bother unpacking, Sophie says, and leans her open suitcase against the dresser. In the middle of the move, Elise sees that Sheba has posted a photo to social media: a lobster head propped in the middle of her plate, the claws fanned to the side, the tail cracked and upturned. Elise double-taps the photo and slides her cellphone into her back pocket.

For the following two weeks, they try to spend as little time as possible at the house. After work, she and Sophie buy pizza slices for dinner and sit on the wharf, watching catamarans skate through the water. They return to Sheba's after the sun has set. Sometimes Elise even shuts off her headlights as she inches up the driveway, trying to get by unnoticed.

It's Saturday, a week before they're supposed to move, and they have not secured another place to live. Sophie is working at the Lunch Counter, so Elise throws a pair of sneakers in her car and drives to the high school football field. The field is an oasis at the center of the island, unpopulated and quiet. She leans against a goal post to tie her shoes, then runs around the track bordering the field, pushing herself to reach the next yellow yard flag, and the next, and the next. When she's slick and bleary with sweat, she climbs the bleachers and lies down, the hard metal impressions digging into her shoulder blades. The town installed a wind turbine on campus several years ago, and the low whoosh is hypnotic. She is sinking into a space somewhere between the sound of the turbine and a dream when she hears a voice call to her from below.

Why do I always find you? Asia shouts from underneath the stands. I swear I'm not a stalker.

Elise glances down between the slats in the steps and sees Asia balancing a soccer ball under her arm.

You play soccer? Elise says, sitting up.

Asia twirls the ball on one finger and catches it as it falls.

You don't remember? I played in high school. Defense.

Asia jogs to the front of the bleachers and hops up the steps, taking two at a time, until she reaches Elise.

We even went to state championships when I was a senior, but no one came to our games. They only went to boys' games, and the boys were terrible. She sits next to Elise and rests the ball in her lap. Now I play in a rec league that meets here once a week.

Elise rubs her forehead. The scoreboard is locked at zero-zero, its blue paint chipped and weathered.

That was a fun party the other night, Asia says. I can't believe Rahul and your friend hooked up. I was sort of shocked, because he was all over you, and he's been in love with you for like ever. I saw him the other day and told him he's a dipshit. I mean, he could have had *Elise,* the hottest girl from our high school, and he hooked up with some summer girl?

Elise keeps looking out at the scoreboard, nodding.

What's your friend's name again? Asia asks.

Sheba, Elise says, and glances at her fingernails. Did Rahul say anything in response?

He said he was drunk, he regrets it, he wants to call you but he's afraid you hate him.

I don't hate him, Elise says and sighs. I wish I did. There's a part of me that wants to forgive him and try again.

I get it, Asia says and bounces the soccer ball on the seat in front of them, the noise echoing across the field. Did your friend apologize?

Elise rubs her face with two hands. She's texted me a couple times saying she's sorry. I haven't responded yet.

Asia nods, bounces the ball again, and then rests it in her lap. I don't know if you heard, but Drew and I broke things off.

I hadn't heard, Elise says. I'm sorry.

Thanks. It's better this way. He was so noncommittal, and it was giving me a lot of anxiety. She pauses, tucks her hands behind her knees. I wanted to say sorry too, by the way, for getting so upset at you that night.

Don't worry about it, Elise says. I would have been upset too if my hair caught on fire.

Yeah, well, still. It wasn't cool of me to snap at you like that.

As she says this, she rests her elbows on the soccer ball and rubs her eyes with two fists.

I don't think I should drink anymore, she continues, and Elise realizes she's tearing up. It's not good for me. I think if I keep drinking, I'm going to be stuck on this island forever. I want to travel and live somewhere new. Maybe get my degree.

Elise collects Asia's hair off her back and places it over her shoulder. A breeze moves across the nape of her neck.

You will, Elise says. You're such a hard worker, Asia. I'm sure you'll accomplish what you want.

I hope so. She pulls a paper napkin from her pocket and blows her nose. Like, I've never even been to Asia. And my name is Asia.

Elise laughs. A wind picks up, making her shiver, her sweat cool and dry. We're moving out of Sheba's house next week, she says. Her mom kicked us out after that party.

Seriously? Asia says. You'll never find a place to live with that short notice.

I know. Elise folds her hands in her lap. I may ask if we can stay a bit longer, but I don't know. I think we have to go.

Asia shakes her head. Worst case scenario, you can come stay with me, she says. I've had five people stay in the shed before. It's actually pretty cozy.

Elise smiles and gives her a hug.

Thanks. I may take you up on that.

The wind turbine thrums at a steady beat behind them, pulsing with the strengthening wind. Elise takes the ball from underneath Asia's arms and tosses it into the air.

You want to play for a bit? she asks. One-on-one.

You're on, Asia replies, and they race each other down the steps, running onto the open field, the two of them, like children, taking flight.

◆

They decide to go for a drive, Elise and Sophie, because the late-August air feels pleasantly fragile and the sky is stretched into a seamless cover. Sophie has her arm out the passenger-side window, the breeze rippling her shirt sleeve. Where should we go next? Elise asks. The question has an existential tone but manifests in the practical turn of the steering wheel, down unpaved roads and dead-end cul-de-sacs. They're trying to be spontaneous, searching for places on the island they've never been before, but the grooves in their memory are well-worn, making it difficult to veer off track. They don't intend to, but their decisions lead them home, their old house, the place they remember best. They approach from the opposite side of the road and park behind an overgrown rose of Sharon bush, its purple petals pressed against the windshield. Elise retrieves her binoculars from the glove box and hands them to Sophie.

The renovated version of their old house looks like a digital rendering of itself: contrast and saturation up, lower warmth, sharpen, no shadows, brighter, brighter. They painted the trim green, Sophie says, adjusting the zoom. And the window boxes are filled with marigolds.

Can you see anyone through the windows? Elise asks.

Sophie leans closer to the dashboard.

I see someone, but it's hard to make out.

A car drives by and they pretend to search through the center console. When the car turns at the end of the road, Sophie picks up the binoculars again.

Mrs. Wagner is home, she says. I can see her sitting at her computer.

Weird, Elise says. Should we knock on her door? All of our stuff is still in their basement.

No way, Sophie says. They should live with it for a while longer, to remember what they did. She presses the lenses against her cheekbones and travels back to their house. They built a porch in our backyard. I always wanted a porch.

Two young children, a boy and a girl, swing open the front door and run onto the lawn. The boy jumps inside a miniature plastic Humvee parked beside the house. He presses on the accelerator and the girl runs in circles ahead of him, shouting, Don't run me over, Jack! Don't run me over! He follows her in the car until the mother—a young redheaded woman wearing capri pants—pokes her head out the screen door and shouts, Jack, don't run over your sister, and closes the door again. The children wait motionless, their tight-lipped mouths wiggling with anticipation, and then proceed with the car chase again.

These kids kind of remind me of us, Sophie says. Skeptical of authority.

Sophie passes Elise the binoculars. She focuses on the attic window, trying to discern if they've transformed it into a proper bedroom or back into an attic. In the window is a dinosaur sticker, and she can faintly see that the rafters have been covered with light blue walls.

Do you still think of it as our house? Elise asks, lowering the binoculars. Even though so much has changed?

Yes, Sophie says. Even if everything about it changes, it will still be our house. She pauses, looks out the window. Elise, I have to tell you something, she says after a moment. And I don't want you to freak out. She waits for Elise to promise, but Elise presses her to continue. Earlier this year, I applied to some colleges. And yesterday I found out I got into one.

Sophie—what? Elise unbuckles her seatbelt and faces her. I didn't even know you had applied.

I got rejected from most, but Berkeley wait-listed me back in April. I basically wrote it off and forgot about it. I figured they would only take me if someone decided to go to like Stanford instead, and by that point the aid money would be gone. But I found out yesterday I got in. And they're giving me money too.

Elise leans over and they give each other a slanted hug, the hard plastic car parts digging into their hips.

You were accepted just like the rest of them, Soph. It doesn't matter how you got there, by wait list or not.

Thanks, Sophie says. But I feel bad leaving you behind.

Elise clings on to Sophie's hand. Don't worry about me. I'd sooner drive this car to Berkeley than prevent you from going to college.

Sophie smiles. I still can't believe it. I'm moving to California. I've never been farther west than our school trip to Washington, D.C.

When's your first day? Elise asks.

I have to be out there next week for orientation.

Next week? That's so soon, Elise responds. Do you have a place to stay? Have you looked at plane tickets?

Actually, Jacqueline said I can stay with her until I find my own place. And I saved a bunch of money this summer, so I can afford the flight.

Elise rests a hand over her mouth and glances out the windshield. She's holding back the urge to warn Sophie not to let her romance with Jacqueline guide her decision-making. This is Sophie's chance to make her own decisions, to develop painful crushes and change her mind, to bleach her hair until the ends are dead, to cram in study sessions until four A.M. and, still, it won't be enough time for all the books she'll need to read. She'll meet mentors and idols and new friends. She'll forget to call her mother and sister back.

Jacqueline knows you're going, Elise says. And now I know. Does Mom?

Not yet. Sophie pauses, stares down at her hands. I'm worried she's going to be upset.

Why would she be upset?

I don't know. Because I'm moving farther away from her.

She'll be proud, Elise says. We're always proud of you, Sophie.

The mother inside the house that used to be theirs opens a window and calls for the children to come inside for dinner. They plead for a minute longer, but the mother insists. The boy abandons his car in the middle of the lawn, its reflective strips faintly glimmering under the dusking sky, and helps his sister climb the front doorsteps. Elise turns on the ignition. She drives through the overgrown rose of Sharon, the branches brushing up against the windshield and over the roof. She and Sophie take the long, familiar route back home.

The birds are grown, plump and gray-feathered, ready to fly for the Gulf of Mexico before the air turns frigid and the nor'easter gales rage. Elise is scooping sand into her palms and releasing it through her fingers, as though she can train time with her hourglass hands. She imagines Sophie sitting in her window seat on the airplane, clicking photographs of the white clouds beneath the wing. Elise had given her a cheddar-and-avocado sandwich for the overnight flight before she went through airport security, and waited until she could no longer see her beyond the metal detector, her heart so full it felt too heavy. She'll be landing in San Francisco any minute now, Elise thinks, where Jacqueline will pick her up in her red sedan, the one she's so proud of, with daisy-chain stickers covering the back bumper.

She reaches into her windbreaker pocket for her phone, checking for a message from Sophie, but there's nothing. I should call my mom, she thinks. I want to tell her I'm coming to see her. I want to go to Brazil to study pink dolphins in the Amazon River. I want to meet my family.

The tips of her fingers are cold from when she rinsed them in the ocean water moments earlier. She presses Gilda's number, and it rings a few times, but the connection cuts and the screen goes blank.

No service. She drafts a text message.

Mãe, estou indo.

I'm coming for you.

She hits Send, and she can feel the message stalling, fighting to push through, until a red triangle appears and it fails.

Gilda is at home in Atibaia having lunch with Beth and Manuel. As a gift, her father brought her his battered copy of *Love in the Time of Cholera* by Gabriel García Márquez—a book he has read at least a hundred times, he tells her. She's learning that her father is as sweet and as easily bruised as a ripe banana, the world too jagged for his inquisitive soul. He arranges a bouquet of tiger lilies at the center of the kitchen table and uncorks a bottle of white wine. Beth has prepared estrogonofe de frango, and even though it isn't Gilda's favorite, she's overjoyed to have her sister cook for her. I don't care if distance makes the heart grow fonder, Manuel says, tipping his wineglass. He always likes to make um brinde before a meal, his version of a prayer. To closeness, he says. Bon appétit.

What does it mean that Gilda hasn't sensed her daughter calling out from the beach, trying to reach her? A bird perches on a branch of driftwood and propels forward, frictionless, over the sea. One follows, then another, until Elise is left alone on a stretch of sand. Wait. She extends her hand to them, attempts to affix her gaze to their wings, flapping, shrinking, but soon they're too far and they disappear from her reach.

The ocean stirs and sinks around her ankles, ingesting a reflection of clouds. Elise bends forward to peer into the water. A wave rushes ahead and pulls back, leaving a thin puddle in its wake. For once, she sees something: a face, hers, older, still young. For once, she sees something, but then another wave comes, and she's gone.

ACKNOWLEDGMENTS

I started writing *Wait* at MacDowell in February 2020. It was my first-ever writing residency; I spent most of my days on long hikes feeling like an impostor, fretting over my debut (which would publish that summer), and teaching myself how to build a fire in my cabin.

By mid-March, of course, everything changed. I begged the residency directors to let me stay. But they couldn't. We evacuated. I returned to New York City, quarantined, and vowed to finish the book that I started in those New Hampshire woods.

A year later, I brought a draft to Yaddo, my second-ever writing residency. I am so grateful to the group of ten artists with whom I spent a glorious month, the snow falling, geese migrating overhead. Without these two bookended residencies, *Wait* wouldn't have the breadth of nature infused in its pages.

Thank you to the people who helped carry *Wait* into the world:

My editor, Nicole Counts. Every time I think I've reached my limit, you remind me of my intentions and push me in a way I could never do alone. It is a bonus that you are funny and passionate and a joy to have breakfast with. Thank you for staying by my side.

My agent, Marya Spence, who is everything and everywhere at the same time. Thank you for your tenderness, determination, loyalty, and compassion. I can always rely on you and your immaculate taste and sensibility.

Thank you, Oma Beharry! Thank you to Nicole for bringing Oma to this book! What a talent, what a pleasure, what a superhuman. I truly hope that you will read drafts of every book I write from now on. No pressure.

Thank you to the One World team, the copy editors, proofreaders, designers, marketers, publicists, and sales teams. Thank you to Andrea Pura, Carla Bruce-Eddings, Tiffani Ren, and Lulu Martinez. Thank you to Mackenzie Williams for jumping in during Marya's maternity leave! Thank you to Chris Jackson—your early feedback on *Wait* shook me to my core and made me realize I am not the genius I think I am, which is exactly what I needed to make the book better.

To those who read *Wait* in its infancy, especially Kayla Maiuri, Ethan Philbrick, Flora Medawar, Sumitra Rajkumar, and Sanaë Lemoine. Thank you for your kindness and gentle nudges.

Flora, thank you for highlighting (with color-coded markers) the parts you thought were funny, the parts that made you teary, and the sentences where I got a plant fact wrong. You're the kind of friend every writer should have, or every nonwriter, or any person, really. Everyone should have a Flora in their life.

Sumi, I can't imagine that anyone else would sit outside with me in subzero temperatures, in the middle of the pandemic, for hours upon hours, talking about literature and films, laughing, gossiping, teasing Rob and Emil. Thank you for being a muse, a rare gem, the person I want to impress when I write.

Thank you to the Hafeez family, Ulla, Rohil, Dano, Faria, Noni, Karina, Omar, and Maria, my home away from home.

A huge thank-you to the Nantucket community for showing me so much support and love during a very difficult book release in the summer of 2020. It made me proud to be an island kid. I hope I've made you proud with this book.

To my Nantucket friends, especially Blakney Young, Amelia O'Connor, Claire Minihan, Tracy Long, and Mira Jube. When I envision a perfect hang, it's with this group.

A special thank-you to Anne Phaneuf, Wendy Hudson, Tim Ehrenberg, and Joshua Gray for your generosity.

I would be remiss not to thank Harvey Young, who picked me up at seven A.M. in his Jeep and took me birding on Nantucket for the first time. I had a terrible pair of binoculars and could barely see anything, but his enthusiasm and knowledge provided the foundation for the bird research I would do for this book. He also showed me that the landfill is one of the best birding locations on Nantucket!

The original birder is my sister, Anna Burnham, who was an endangered species monitor for the piping plovers on Nantucket in the early 2000s. Anna, in writing this book, I realized how much you have taught me as my sister. It is a gift that we get to grow up together. Thank you for being a constant source of inspiration.

And to Emil. You have given me a love and stability I never thought I would find in my life. I am so grateful I don't have to do any of this without you.

ABOUT THE AUTHOR

GABRIELLA BURNHAM's debut novel, *It Is Wood, It Is Stone,* was named a best book of the year by *Harper's Bazaar, Marie Claire, Publishers Weekly,* and *Good Housekeeping.* She holds an MFA in creative writing from St. Joseph's College and has been awarded fellowships to Yaddo and MacDowell, where she was named a Harris Center Fellow. Her nonfiction writing has appeared in *Harper's Bazaar.* Burnham and her partner live in Brooklyn with their two rescue cats, Galleta and Franz.

gabriellaburnham.com
Instagram: @burngabiburn

ABOUT THE TYPE

This book was set in Bembo, a typeface based on an old-style Roman face that was used for Cardinal Pietro Bembo's tract *De Aetna* in 1495. Bembo was cut by Francesco Griffo (1450–1518) in the early sixteenth century for Italian Renaissance printer and publisher Aldus Manutius (1449–1515). The Lanston Monotype Company of Philadelphia brought the well-proportioned letterforms of Bembo to the United States in the 1930s.